Pel and the Missing Persons

Previous Inspector Pel mysteries:

Pel and the Party Spirit
Pel and the Picture of Innocence

PEL AND THE
MISSING PERSONS

Mark Hebden

St. Martin's Press
New York

Library of Congress Cataloging-in-Publication Data

Hebden, Mark.
    Pel and the missing persons / Mark Hebden.
        p.   cm.
    "A Thomas Dunne book."
    ISBN 0-312-06441-1
    I. Title.
    PR6058.A6886P452   1991   91-745
    823'.914—dc20   CIP

First published in Great Britain by Constable & Company Limited.

First U.S. Edition: December 1991
10 9 8 7 6 5 4 3 2 1

AUTHOR'S NOTE

No writer of detective stories can do the job without reference to the experts and for the technical details on ballistics in this book, I feel I ought to acknowledge my debt to *Mostly Murder*, by Sir Sydney Smith, which devotes a chapter to this subject.

Though Burgundians may feel they recognize it – and certainly some of the street names are the same – the city in these pages is meant to be fictitious.

Pel and the Missing Persons

1

Two days, six hours, fourteen minutes and – a quick glance at the dashboard clock – sixteen seconds. Evariste Clovis Désiré Pel, Chief Inspector of the Brigade Criminelle of the Police Justiciaire of the Republic of France, managed to look at himself in the rear mirror of his car and what passed with him as a smile crossed his face. He was pleased with himself. Two days, six hours, fourteen minutes and – he looked again at the clock – twenty-five seconds since he had last smoked a cigarette.

For Pel it was a monumental achievement, roughly equivalent to one of the labours of Hercules. The fact that he felt dreadful was beside the point. Pel *expected* to feel dreadful. Life for Pel was real and earnest; for anyone who took it as seriously as he did, it was bound to be hard work. And at the moment it was cold and the wind buffeting the car set it staggering as it whirred down from Leu where he lived. It wasn't the sort of weather one expected of Burgundy. The wind was coming direct from Siberia and, being a cautious type, he had put on so much clothing he found it hard to move his arms.

He would have been better, he thought, to have directed his energies on leaving school not to police work but to being a crook. That way he would have lived in St-Trop' where the weather was warm and, surrounded by film starlets, he would have driven about in a gold-plated, steam-heated Cadillac. On the other hand, St-Trop', pleasant as it was, wasn't Burgundy, and Burgundy, to Pel, wasn't a province of France, it was a religion.

Rain slashed against the window by his elbow and he decided sadly that at that moment it was a very chilly religion. Especially since he was suffering from a heavy head cold with catarrh, painful sinuses and watery eyes. His wife, Geneviève, had tried to persuade him to stay in bed but he felt the Hôtel de Police couldn't function without him and preferred to be a martyr, anyway. And the head cold, which refused to go away, took all the taste out of cigarettes, so that his achievement in giving them up wasn't all that splendid in the end.

However, his wife was being doubly attentive, and he had noticed that Claudie Darel, the only woman member of his team, had also been showing concern for him over the past few days, so that he had come to the conclusion he must be looking pale but interesting, and had decided to prolong his suffering as long as possible. Pel liked attention, and even Madame Routy, who had been his housekeeper in the days before his marriage, after which she had been taken on with Pel by his new wife, had begun to show an interest in his condition. Since he had been conducting a vendetta with her for years, perhaps her concern was with how much longer he had before – according to taste – he passed on, passed over or passed out and she was finally shot of him.

She had handed him his briefcase as he had left the house. His wife had put into it a flask containing a mixture of glycerine, lemon and rum that she had prepared – she considered Pel about as capable of looking after himself as a one-armed orang-utan – and Madame Routy had handed it over as if she hoped it would poison him.

His mind busy, Pel was just on the point of reaching for the glove pocket where he kept his Gauloises when he remembered he had stopped smoking. He had been reaching for Gauloises ever since he had left school. He had been tempted by a fellow schoolboy to try one at the age of thirteen and, because he had just been crossed in love – the girl had laughed outright when he had told her his Christian names – he had taken to smoking like a duck taking to water. He had been trying to give it up ever since.

He'd taken snuff, chewed gum and eaten sweets. He'd even been to a meeting of smokers who had got together in the city in a joint effort to give up. But he hadn't been able to concentrate for the coughing and because, between the recounting of

8

individual catalogues of failure, they had all been smoking like maniacs. He had left before the meeting had even started.

Now, however, he felt he had kicked the habit. Two days, six hours, twenty minutes and four seconds. Mind you, he had a feeling it was only because of his cold that he had held out so long and he sensed that as soon as the cold was better he would grab for his Gauloises like a drowning man grabbing at a straw. Though his wife was encouraging him to stick with it, he had a feeling she had long since come to regard him a lost cause. He was under no delusions really. It was only because the area's criminal fraternity seemed to be taking a holiday that his campaign was succeeding. When they all came out of their holes again, he had really not much hope.

He glanced at himself in the mirror. He was looking old, he decided. There were new lines round his mouth and the bags under his eyes now had bags on *them*. He ought to take exercise or something, a few days at a health farm,perhaps, as his wife had once suggested. But the meals would consist of soda water, bean sprouts and wheatgerm biscuits and there would be callisthenics, aerobics and steam baths. Pel's idea of exercise was watching other people exerting themselves. Or winding up his watch. But even that had disappeared since he had acquired a battery-operated one. For more violent pastimes, this left him only a game of boules or an afternoon's fishing, preferably with the fish not too active.

He took another quick glance at himself as he reached the bottom of the hill where he joined the main road and, as he did so, through his musings he became aware of a shadow on his left. It was a lorry and trailer carrying washing machines. It had about fifty wheels and weighed around a million tonnes. It shot past him with a roar and a whoosh that shook his car. Because he was on the mean side, it was only a small car and shook easily, but joining the main road was Pel's daily dicing with death. About three times a week, absorbed by his thoughts, he came within an ace of being smeared by passing lorries.

He sat up straight, concentrated fiercely, and drove into the city without taking his eyes off the road. Near the Place du Rosoir there was a poster encouraging the ecological way of

9

living. Near it was another advising that whales shouldn't be killed and seals should be spared. Alongside that was an advert for tomatoes. 'Rich in vitamins and mineral salts,' it said. 'Efface stomach maladies and fight arthritis and rheumatism.' It came at you from all angles. The world, Pel felt, was full of clever dicks all telling you what was good for you. If they weren't politicians or trade union leaders, they were health experts and ecologists. He was so lost in this idea he almost hit the police-man on traffic duty at the Porte Guillaume.

French traffic policemen don't take kindly to drivers who jeopardize their lives. One once even put an advertisement in the newspaper saying 'I have a delicate temper. Please don't irritate me.' This one had the same short fuse and, dripping with rain, was just about to stop Pel dead in his tracks and tear him off a strip when he realized who he was. The mouth that opened to let out a roar of rage switched to a beaming smile, and the hand that was about to indicate a halt changed hurriedly to a sloppy salute.

'Silly old con,' the policeman thought. It was a pity he was the best cop they had, or he'd have been run in long since for his driving. He spat water off his lips and studied the rain; '*Comme une vache qui pisse,*' he said disgustedly.

The Hôtel de Police seemed quiet. The man on the front desk looked up, saw it was Pel and hurriedly looked down again. Like everyone else in the building, he'd heard of Pel's attempt to stop smoking and was aware of the tension that permeated the whole building.

Reaching his desk, Pel glanced at the reports placed there for him to see. The top one concerned a bribery case among police in Lyons where two senior officers were being investigated. He knew one of the men because when he had been a sergeant the man had been his superior officer, but he had got himself posted to Lyons in the belief that there were better prospects there. He would undoubtedly go to prison for his efforts.

Pel's deputy, Inspector Daniel Darcy, arrived. He had an open file in his hands and was reading it as he appeared. Pel nodded and Darcy smiled, flashing his teeth at him. Pel envied

Darcy. He always looked as if he'd just come out of a bandbox, dusted, polished and set in motion. He was a good detective but he made Pel feel like the man who had come to mend the lavatory.

His team were a mixed bunch. After Darcy came Nosjean and De Troq', the most reliable of his men, and after them Bardolle of the bulging muscles and the iron voice, who was on leave at the moment – fortunately, because he gave Pel a headache just by being around. Then came Aimedieu who had a face like a choirboy – at that moment an angry choirboy, sounding off about Pel: 'He's always in a bad temper and taking it out on me,' he was saying. Then there were Brochard and Debray, and finally Lacocq, Morell, Cadet Darras; and the golden oldies, Lagé and Misset, both slowing down, Lagé because he was growing fat and looking forward to retirement, Misset because he was just naturally lazy. On the whole they had their good points and their bad points and Pel knew how to use them to advantage. Aimedie, for instance, was useful where cool cheek and a choirboy's face were needed. Brochard made women want to mother him. Lagé was dogged and always sure where long-winded enquiries had to be made, though he had lately taken to complaining about his feet. Pel didn't even think of Nosjean and De Troq'. They could be safely left to work on their own.

As he started divesting himself of clothing, flapping his arms to restore circulation, Darcy watched him with amusement. He allowed him to gather his wits before he spoke.

'How are you, *patron*?' he asked.

'My ribs feel rusty,' Pel growled.

Darcy grinned. It always took Pel a little while on a cold day to come to life. As he stood flapping, Darcy decided he had been born middle-aged, complete with thinning hair and specs.

He waited until Pel was about to sit down, then stopped him with his backside poised over his chair. 'The Chief wants us,' he said.

Pel scowled and Darcy's hand went to his pocket for his cigarettes. For a long time Darcy had been spiriting away Pel's bad tempers with a Gauloise. This time, however, his hand stayed in his pocket. The offer of a cigarette would have produced an eruption of cataclysmic proportions. Like Madame Pel, Darcy had a feeling that Pel's campaign had been a lost cause from its inception but he wasn't prepared to be the one to end it for him.

Pel said nothing as he headed for the Chief's office, Darcy trailing behind him with his arms full of files. Coffee was called for and the Chief was about to offer cigarettes when he saw Darcy silently shaking his head. The Chief was a big man who had been noted as a boxer in his youth but he was always a little scared of Pel. Not physically. He could have eaten Pel for breakfast. But Pel, he always felt, was an awkward little bugger, though fortunately he had nerve ends that reacted to crime. He could smell it – the Chief was convinced of it – and, because his successes reflected on the Chief, he was best kept in a good temper.

There were those who claimed that Pel had mellowed since the Widow Faivre-Perret had got him to the altar, but the Chief wasn't so sure, and for safety he brought out the brandy bottle. Pel sat opposite him, his spectacles on the end of his nose, his thinning hair brushed across his scalp like disturbed cobwebs on a Second Empire glass dome full of wax fruit, his expression one of prim gloom, looking as though he'd been too often to the laundry and shrunk in the wash.

'What have we got?' the Chief asked.

'The usual,' Darcy said. 'Paperwork.'

The Chief frowned. He knew all about paperwork. It had expanded a thousandfold since he had been a young cop. Nowadays it took a couple of minutes to arrest a wrongdoer and a couple of weeks to fill in the forms.

'Crime-wise,' he pointed out.

'Nothing big. Enough to keep everybody busy but not enough to give anyone a heart attack. We've sorted out those thefts at Metaux de Dijon. It was one of the security men. He's up before the beaks tomorrow. We've also pulled in Pierre la Poche. He's been running a gang of kids picking pockets round the Place des Ducs. Tourists mostly. There's also been a complaint from Couchy. Type there says the man next door's killing off his garden by sprinkling something on it at night. Misset's been keeping an eye on the place. He's seen nothing.'

12

'Misset,' Pel observed, 'wouldn't see anything even if it were stuck up his nose. He ought to be retired.'

The Chief consulted a sheet on his desk. 'Several more years to go,' he said.

'Sacked, then.'

'We can't sack him. He's pulled off one or two things.'

'Sheer luck.'

The Chief sighed. The argument about Misset had been going on for a long time. He tried to change the conversation. 'What about those armed robberies?' He crossed to a map on the wall. It concerned a new gang that had appeared in the neighbourhood. They used fast cars, held up shops, jewellers, any premises that might carry large sums, and disappeared again at once. It was headed 'Les Tuaregs'. It was a name that had been given to them by Henriot, of the local rag, *Le Bien Public*. Henriot wasn't noted for his imagination or skill as a journalist, but this time he had hit exactly the right note. 'They come from nowhere,' he had written, 'masked like the Tuaregs of the desert, take what they fancy, and vanish just as easily.' The name had stuck.

'Chateaurenard,' the Chief said. 'Brière. Eglise St-Georges. Fleurs. Etuf-le-Cascade. Martour. Pouges. Six places. One this week. Small supermarkets. Hotels. Places likely to have full tills. Held up by men with sawn-off shotguns.'

'We've got Nosjean and De Troq' on it,' Darcy said. 'They're a good team.'

'They've produced nothing yet. The gang seems to have grabbed the initiative. Why aren't we one step ahead of them?'

'Because,' Pel said, 'we don't know where they're going to strike next. It's a bit of a disadvantage.'

'Don't we have any information? Fingerprints, for instance.'

'None. They use gloves. Like everybody else, they watch the television and read all the books. They know what to do. We've dusted the cars they use. Always fast but never new. Nothing to attract attention. They steal two or three, use one for the job and switch to the others until they're clear to pick up their own.'

'Haven't your informers got anything?'

'They know nothing. We think they're youngsters. Early

13

twenties. That age. Informers don't pick up anything on that sort.'

'Perhaps you ought to extend your information service.'

Pel scowled. 'Information doesn't come cheap.'

Darcy was trying to hang on to his smile. The Old Man was fighting back. Nobody bullied Pel, not even the Chief, who bullied everybody else. There wasn't much of Pel and most of the time he looked like something the cat had dragged in but so long as he was on his feet, no one was going to push his people around.

The same idea had finally occurred to the Chief so he changed the subject. 'You know Judge Polverari's on a long leave of absence. He's not been well.'

Pel nodded. He knew all right, because Judge Polverari, an old friend of his, had celebrated with him only two or three days before. Small, fat, good-natured and married to a wealthy wife, he had spotted Pel's potential long since and had supplied him with good meals and brandy when he was just a poverty-stricken inspector in the days before he had met the Widow Faivre-Perret.

Pel knew he would miss him. *Juges d'instruction* could be important. They could be a help or an impediment, according to their character. When anything happened, the police interviewed witnesses, took statements and passed the documents to the *Procureur* who decided whether there was or was not a case to answer and named an examining magistrate to build up a dossier. These *juges d'instruction* could summon witnesses and interrogate them, and according to temperament, could be a great help or a pain in the neck. Polverari had been good at his job and Pel could only hope whoever came as his relief would be as good.

The Chief watched him. 'I saw Philippe Duche in town,' he observed quietly. To his surprise Pel showed no concern.

'I know,' he said calmly. 'He's out of gaol.'

'He once wanted to kill you. For sending him down over that Zamenhoff robbery attempt.'

'He doesn't now,' Pel said.

The Chief raised his eyebrows. 'Oh?'

'He's gone straight. He got married.'

14

'Who'd have Philippe Duche?'

'Woman called Solange Cardillac.'

'I've heard of her.'

'I expect so. She's a prison visitor.'

'And she married Duche?' The Chief looked startled. And well he might, because Philippe Duche had inherited the Duche gang when his older brother, Edouard-Charles, had been murdered.

Pel nodded. 'He bought a truck and started in haulage. He's got four now and doing all right. I think he's discovered to his surprise that being honest's easier than crime. He's living at Benois de l'Herbue.'

The Chief knew the place. It was just off the N74 on the lower side of the slope of the land. It was said that the right of the road was entirely conservative and the left entirely socialist and that it showed in the wine they produced.

'It was the gang's headquarters in the old days,' Pel said. 'He lived there with his mother but she died and his girl-friend married someone else while he was in gaol. He was all set to kill her when he came out, but fortunately he met Solange Cardillac.'

'What's she like?'

'No longer young. But these days neither is Duche. She's a bit of a saint. He goes to church now.'

'Well, give him a chance. Keep out of his hair. See what happens. He's less trouble to us this way. Who's running his gang?'

'Nobody. It vanished. We put most of them in Number 7, Rue d'Auxonne.' Number 7, Rue d'Auxonne was the local gaol. 'When they came out, two of them went south. Marseilles has them now. One went to Paris. One died in prison. The rest decided it wasn't worth the candle.'

The Chief beamed. Things seemed to be under control.

'Anything else?'

'We could do with more men,' Pel said. 'They're all handling half a dozen cases at once.'

The Chief pretended to be deaf. 'By the way,' he said. 'I'm taking away Cadet Darras and Detective Officer Morell.'

15

It was unexpected and brought Pel upright in his chair at once.

'Why?' he snapped.

'Take it easy.' The Chief held up a calming hand. 'It's only temporary. There's been a complaint from Missing Persons Bureau. They say there are too many names on their computer. It's a request to all areas to try to clear a few up.'

Darcy gave Pel a weary look. The Chief was known for the blitzes he had from time to time: the traffic round the Porte Guillaume; drugs in bars; the crowds of youngsters who gathered in the station forecourt on skateboards, mopeds and motor bikes.

'Missing persons,' Pel observed, 'include kids who don't like their parents, parents who don't like their kids, husbands who don't like their wives, wives who don't like their husbands, old people who are fed up, and schoolchildren who object to their teachers. Most of them prefer to stay missing.'

'A few don't,' the Chief said mildly. 'In 1986, for instance, it was discovered that quite a few missing geriatrics from a private hospital overlooking the sea near Brest were being bagged up like fresh groceries and dropped into the Atlantic weighted with stones. Five, I think it was. They were only discovered when one of them, rather carelessly weighted, turned up in the water just outside – knocking at the door, so to speak, and asking to be let back in.' The Chief grinned. 'We aren't expecting anything quite so spectacular as that but we hope to sort out a few for their worried relatives. I'm making up a team. Two of headquarters staff, one of Nadauld's men from Uniformed Branch, one of Pomereu's from Traffic, and Morell and Cadet Darras from your department.'

'Why *two* from me?'

'One,' the Chief corrected. 'Cadet Darras is only used to run errands and fetch the beer and sandwiches.'

'I've been doing some checking,' the Chief went on. 'We can't expect to sort out missing children, wives and husbands because, as you say, some of them don't want to be found. But we have thirteen missing old age pensioners. I think we ought to be able to find one or two. In fact, we've already found one.

16

She'd gone to live with a cousin and forgot to tell her family. That's the sort of thing we want to sort out.'

Pel said nothing and the Chief went on cheerfully. 'I'll get the team making enquiries. It'll please Central Records, ease the strain on the computer – if computers feel strain – and, above all, it'll please me.'

There was no more to be said. The Chief had made up his mind and he was the boss. Pel studied him carefully. He had a feeling he had something further up his sleeve and he was keeping it until last because he knew it wasn't pleasant.

The Chief sighed. He knew Pel had guessed there was more to come. The cunning little bugger, he thought, always did. He drew a deep breath.

'How well did you know Inspector Goriot?' he asked.

'Too well,' Pel said bluntly.

'Get on all right with him?'

'No. He had as many opinions as a caterpillar has legs.'

'He was badly injured in that bombing business in the Impasse Tarien.'

'Four dead,' Pel said. 'Three of them cops.'

'He's back.'

'I hadn't noticed he'd been away.'

'Well, they made him co-ordinator for the area. Light duties until he recovered. He's back in harness.'

'Doing what?'

'Working. With you. *Under you*,' the Chief added hastily.

'I expect his great-uncle, Senator Forton, pulled strings.'

He didn't miss a trick, the Chief thought. Because that was exactly what had happened. Goriot had had a word with his great-uncle, who had had a word with the Prefect who was selected by Central Government to see that the Maire, who was elected by the people to do what they wanted, did what Central Government wanted instead. The Prefect was important and could fix things. 'Goriot will do as he's told,' he said.

'He'd better,' Pel said darkly. He didn't like people who might usurp his authority – especially people who had great-uncles with influence. He had always considered Goriot pompous and not very bright, and to have him back after so long was enough to make a man worry rats. It completely cancelled the satisfaction that came from Philippe Duche's turning over a new leaf. He sighed. Burgundy wasn't what it was, he thought.

'You'll have to work with him,' the Chief said.

Pel made no promises.

'He's due for retirement soon.'

So, Pel thought, am I. He was, he considered, overworked, underpaid and unappreciated, and in his old age would have ended up in the poorhouse at Beaune but for the fact that he had contrived – he still didn't know quite how – to marry a woman who not only had money but knew how to use it to make more money. She ran the best hairdresser's salon in the city – the way they charged, it could only be the best – and now was branching out in other directions with a boutique next door, a sportswear shop and a children's shop in the Rue de la Liberté. Pel often wondered what it would be like to be married to a millionairess, because every one of Madame's enterprises seemed to be making money hand over fist and, into the bargain, she had recently once more come into money on the death of an aunt. She belonged to a family of ancients who, because she was the only youthful member, left her all their money when they died so that she increased her wealth without even trying.

'I suppose he couldn't take over these smash and grabs?' the Chief asked.

'No,' Pel said. He paused. 'I could put him on to the type who thinks his garden's being damaged by the man next door. Misset should be able to give him a few tips.'

Since Misset was the one man in his team Pel didn't trust, it was no compliment.

Pel left the conference feeling worse than when he had entered. His cold seemed to have increased and his head ached. He wished he were a sewage inspector. As he stalked back to his office, his eyes were feverishly bright.

'Let up, *patron*,' Darcy advised.

'Shut up,' Pel snarled.

'Yes, *patron*.' Darcy used the most pained voice he could produce and Pel immediately felt guilty. Darcy was as modern as a rocket to the moon, and when his profile and personality were in top gear, could collect girls as if they were wasps round a honeypot. It made Pel sick with envy.

'Not your fault,' he managed to growl.

They ate lunch together at a small restaurant near the university. The steaks were tough enough to sole your boots with, the wine tasted like paint-stripper, and the waitress had so much mascara on her eyelashes, they seemed in danger of dropping off into the hors-d'oeuvres.

When they returned to the Hôtel de Police, Claudie Darel was waiting. She looked like a grave Mireille Mathieu. 'Bad news, *patron*,' she said.

Pel's eyebrows rose. 'The government's fallen? War's broken out? We've been invaded by Mars?'

'Worse,' she said. 'The Tuaregs again. The supermarket at Talant.'

Pel sighed. What with the Tuaregs, Goriot and the Missing Persons Bureau, it was more than a man could stand. He finally gave up. Where not smoking was concerned, he gave up easily.

'You carry on with the paperwork,' he said to Darcy. 'I'll go. But first I'd like a cigarette. I threw all mine away.'

Darcy handed over his packet. 'I thought you'd given them up,' he said mildly.

Pel lit the cigarette and dragged smoke down to his socks. 'I've started again.'

'How long was it?'

Pel gave vent to a triple grandsire peal of coughing. As he recovered, feeling better, he looked at his watch. 'Two days, eight hours, fourteen minutes and a few seconds. It was a good try.'

'It didn't last long.'

'I didn't expect it to.'

'Won't Geneviève mind?'

'I don't suppose so. She didn't expect it to last long either.'

2

Sergeant Josephe Misset leaned on the zinc of the Bar de la Petite Alsacienne in the suburb of Couchy. He was supposed to be watching a house in the street that ran at right angles away from where he stood. It was about as exciting as watching paint dry. A man called Raymond Jouet had been complaining that his next door neighbour, one Aloïs Ferry, was deliberately ruining his garden. Misset had talked to Jouet and certainly the garden looked as though *something* had attacked it.

'I think he's putting something on it,' Jouet had said. 'They use things to get rid of grass in crazy paving, don't they? Perhaps he's scattering it on my garden.'

'Why?'

'I don't know.'

'Have you quarrelled?'

'No.'

'Have you seen him scattering anything?'

'No.'

'Perhaps he's trying to do you a favour. Getting rid of the weeds for you.'

Jouet had given Misset a look that would have shrivelled an elephant.

'Well,' Misset had said, 'what proof have you? You haven't quarrelled with him. So why should he do this to you?'

'I don't know.'

'What's he like?'

'He's a funny type.'

'What do you mean by "a funny type"?'

'Well, he keeps himself to himself.'

20

Misset had often wished *he* could keep himself to himself – especially when his wife was on at him. Women, he felt, got married to have a house-trained pet. Men started as husbands but gradually got themselves moulded until they were something else entirely and, when they were finally thoroughly mouldy, the wives decided they didn't like what they'd made and started looking elsewhere. Not that Madame Misset looked elsewhere. Sometimes Misset wished she would. But she was determined to hang on to him, in spite of the fact that she didn't trust him. She didn't understand him, he felt. She never had. His spirit, he considered, was a wild, free one that couldn't be fastened down; though Misset felt sometimes he had a nail through one foot into the floor. Even the kids didn't understand him. They always took his wife's side. It would be nice, he thought nostalgically, if he could stuff the lot of them – the family dog, too, for that matter, because even that took sides – into the nose cone of a rocket and fire them off into outer space. They'd look fine on Mars wondering what had happened. He didn't think they'd get on with the Martians any better than they did with him.

They always, he decided, seemed to be in his hair, which was why Misset spent all his time on duty – at least, so he told his wife. Most of it, in fact, he spent standing at the zinc in bars, just as he was doing now. There had been a time when he had chased girls. But they didn't seem to notice him any more. He wondered if it was the dark glasses that put them off. He had started wearing them when his eyes had begun to go, trying to look as though he were a danger to his fellow men and a devil with women. It didn't seem to work. Nobody seemed to feel threatened and women preferred younger, slimmer men. Once Misset had been good-looking; now he was just fat from too much beer-drinking and too much dodging work.

'Does he mess about with chemicals?' he asked.

'Not to my knowledge,' Jouet said.

'Why would he want to ruin your garden?'

'I don't know.'

'Does *he* do any gardening?'

'Never. His place's a pigsty.'

21

'And yours isn't?'

'I take a lot of trouble with my garden.'

Misset often wished someone would take a lot of trouble with *his* garden. Gardening wasn't something that roused in him a deep emotion. He could just as easily look at a bare patch of scrubby lawn as a bright green sward surrounded by flowers. He never sat in the garden, except on a summer evening with a beer when his wife and family were out visiting, and he couldn't rouse any enthusiasm for working in it.

He stared at Jouet. He seemed to have run out of questions. He couldn't think what to ask next. He'd been given the job chiefly because everybody else was engaged elsewhere and there was no one else. Normally Misset's job was handling the telephone but occasionally when the cases piled up he was sent out to do his stint – usually on piffling enquiries like this one. It didn't worry Misset. There had been a time when he had hoped to hold the Chief's job or that of Commissioner for Paris, but he had perpetrated too many mistakes and he knew he'd never make it now.

He finished his beer but was reluctant to leave the bar. It was run by a barmaid with blond hair and a bust like two buns bursting out of a bag. Misset found it hard to keep his eyes off them. As he stepped into the sunshine he spotted a big Citroën parked in the street. Alongside it were two men. Misset recognized them at once: one was Councillor Auguste Lax, who represented the area on the Communal Council. He was a harsh-voiced, abrasive character who spent most of his time attacking people more able than himself. Known as 'The Rasp' for his voice as well as for his tactics, he was far from popular in the Council Chamber, where he was known for always going over the top in his criticisms.

The other man was Senator Forton. Misset knew Senator Forton well. He was Inspector Goriot's great-uncle, and until Goriot had been injured in a bombing affair in the city that had made the storming of the Bastille look like a Saturday night fight outside a bar, he had benefited greatly from Senator Forton's patronage. Senator Forton liked to interfere, and Goriot had always been willing to supply him with information. It had once resulted in Misset's being hauled up before the Chief for

22

neglecting his duty. He hadn't neglected his duty – well, a little bit, he conceded – but a villain they'd had under surveillance had managed to make an escape while Misset had been eyeing a girl. It had reached Senator Forton's ears and he had asked questions of the Chief who had taken it out on Pel, who had gone for Darcy, who had bawled out Misset, whose only option, being as low in rank as he could be for the job he was doing, was to kick the cat when he got home. Misset had no love for Senator Forton, or for that matter Inspector Goriot or Councillor Lax. It was always easy to be wise sitting on the sidelines – a bit like football commentators indicating what a player should have done when he'd been more concerned with being up to his neck in flying boots and pounding heels. It was time, Misset decided, to move from the bar. He didn't expect either Forton or Lax to remember him, but they might if they saw him hanging about.

Walking to the house next to Jouet's, he studied it from the roadway. It was small and detached and looked exactly like Jouet's. It had an attached garage with a roof that sloped towards Jouet's property, which was only the width of the path that ran alongside the garage away from it. In the drive was the owner's car. It was a blue Peugeot of not very recent vintage and was patched with rust.

As he knocked on the door, it was opened by a man with a face that looked as if he could well have been used pushed down holes to chase rabbits. But he was small and he looked harmless. Misset liked harmless types.

'Monsieur Ferry?' he asked.

'That's right.'

'First name?'

'Aloïs. Why?'

'There have been complaints about gardens being damaged in the city. We're running a check. There's talk of acid rain coming down. I expect it's the English. They're always at it. Or else it's the fag end of Chernobyl.'

'That was years ago.'

'It's been floating round in the upper hemisphere for a long time and the weather patterns have finally brought it this way.' Misset thought this brilliant. 'At least, that's what they say.'

23

The little man stared at him through glasses as thick as the bottoms of wine bottles. 'Who're you?'

'Misset's my name.'

'I mean, who do you represent?'

'Er – the National Meteorological Department. I've been given this district. We just want to know if you've had any trouble with your garden.'

The little man gave a sly smile. 'I never have trouble with my garden,' he said.

'You don't?'

'No. I never even look at it. Jouet next door says it's full of weeds and the seeds blow into his garden.'

'He thinks something's killing his flowers.'

'He's a nut about his flowers.'

'Yes, well – where do you work?'

'Why?'

The little man was sufficiently aggressive in his replies to put Misset off his stride. He clearly wasn't disturbed by Misset's size.

'It's part of the questionnaire,' he said.

'I'm a truck driver,' Ferry conceded. 'I'm also a writer. Part time.'

'Novels?'

'Political pamphlets.'

'Any special party?'

'No. I don't like any of them. All politicians are liars. I bet you've come from a political lot. It's a poll, isn't it? To see if I like the government or something?'

'No, it's not that.'

'Well, I'm not interested. I don't give opinions. And I don't use my vote. Politicians are all hypocrites. I prefer to keep myself to myself.'

'Do your writing at home?'

'Yes. I've got a room upstairs.' Ferry gestured and, stepping back to look, Misset saw a window over the sloping roof of the attached garage. It seemed to have paper plastered to the glass.

'What is it?' he asked. 'Photographic dark room?'

'It's a study and workroom. The paper on the window's to

24

stop that nosy con next door staring in. I spend a lot of time up there.'

'Doesn't your wife mind?' Misset's wife would have, he knew.

'I haven't got a wife,' Ferry said. 'She left me.'

Misset wasn't surprised.

'She said I never showed any interest in her. She believed in Women's Lib, racial equality, health food, and all that. She took the children with her. I wasn't sorry. I didn't like them either. None of them.'

'How many were there?'

'Five. They were all against me.'

Misset ended up swapping woes with him.

The supermarket at Talant was the *bête noire* of Pel's team. It was regularly broken into; once it had caught fire; once it had been the site of a gang fight. Policemen were always being called to sort it out. They had never been summoned there for a hold-up, however, so at least this time it was different.

When Pel arrived, it was to find the place in an uproar. Nosjean had arrived just ahead of him and was handling things. Two policemen from the Talant substation were also there, watched over by their *sous-brigadier* who announced that he'd sent for the dog-handler.

Pel didn't think much of dogs as aids to police work. He'd once been bitten by one. 'Why dogs?' he asked. 'The gang's gone, hasn't it?'

The *sous-brigadier* looked surprised. 'Well, yes, sir,' he said. 'But we always have the dogs in. They might turn up a scent.'

A crowd had already gathered, all staring at the police cars. Crowds gathered automatically when anything happened. A dog depositing a turd on the pavement could bring a crowd, so could a man staring at a flat tyre on his car, a woman cuffing a difficult child. A girl adjusting her stocking could stop traffic. If the plague had arrived, a crowd would have assembled to see what it looked like.

Talant supermarket was a modern building with a glass front showing its interior, and inside, on easels, hanging from the roof and plastered on the doors were large fluorescent notices for special offers, foods at low prices, and – a new thing – suggestions for good health! Cholesterol-free polyunsaturated sunflower margarine. Additive-free meat. Healthy hamburgers full of monosodium glutamate. Organically grown vegetables. Free-range eggs devoid of botulism, salmonella, listeria and all the other desperate diseases that had recently emerged. Wheatgerm bread. Pasteurized milk. Tuberculin-tested cream. Caffeine-exempted coffee. Low-fat biscuits made of oats, bran and sand. Where, Pel wondered, had all the Norman butter gone? The pâté de foie gras from Alsace? The cheese? Where, for that matter, courage in eating. Perhaps it was a Russian plot.

The French, he decided, had become a race of hypochondriacs. Still, he thought, perhaps they always had been. Pel certainly was. Dinner table talk these days was always about things that were good for migraines, the intestines, the liver, the kidneys, the bones, the blood. Even bottled water was good for you. Adverts regularly appeared in magazines showing a cartoon figure of a nude male, complete with family pride and joy, holding a bottle of clear spring water, a stream of urine cutting the air in a perfect arc and a balloon issuing from his mouth announcing 'C'est bon pour la santé'.

As he pushed through the glass doors, the manager was in a state of panic at the way the police had closed the premises. 'We've got to keep the place trading,' he was wailing. 'It'll bring the takings down. The owners will want to know why.'

'Won't they be more interested to know what's happened to the money from the till?' one of the Talant policemen asked.

There had been only one cash desk working when the raid had taken place, and the girl who had been operating it was sitting in the manager's office clutching a brandy. She was small and blonde and her jaw worked at a wad of chewing gum. Near her was another girl holding a glass of water and a packet of aspirin.

'Which is the one who was robbed?' Nosjean was asking.

'That's her,' the manager said, pointing to the girl with the brandy. 'Janine Ducassis. She's a good girl. Due for promotion. Been with us three years. Very responsible. I'm Georges Blond,

26

by the way.' He indicated the girl with the glass of water and the aspirin packet. 'This is my secretary, Pascal Dubois.'

Nosjean noted that, while Janine Ducassis looked efficient, Pascal Dubois looked both efficient *and* beautiful. She had a splendid figure and a mass of dark wavy hair. Nosjean never failed to notice such things.

He bent over Janine Ducassis and she stopped crying and looked up with interest, because Nosjean was good-looking with a beaky nose that made him look a bit like the picture of Napoleon on the bridge at Lodi.

'All right, Janine,' he said gently. 'Tell us what happened.'

She blinked away her tears. 'Well, there weren't many in the store,' she said. 'The first rush had finished. We always get a few in first thing. Buying things to eat at work. Things like that. Then it goes quiet for a while and then the women come to buy for their midday meal. After that it goes quiet again. That's when they came. The other girls had gone for coffee and I was on my own.'

'At the cash desk?'

'Yes.'

'Perhaps we'd better have you there now. So we can see things as you saw them. Think you can manage it?'

She could have managed anything for Nosjean. He was as good as Robert Redford. They trooped out to the cash desk and she sat down on the stool.

'This is where you were?'

'Right here.'

'Anybody else near you?'

'No. There were a few people in Paperware and Kitchen Goods. I saw them. But nobody round here.'

'Go on.'

'Well, I saw this car draw up outside. There were only a few people about and they were all at the other end in Fruit and Vegetables. There weren't more than three or four cars in the car park so this one was able to park right outside. Two men got out and another one stayed in the car. I thought they were workmen come to buy sandwiches. We sell them. Ham with lettuce. Cheese and lettuce. Ham and cheese with – '

'Go on about the man,' Pel interrupted.

The girl looked at him. She didn't like the look of him, especially when he interrupted Nosjean.

'Who's he?' she asked Nosjean.

'It's all right,' Nosjean pointed out. 'He's a policeman.'

She seemed satisfied. 'Well,' she said, 'they came through that door there. They had on these Canadienne things. You know, those big checked coats workmen wear in winter. They had caps and dark glasses.They went through the turnstile, but instead of going down to Tinned Fruit and Speciality Foods where most people go, they just turned round and stopped in front of me. And then – ' she stared at Nosjean with big eyes and started to cry again – 'this one pointed this gun at me.'

'What sort of gun?' Pel asked.

'A gun sort of gun,' she snapped.

She turned her back on Pel and looked at Nosjean. 'It had a big barrel. Do they call them sawn-off shotguns? It had a big hole in the end. It must have had a big bullet in it.'

'If it was a shotgun,' Pel said, 'it would have lead shot. A lot. You did right not to resist. It could have made a mess of you. That would have been a pity.'

'Why?'

'Pretty girl like you.'

She looked much more warmly at him.

'This is Chief Inspector Pel,' Nosjean introduced. 'He's my boss.'

'Oh!' The girl was obviously impressed.

'Tell him what happened.'

'Well, then I saw they both had – well – these gun things. One of them had his almost up my nostril,' She was recovering rapidly. 'The other held out a bag and told me to put the money in.'

'What sort of bag?'

'One of ours. Plastic. It says *Supermarket Talant* on it. In red letters. We give them to our customers. He held it out and said to open the till and put the money in. I didn't argue. Would you have?'

'No,' Pel said.

'So I put it in.'

'How much was there?'

'Well, we'd been open since eight o'clock so there – '

'Six thousand, three hundred and twenty-four francs,' the manager interrupted.

'That's not a lot.'

'That's not all. They opened the till on the next desk.'

'The girl had left her key in it when she went to get her coffee,' Pascal Dubois said.

'It's against the rules,' the manager added. 'She'll have to go. Rules are important. What's the good of having rules if – '

Ignoring him, Pel turned to Janine Ducassis. 'And what were you doing while this happened?'

'Well, I was sitting on my stool, with this gun up my nostril, wasn't I? I heard one of them say, "The next till." The key was in it so the one with the bag went round there and emptied it. Then I saw someone coming. They'd reached Health and Babycare. That's usually the last call before they stop at Wines and Spirits on the way out. The man with the gun said, "Let's go." So they went. They went out of the door and got in the car and it drove off and I started screaming. I didn't move while they were here.'

'Very sensible,' Pel said. 'Or we might have had a murder on our hands. Did you catch the number of the car?'

'No.'

'What sort was it?'

'It was grey.'

'I mean, what make?'

'I don't know. It had four wheels. I know that.'

Pel turned to the manager. 'Did you see it?'

The manager shrugged. 'I saw nothing. I just heard the screaming and ran out. It had gone by then.'

'Anybody else in here see it?'

'I've asked. No.'

'Any of those people outside see it?'

'I asked them, too. They hadn't arrived when it left.'

'Just one old woman,' Pascal Dubois put in. 'Madame Folieux. A regular customer. She said she was driving in as it shot out.'

'Did she notice anything about it?'

The manager struggled to produce a tired smile. 'She said it was grey.'

29

'We'll ask her.'

'She's seventy-five. She'll probably say it had four wheels.'

She probably would at that, Pel thought.

'Have you checked the amount taken from the other till?'

'Yes. Four thousand and seventy-four francs.'

'Not a big haul,' Pel said quietly to Nosjean.

'They don't seem to go in for single big hauls,' Nosjean agreed. 'They seem to prefer to do a lot of small places like this where there isn't a sophisticated security system. But they're doing all right. This is the second this week. With today's, they've netted forty thousand francs. That's not bad business in anybody's language. Especially since they don't have any overheads. No rates. No taxes. Not even the cost of the cars they operate, because they're all stolen.' He looked at the girl. 'Could you describe them?'

She shrugged. 'I didn't look at them much. I kept my eye on the gun, ready to duck.'

'Have a try.'

'Young.'

'How young?'

'Twenties. Both big. I couldn't see much. They had on these heavy coats with the collars up, caps over their eyes and dark glasses. About all I could see were their noses.'

They ascertained that one of the men seemed to have a thin hooked nose and the other a short turned up one. Both were dark, and one Canadienne was reddish, the other brown and white. From what they could make out, the driver had been small and red-haired.

'Anything else?' Nosjean asked. 'Voices for instance.'

'They didn't say much.'

'Did they come from round here, do you think?'

'I didn't ask them. Would you with a gun up your nose?'

'I mean, had they local accents?'

'I didn't notice.'

'Touch anything?'

'Well, they didn't touch me. I might have moved if they had. All they did was stick this gun up my nose.'

'I'm thinking of fingerprints.'

'Oh!' The girl smiled. 'Well, they wore gloves.'

30

'That doesn't help us.'

'Except when they opened the next till.'

'What happened then?'

'The one with the thin nose couldn't scoop the money out with his glove on, so he took it off.'

'And touched something?'

'I don't know. I only saw out of the corner of my eye. I had this gun up my nose, remember.'

Nosjean smiled. 'I remember. We'll have it checked.'

'My nose?'

'No. The till.' Nosjean turned to the *sous-brigadier* from Talant and gestured at the next till. 'Have that thing taped off. We don't want anyone touching it.' He turned to the girl. 'Thank you. You've been very helpful.'

She beamed at him, fully recovered now and sorry to lose him. She even managed a smile at Pel.

Pascal Dubois offered them coffee. 'Not from a machine,' she smiled.

When they went outside to talk to the local policemen, the crowd had grown and now included a few women who were complaining that they couldn't get into the supermarket to do their shopping, a few children on their way home from school and one or two old men taking their morning constitutional with their dogs. They had just stepped through the doors when the dog handler arrived in a rush. His dog was an alsatian and, as soon as he opened the door of his van, it shot like a bullet from a gun in the direction of the crowd where it promptly set about a large poodle which was innocently cocking its leg up at a lamp-post.

The victim was promptly supported by a labrador and a collie which must have been friends, with a mongrel that looked like a shaggy rug dancing round on the outside seeking something to bite. Women screamed. The owners of the dogs swore and lashed out with walking sticks and dog leads.

'Holy Mother of God,' one of the local policemen said. 'There's blood everywhere.'

The dog handler managed to grab his dog and drag it away, snarling, to fling it into his van. 'It always does this,' he said bitterly. 'I don't know what to do with the damn thing.'

31

'Try shooting it,' Pel suggested.

With peace restored, the local men were questioned about the raiders.

Canadiennes? Brown and white checked? And red? They looked at each other and shrugged. They had seen no one about answering the descriptions and they knew of no one who might fit.

'It's the first decent description we've had,' Nosjean said. 'They always wear scarves covering their faces. Once ski masks. They seem to like to vary it a bit.'

As they talked, another police car arrived. The man who climbed out was Inspector Goriot. He was a tall man, with grey hair, handsome features and a statuesque appearance, which was one of the reasons Pel didn't like him. In Pel's book, anybody taller and better-looking than he was, was suspect. Anybody taller, better-looking, with influence and after Pel's job was beyond the pale.

He shook hands reluctantly. Goriot stared round him as if he were discovering unexplored territory.

'Got it sized up?' he asked.

'It's a habit of mine,' Pel said.

'Thought I'd come out and have a look.'

'Why?' Pel asked disconcertingly.

Goriot coughed. 'Just thought I'd start getting into harness again.'

'Find the saddle chafes?'

Goriot pretended he hadn't heard. 'We ought to be able to nail this gang,' he said.

'If nobody interferes we shall.'

'Had a word with Philippe Duche?'

'No.'

'He's out of gaol. He's probably getting his team together again.'

'Leave him alone,' Pel said.

'Why? He's a criminal.'

'It's the Chief's wish.'

Goriot frowned. 'You leaving now?' he asked.

'Yes. Nosjean's in charge. Fingerprints and Forensic are on their way.'

'I'll stick around a bit.'

Pel scowled. 'I shouldn't,' he advised.

Goriot looked surprised. 'Why not?'

'Because,' Pel said pointedly, 'it's not your case. It's Nosjean's.'

3

'Bomb,' the Chief said.

They had been called into his office and were all sitting round when he sprang his surprise.

'At the airport,' he said. 'Last night. It was in an outbuilding,' he explained. 'It was home-made and did little damage.'

They waited for further enlightenment. The Chief obliged. 'As you know, the city airport is shared with the military. It doesn't receive much in the way of civil traffic but the Armée de l'Air, which uses the eastern side, is always nervous. That's why the incident was reported to me quietly. I was asked that no fuss should be made. I pass it on to you in the same spirit. There is to be *no* fuss.'

'We should have men out there,' Goriot said.

'*They stipulated no fuss*,' the Chief insisted firmly. 'I say the same. It did little but make a noise. It was the usual thing – sodium chlorate, the main ingredient, packed into a tin. But it wasn't very well sealed. You could use the mixture in one half of a two-battery torch and use the other battery to set the thing off and the pressure could be tremendous if it were properly packed.'

'The one in the Impasse Tarien was made of torches,' Goriot said and they were all silent because if anyone knew of the effects of home-made bombs, surely Goriot did.

'Exactly,' the Chief agreed, his expression sympathetic. 'But this was a tame effort – somebody who didn't know a lot about it. And I agree with the Air Force. It could start copycat bombs.These days people know how to make them. The army

34

from the Avenue du Drapeau are doing the investigation and they have their own bomb experts.'

'We *should* be involved,' Goriot insisted.

'I think we should not,' the Chief said mildly. 'It was small and crudely made and the Air Force even have the feeling it might have been a lark or a bit of spite by a conscript. It was clearly not a serious attempt to damage aircraft or installations. They prefer to keep it quiet and handle it themselves, and not invite any more.'

'Where was it?' Pel asked.

'In an outbuilding near the perimeter on the civil half of the field. It didn't do any real damage.'

'Terrorists would have chosen somewhere more important. Hangar. Aircraft park. Officers' mess. Armoury. Something of that sort.'

'That's what the Armée de l'Air decided,' the Chief agreed.

'Could it be a protest of some sort?' Darcy suggested.

'It could.'

Goriot, who had been writing furiously in his notebook, looked up, bright-eyed and bushy-tailed, to indicate he was on the ball. 'Has anybody investigated what Philippe Duche's up to?' he asked.

'Philippe Duche,' Pel said patiently, 'is running a haulage company.'

'He was going to use explosive on the Zamenhoff robbery.'

'He was going to ram the door open with the scoop of a digger,' Pel corrected. 'And anyway, Philippe Duche would have used something more sophisticated than a home-made bomb. He'd have got some type from Marseilles.'

'We should watch him.'

'We'll leave him alone,' the Chief said firmly. 'I've talked to the prison governor and the prison visitors about him. We'll give him his chance. If he takes it, so much the better. Leave him alone.'

As the conference broke up, the Chief drew Pel aside.

'Keep an eye on Goriot,' he said quietly. 'I don't entirely trust him. He behaves a bit oddly. I think he's determined to get back his seniority no matter who suffers. Perhaps that bomb in the Impasse Tarien did him more harm that we thought.'

Pel gave him a warm glance. It was the sort of hunch he admired and the Chief, shrewd as he was, wasn't the type to go in for hunches as a rule.

'By the way,' the Chief said as they parted, 'we've turned up two more missing persons. One was a girl of fifteen who ran away from home, regretted it and didn't dare go home. She was living with a man of thirty. She's home now, forgiven, and content – until she does it again. The other was an old woman who wandered off. She's been found in hospital at Beaune.'

'Goriot's determined to have Philippe Duche behind bars again,' Darcy said as they left the Chief's office.

'He's eager to make his mark,' Pel agreed. 'He probably feels he's lost of lot of leeway with all the time he's had on light duties.'

As they left the Chief's corridor, Inspector Nadauld of Uniformed Branch touched Pel's arm.

'Friday evening,' he said. 'We're having a few drinks at the Bar Transvaal. My son's wedding. The fact that he's getting married to a girl from Avallon – in Avallon – doesn't mean we can't have a few drinks here to celebrate. Sergeant Gehrer, my deputy, is celebrating too. He finishes his time tomorrow. His successor – chap called Lotier – will be there. You'll get a chance to meet him. You, too, Daniel. The Chief's promised to look in.'

'Goriot's trying to shove his oar in,' Pel said.

Madame Pel, who was seated at her desk busy with her accounts, looked up, her eyes amused. She wasn't very worried about Goriot. After a year or two of marriage, she knew her Evariste Clovis Désiré enough to believe he could handle Goriot and several more like him if necessary. There wasn't much of him but she would have backed him against Goriot any day, even with an uncle who was a senator.

'What will you do?'

'I've done it already. I told him to get lost.'

Madame smiled. 'I thought you might,' she said.

36

Pel sat back. He liked to see Madame handling her money. She did it expertly and with a quiet confidence that reassured him. The days when he had expected a poverty-stricken old age had gone. With the skill she showed over finance, he felt he might manage now, if he were careful, to survive in reasonable comfort to the end of his days.

'He tries to interfere with Darcy,' he said.

'I'm sure you'll persuade him not to.'

Pel picked up the paper. It was *Le Bien Public*. The headline concerned the supermarket hold-up and his face was plastered all over the front page.

'Why is it I always look as if I'd been struck by lightning?' he mused.

'Oh, you don't,' Madame said. 'You're really very handsome.'

It was balm to Pel's heart. 'I am?'

'Of course.' Madame didn't really think so but she knew Pel liked a little flattery now and again and she was more than prepared to offer it. She knew he was good at his job – one of the best – and that policemen were always underpaid for what they did, and was more than prepared to make up for it by dishing out soft words.

She began to put her account books away, singing to herself as she did so.

Où est donc l'évêque d'Odon?
Il est parti à Loudon
Manger du pudding.
Dong et dang et ding.
Il est parti à Lou-don.

'Where do you find them?' Pel asked wonderingly.

'My Great-Aunt Jeanne used to sing them to me when I was a little girl.'

'Which one was Great-Aunt Jeanne?'

'She died last year. She left me some money.' Madame spoke as if it would have been odd for someone in her family *not* to leave her money.

Under the circumstances, Pel felt they ought to be able to eat out. He decided on the Relais St-Armand and pretended it was

37

because that was where he had first met Madame. Actually it was because they served excellent andouillettes, the chitterling sausages of the region, with a chablis that took the roof off your mouth. Madame wasn't fooled for a minute.

The place was full and she glanced around her, interested – not only as a woman but also as the owner of a business concerned with women – in what people were wearing and how they had their hair done. Near the window, half hidden from Pel by a wilting palm, was a woman in a red polka-dotted dress. The lights were low but he could see she was a big woman with blond hair. Accompanying her was a man who seemed to have been chosen to match her in every department. He had his back to Pel but he was large with powerful shoulders, good features and strong dark hair that curled round his ears. Madame was watching them closely.

'Something of interest?' Pel asked.

Madame smiled. 'Only the dress,' she said. 'It's one of ours. An exclusive model. She looks well in it. She has one of our handbags, too.' She smiled again. 'In fact, she has one of our hair styles. It was done by Sylvie Goss and I can recognize her work anywhere.'

Returning home, they watched opera on television. Pel didn't go much on opera on television. In fact, he didn't go much on anything on television. During the days when he had had only Madame Routy to keep him company, he had endured night after night of it with the volume turned up from *Loud* to *Unbelievable*. But his wife liked music so he sat through it patiently, dozing at intervals, watched fondly by his wife who knew his views.

The opera went on later than they expected and Pel was just doing what he called his exercises before getting into bed when the telephone rang. Pel's exercises wouldn't have strained an eighty-year-old but at the sound of the bell he was only too happy to pause, his knees bent and his arms outstretched as though he were about to take off and loop the loop.

Madame watched him cheerfully. She had long been aware that she was married to an oddity who would probably descend into raving eccentricity as he grew older. But she felt she could cope and was always delighted.

Pel was staring hostilely at the telephone as though he expected it to explode. Frowning, he rose and snatched at it. It was Darcy.

'Thought you'd like to know, *patron*,' he said. 'There's been a body found on the motorway. Near Mailly-les-Temps.'

'Murder?' Pel asked.

'Could be. Cruising patrol car found him.'

'I'd better come.'

As he put the telephone down, Madame Pel looked up. 'You've got to go out?' she said.

'Yes. I'm sorry. I don't want to.'

'Don't be silly. Of course you do.'

Amusement bright in her eyes, Madame put her spectacles on to see him better. Pel had often felt that, but for feminine vanity and her dislike of being seen in spectacles, he might never have got her to the altar. God knew, in spite of what she said, he was no Adonis and he could only put it down to the fact that she hadn't been able to see him properly.

'You love your work,' she said. 'It comes first and I come second.'

'Never!'

'But yes. If I died or disappeared, you'd mourn me, I suppose, but you'd still go on catching criminals. But if you were to be told tomorrow you had to give up police work, you'd die.'

There was no answer because it was true. 'That's not fair,' Pel said.

Madame smiled. 'Go on. Off you go. Take your warm coat. It's cold. And don't forget your cigarettes.'

Pel managed to look shamefaced. 'I gave them up,' he said.

'But now you've started again.'

'You knew?'

'Of course.'

At the door, she handed him a small leather-covered pocket flask. 'Brandy,' she said. 'Against the cold air.'

'It'll give me indigestion.'

'Indigestion's better than pneumonia.'

39

Darcy was waiting for him at the Hôtel de Police and they drove off together.

'Everybody's been called out,' Darcy said. 'Forensic. Fingerprints. Doc Minet's deputy, Doctor Cham. Minet's in bed with influenza. There's a lot of it about.'

'I think I've got it.'

Darcy grinned. If there was *anything* about, Pel immediately assumed he was about to die of it.

'Cham's bright,' he observed. 'I expect he'll take Minet's place when he retires.'

'Everything's changing,' Darcy agreed. 'Judge Polverari's relief's arrived. The Palais de Justice told me.'

'Anybody we know?'

'Name of Castéou. Claudie Darel got the name from that barrister she's going around with – Bruno Lucas. I expect she'll be the next to go.' Darcy suddenly realized he sounded like Pel. Having for years listened to Pel being Pel and finding it amusing, he was alarmed to discover he was becoming like him. Good God, he thought, perhaps it goes with the job.

'Goriot was at Talant,' Pel said. 'Trying to worm his way in.'

'He seems round the bend a bit these days,' Darcy said. 'He was always a bit self-important, with that great-uncle of his. Since he got blown up in the Impasse Tarien he's become worse. He's started demanding his old team back.'

Pel snorted. 'All his old team but Aimedieu were killed, chiefly because Goriot didn't think ahead.'

'The Chief's assigned him Aimedieu,' Darcy said.

'What?' Pel nearly went through the roof of the car. Despite his choir-boy face, Aimedieu had become one of his best men.

'Aimedieu's furious,' Darcy said.

'I'll bet he is.'

'The Chief says it's only temporary. Aimedieu's afraid it won't be.'

'So am I. We need Aimedieu. He's bright.'

'Bright enough not to be attached to Goriot. Goriot's going to be a nuisance.'

'Goriot was *always* a nuisance.'

Darcy said nothing for a moment. 'He tried to bring a charge against Philippe Duche,' he said eventually. 'Said one of his trucks had faulty brakes. It was nonsense. Pomereu, of Traffic, was furious. It's his department, not Goriot's.'

'I think Goriot's got it in for Duche.'

'He's got it in for me, too, *patron*,' Darcy said.

'Been having words with him?'

'Not pleasant ones. I think he'd like my job.'

'He's got a hope.'

'He's senior, *patron*. By many years.'

'That's because he stuck at inspector. You won't.'

'I think Judge Brisard's ganging up with him.'

Pel frowned. Judge Brisard was one of the examining magistrates. He was young, aggressive, and anathema to Pel. He and Pel had disliked each other from the day they had met. Brisard was tall and plump, with a big behind and hips like a woman. He had a nice line in family togetherness which Pel knew was phoney because he had learned that Brisard kept a policeman's widow down the motorway in Beaune.

'You've never quarrelled with Brisard, have you?' he asked.

'*You* have, *patron*,' Darcy said. 'And anything they can lay on me reflects on you. Goriot's also got Senator Forton behind him, remember.'

Since Senator Forton spent most of his time in Paris, Pel couldn't imagine what he could possibly know about Burgundy. As different from the areas that surrounded it as chalk was from cheese, it was noted for its courage, character and strength, and had defied the French kings and produced Vercingetorix and Philip the Bold. It had even produced Evariste Clovis Désiré Pel.

He sighed. Office politics were always with them. There were always men who relied more on being noticed by their superiors than on what they achieved, pushy men who manoeuvred rather than worked their way to the top. They occurred in every office where people operated in groups.

'All the same,' he said, 'we've got to work with him. It's a measure of a man's fitness for the top jobs that he can work with someone he doesn't like.'

Darcy grinned. Pel had never made concessions to anyone.

Because of the hour, it was quiet and only one car passed them, going at a speed well above the regulation. On the southbound carriageway near Mailly-des-Temps they began to see warning cones on the road and signs indicating that the inside track was closed. Finally, they began to see the flashing lights of police vehicles and eventually came to an area where the three tracks had been cut to one. The other two tracks had been blocked off and cars and vans were parked to force any traffic that appeared away from the scene. Policemen with handlamps were there to wave vehicles down but, at that hour, the motorway was empty. On the northbound carriageway there was a single 'whoosh' as a late car hurtled past. A police van, its engine running, had its lights directed across a huddle of men in the roadway. Among them, close to the verge, they could see the body.

Doctor Cham was bent over it. He looked like a studious hen, tall and thin with glasses, a high forehead and an Adam's apple that went up and down in his long neck like a yo-yo. He looked up as Pel and Darcy appeared alongside him, his spectacles reflecting the flashing lights of the police vehicles.

'Looks like an ordinary accident,' he said. 'Hit and run perhaps. Severe head injuries. Both legs broken. That's at first glance.'

'What does that mean?'

'I'll be more specific when I examine him on the slab.'

It was something Pel had to accept. A car, slowed by the waving torches of police, growled impatiently past, the beams of its headlights probing the darkness like lances.

'Any indication who he is?'

'None. Pockets seem to be empty.'

'People don't empty their pockets to go wandering along the motorway in the dark.'

'They probably do if they're drunk.'

'*Was* he drunk?'

'He'd been drinking. You can smell it. Whisky. I can check the amount later.'

'Fingerprints been taken?'

Prélat, the Fingerprints expert, standing just beyond the glow of lights, shook his head. 'Not yet, *patron*.'

'Age?'

'Sixty-five to seventy,' Cham said. 'About that. Probably

42

senile. He must have been a bit confused. His waistcoat's inside out and unbuttoned. His shirt and jacket are buttoned in the wrong holes. He's not wearing socks. I'd say he was old and perhaps ill. But he was tall and I imagine good-looking when he was young. I reckon we should be looking for somebody's elderly father.'

What they'd found seemed to be an accident and accidents weren't Pel's line of business. They belonged to Inspector Pomereu, of Traffic, who turned up just as Pel was preparing to leave.

'I'll look after the details, *patron*,' Darcy offered. 'You take my car. I'll get a lift back with someone.'

But Pel was reluctant to leave and stood watching as the tape measures came out and distances were set down; as photographs were taken; as Cham stared up and down the motorway, deep in thought, making calculations in his mind.

'What sort of vehicle are we looking for?' Pomereu asked.

'Squarish bonnet, judging by the injuries,' Cham said. 'He's been hit on the head by something with a corner to it and then again by something long and narrow. One of those arms that hold protruding rear mirrors on trucks, perhaps? So it was a heavy vehicle, but not so heavy it couldn't go fast. Not a truck, I'd say.'

The radio in Darcy's car began to squawk. He leaned over and spoke into the microphone. Slamming it back into place, he crossed to where Pel was standing, huddled in his coat against the wind and the rain.

'Another raid by the Tuaregs, *patron*. All night garage at Saint-Blas. That's just north of here. It could have been them who did this – in a hurry, heading down the motorway to make their getaway.'

The wind dropped during the night, and the next morning was bright but cold enough for Pel to look like a polar bear wearing woollies. He already had Cham's description of the victim of the motorway. It had been on his desk when he arrived. 'Height

43

– one hundred and eighty centimetres. Slightly built. Age sixty-five to seventy. Thinning grey hair. Blue eyes. False teeth. Narrow nose. Appendicitis scar. Arthritis in joints.'

It was difficult to know which of the two cases that had come up to go for first – the hit and run or the hold-up at Talant – so they left Cham to complete his checks on the motorway victim and went to Talant.

As the manager of the supermarket had suggested, Madame Folieux, the old lady whose car had been almost run down, was able to tell them nothing.

'It was a car like mine,' she said.

'What sort have you got?'

'I don't know. My son bought it for me. He had to go to North Africa for a year on business, so he put me on the telephone and bought me a television and a new car.'

'What sort is it, Nosjean?' Pel said.

Nosjean grinned. It was a tiny Peugeot 205.

'Well, it was the same colour,' she said.

The car used in the raid on the all-night garage at St-Blas had been found abandoned at Goray just off the motorway. There it was, a Peugeot 604, standing in the square underneath the trees.

'Get anything from it?' Pel asked.

'A lot of fingerprints, *patron*,' Prélat said. 'But it's my guess they all belong to the owner and his family. There are too many for them to belong to the Tuaregs.'

'Whose is the car?'

It turned out to belong to an architect in Dijon and it had been stolen from outside his office in the Rue Général Leclerc. It was undamaged.

'Village cop found it,' Nosjean reported. 'From what Cham said, I'd have expected smashed headlights, a dent or two, a spot of blood. But there's nothing. It's clean. It wasn't the car that killed the old boy at Mailly-les-Temps. Prélat says there are marks that indicate they were using gloves.'

"That fits with what the girl at Talant said. How about the till there? Did he find anything?'

'A single print. But badly smudged. I've put it into the computer but I don't expect anything. I feel certain they're young-sters and new to the game, though it's only a hunch.'

Pel nodded. He had a great respect for hunches when they came from someone as bright as Nosjean.

'It looks as though we've got to think again about the old boy on the motorway,' he said. 'I'll see if Cham's come up with anything new.'

Cham had.

When Pel arrived in his office, he was just taking off his coat. He had been down the motorway again to look at the scene of the previous night's incident.

'What were you expecting to find?' Pel asked.

'I don't know.' Cham shrugged. 'Something, perhaps.'

'Isn't that Forensic's job?'

Cham smiled. 'Probably it is. But two heads are always better than one.'

'Find anything?'

'I don't know. There wasn't much blood. I noticed that last night. That's why I went to have another look. There should have been some and I'd have expected to see signs of smearing if he'd been dragged or flung along the road for instance. Something like that. I'd have expected to find traces.'

'What's all this leading to?'

'Not to. From. It's leading from the way I've been thinking. I'm having second thoughts. He was hit by something, that's a fact. I found tiny fragments of glass embedded in his scalp. That indicates headlights. His skull was fractured. He also had two broken legs. I'd have expected more if he'd been hit by a fast-moving car. Broken shoulders. Broken neck. Heavy graz-ings on the face. After all, a fast-moving car hitting a man would break bones to start with, then there would be more broken when he hit the road after being flung into the air. There would also be multiple grazing and contusions.'

'And there aren't any?'

'Nothing that would fit with a fast-moving car hitting him. There was one other thing. As I've said, he had two broken legs. Both tibiae. And both in the same place. And that's odd. You'd expect in a hit and run for them to be broken in different places. But they weren't. I think his legs had been run over.'

45

'Run over?'

'One of his shoes was wrenched off – it's disappeared – but there are also tyre marks on his trousers. Below the knee. I'll let you have photographs. I think you can identify the type of tyre even.'

Pel frowned.'How does a hit and run driver manage to run over a man's legs? They usually knock them flying.'

'I don't think now it *was* a hit and run,' Cham said doggedly. 'He was run over by a car, certainly, but he must have already been lying in the road. Drunk, perhaps? He had a fair percentage of alcohol in him and he smelled of whisky. His hair especially. Why his hair? You don't imbibe it through the ear. But he hadn't drunk enormously. Enough to make him sloshed but not enough to be paralytic. Certainly not as much as I'd have expected. Do you want the exact amount?'

'In the report.' Pel didn't believe in clouding his thinking by having too many details too early in a case.

'There were also traces of nembutal in the stomach. Sleeping tablets, I expect. You're not supposed to take those with alcohol but old people sometimes do. They take them and forget what they've done and take another. That's probably what he did. It would be enough to make him confused. It begins to look as if he was staggering about and fell down and was hit by a car, but though his legs were broken they weren't compound fractures. There was no perforation of the flesh by splintered bone, which I'd have expected if he'd been hit by a fast-moving car. There was one other thing: when we removed his clothes, we found he wasn't wearing underwear. No vest. No underpants. Just shirt, trousers, waistcoat and jacket. All with empty pockets. Shirt and jacket buttoned up wrongly, waistcoat unbuttoned and inside out. No socks. One shoe.'

'Any laundry-marks on his shirt?'

'No. None. He either did his own laundry or took it to a laundrette.'

'Unless some neighbour did it for him. Go on.'

'Suit – good quality. You can tell by the finish. It wasn't off the peg at Nouvelles Galeries. It was made by a good tailor. Probably in Paris.'

'How do you know it was probably from Paris?'

'When I qualified, my father took me to his tailor and had me a suit made. It was a wonderful suit. Cost him a fortune. I dropped a tin of paint down it decorating my house when I got married six months later. Ruined it.'

'Did it have the tailor's name in it?'

'Of course it did.'

'Not yours, the man on the motorway's.'

'Oh! It had had one but it had obviously come away. The remains of the stitching were there. It was an old suit. A very old suit.'

'So what we've got is a man of sixty-five to seventy who could afford – once upon a time, anyway – to wear good suits, probably made in Paris.'

'That's about it. He must have driven to where he was found, too, so his car's around somewhere, waiting to be picked up. Where he was found isn't near anywhere. It's between Mailly-les-Temps on one side of the motorway and Ponchet on the other. But not near enough to either for him to have walked from one of them – staggered would be nearer, because he appeared to have been drinking a lot. Perhaps he found he was too drunk to drive and decided to leave his car and walk it off.'

'Where to?'

'To wherever he was going.'

'Nothing at all in his pockets to indicate who he was?'

'No.' Cham frowned. 'Just a one-franc piece, a few centimes, a dirty handkerchief, and inside the lining of a jacket pocket a bent card which indicated he was a member of the Club Atlantique de Royan.'

'Club Atlantique de Royan? That's on the east coast and miles away. It sounds like one of these summer things where they get people doing exercises on the beach. It won't be going at this time of the year.'

'It looks like an old card.'

'Plastic?'

'Yes.'

'Any fingerprints?'

'Prélat says a few. But they're smeared, and one on top of another. He picked up two. Both the same. They're the dead man's. I suspect it's one he used some time when he was on

47

holiday and it was tucked away in the lining and was over-looked when his pockets were emptied – deliberately in my view.'

'Is there a name on it? These clubs usually demand the owner signs them, like banker's cards.'

'There's no signature on this one. But there is a number – 579.'

'Any year?'

'No year. It'll mean looking up number 579 for a few years back.'

'Charming.' Pel sighed. 'Well, we'll check. We'll check at Mailly-les-Temps too. It's the nearest place. He might have done his drinking there and wandered off in a stupor. Perhaps his home was the other side of the motorway and he was drunk enough not to worry about crossing it.'

'There's just one more thing,' Cham said. 'If he was lying flat in the road – as he must have been to get his legs smashed as they were, how did he get the head injuries?'

'Could the car that ran over his legs have thrown him up underneath? So that his head came into contact with the under-side? It might have, if it were travelling fast.'

Cham frowned. 'In that case, I'd have expected to find oil in the wound,' he said. 'Grease. Dried mud. The sort of things you get from under a car. There was nothing to indicate that was what happened. There were two indentations in the skull. Something more solid than a glass headlight hit him, something hard and heavy. Then something else like an attachment on a car. Yet there are no flakes of paint around the wound as I'd have expected. Yet' – Cham frowned, puzzled – 'there were slivers of glass as if he *had* been caught by the headlights or the windscreen. The injuries just don't seem to match up. And why no underwear or socks?'

'We'll get the local radio to put out a story. We'll need to know if anybody saw this type lying in the road. There couldn't have been many cars at that time of night but somebody might have spotted him.'

'I'll bet we don't get much,' Cham said heavily. 'If somebody did see him, they'd ignore him. They'd think he was a dummy shoved into the road by a hold-up merchant to persuade someone to stop so he could step out from the darkness and stick a pistol up their nose. Or they'd think he was a drunk, and who'd want to pick up a drunk? When you'd got him in the car he'd want to start a fight with you or be sick all over the back seat.'

Pel sighed. It was true enough. You didn't normally find people lying around on a motorway, except when there'd been a million-car pile-up in the fog and then you found you were knee deep in stiffs.

4

Nobody was missing from Mailly-les-Temps. Nor from Ponchet, on the other side of the motorway. And no one appeared to have noticed anybody drunk or getting drunk enough to collapse and be run over. Finally, no motorist had appeared who claimed to have seen the body lying on the road.

Perhaps it just happened that the dead man had fallen on the motorway just in time to be hit and no one had seen him until the cruising police car had found him. On the other hand, perhaps someone *had* seen him and, scared of the things that happened to motorists who stopped to offer help to stranded travellers, had preferred to ignore him.

'So where did he come from?' Pel surreptitiously reached for a cigarette from Darcy's packet that lay on his desk. Darcy saw him and gave the packet a push. Pel sighed, deciding he was weak-willed and probably even feeble-minded. Anybody who was willing to smoke himself to death couldn't be all there.

'Could he have been put out of a car?' Darcy asked. 'Gangsters getting rid of an unwelcome friend? They're the only types I can think of who would empty a man's pockets deliberately. On their way from Paris, for instance, to confer with allies in Marseilles. They do that these days, *patron*.'

They did indeed. In the old days of horse travel you could reckon your killer, even if he were only the driver of a hit-and-run horse and cart, couldn't have travelled far from his crime in twenty-four hours. Nowadays you could kill someone in Paris and be in Marseilles a few hours later. Even, for that matter, in America. Travel was so fast these days, alibis where minutes or hours counted were hard to break down.

'It would account for the head injury, *patron*.'

'Not quite. Cham says there was glass in the wound. And that' – Pel frowned – 'that seems to take us back to a car headlight or a car windscreen. Cham thinks he wasn't dragged by a car – as he would be, for instance, if his clothes snagged on something – and he says there wasn't a lot of blood where he was found.'

'Which seems to indicate that he didn't die there, *patron*. Those injuries to his head would certainly have produced blood. And if it wasn't on the motorway, where was it? There was no rain to wash it away. That, *patron*, seems to indicate he was killed somewhere else.'

'And that,' Pel said firmly, as though it were something they had been working towards for some time, 'seems to indicate that what we've got isn't a hit and run at all. It's murder or manslaughter.'

As they talked, there was a tap on the door. It was Claudie Darel. Both of them smiled at her. Everybody in the Hôtel de Police smiled at Claudie, though by this time everybody had given up hope of winning her.

'It's De Troq', *patron*,' she said. 'He's with Nosjean in Volnay-le-Grand. They were called there by the local police brigadier. They've got a man there. He's admitted hitting the man on the motorway with his car.'

Pel and Darcy stared at each other. Hit and run after all! Back to square one.

His name was Emile Jourdain and he was an estate agent. He had been to a family celebration at Poitonne and had had too much to drink. His friends had tried to persuade him to stay the night but he had insisted on going home. He was a middle-aged man with a fat flabby body, two or three chins and watery eyes. He looked the sort of man who drank too much.

De Troq', slightly built, neat and handsome, met them at the door of the substation and jerked his head in Jourdain's direction. 'He's not one of the Tuaregs,' he observed. 'Those boys move fast and I don't think this type could move fast if he tried.'

'Where's Nosjean?'

'Morbihaux. We think one of the cars that were used in the Talant hold-up's turned up. We'd worked out one of them must have been a souped-up Citroën 19 and there was one standing in the square at Morbihaux underneath the wall of the church. The owner of the bar reported it. It's been there for three days – ever since the Talant hold-up, I imagine. We've asked Fingerprints to have a look at it. There's also an old boy who uses the bar who remembers seeing another car there before it appeared. We think *that* one might have been the car the Tuaregs changed to from the getaway car.'

'Is it a firm identification?'

'Not by any means, *patron*. The old boy noticed a Ford Sierra 2000 parked under the trees. It was there all day. Next day on his way to the bar he noticed it had gone but near where it had stood was the Citroën 19. We've checked it. Stolen in Latou. No fingerprints. It belongs to a lawyer there.'

'And the Sierra?'

'Fawn-brown. They produced a lot that colour. The old boy didn't think to take the number because at the time he didn't think anything of it. Later, he wondered if somebody had driven into the square in the Citroën and left it there and driven away in the Sierra. It's what we think the Tuaregs have been doing. Nosjean's checking if something of the sort was done after the St-Blas hold-up and the other places. He's also checking if the Sierra's been seen anywhere else. It might give an indication of where they operate from.'

Pel nodded and gestured at the man sitting in the police office waiting for them. 'We'd better see our friend there,' he said. 'Has he admitted knocking down the type on the motorway?'

'Well, not quite, *patron*. We got dragged in because we were looking for the Tuaregs after the St-Blas hold-up. He's admitted hitting *someone* on the motorway near Mailly but not to knocking him down.'

Pel looked puzzled. Jourdain, the man waiting in the office, enlightened him.

'I had to get back,' he explained. 'I run a business and my secretary's off ill. She's got this influenza bug that's going around and I couldn't leave the office shut all day. You know how it is when you've got responsibilities.'

Pel said nothing and Jourdain spread his hands as though trying to show he had the stigmata. 'And when you've had one or two drinks, responsibilities seem more important than ever. I decided to drive slowly for safety and I knew if I went down the motorway I'd be home in no time. But you know what modern cars are like. It's hard to keep the speed down. It creeps up, especially when there's an empty road in front and nobody in sight. I wasn't going fast but I wasn't going slow either. I live here in Volnay, which is only about forty kilometres from Poitonne, and I thought I was nearly home.'

He drew a deep breath and blew his nose. 'Then, just after I passed the Mailly turn-off, I saw this thing in the road. I thought it was a dead donkey or something. It was just lying there. I must have dropped off and was half-asleep. You know how these long empty roads affect you. I was over it before I knew what had happened. I felt the bump. Well, two bumps. I'd gone over him.'

'Which wheels?'

'Right wheels. I tried to slow down and swerve at the last minute. He was lying near the verge.'

'Which way round? Head to the centre of the road? Or feet?'

'Feet.'

'He wasn't kneeling?'

'No. Why?'

'He had head injuries. If he were lying flat in the road and you just ran over his legs, how did he get them?'

'I don't know. He was flat when I saw him. I only saw him for a second in the headlights. He wasn't wearing light clothing. Then I was over him and on. I was scared but when I looked in the rear view mirror I couldn't see anything. You can't at night, can you?' Jourdain paused. 'Well, that's not true. I did see something. Just momentarily. But it looked just as it did when I'd first seen it. I was a bit scared and just drove on. I tried to persuade myself it was a tarpaulin that had blown off a heavy truck. They do sometimes. They're quite dangerous.'

'Not as dangerous as drunk drivers,' Darcy growled.

Jourdain gave him a pained look. 'Well, no. But I thought if it were a man there'd have been a bigger bump.'

'So what did you decide it was in the end?'

'Somebody's goat or something like that. A big dog that had wandered on to the motorway.'

'But you knew it wasn't a goat or a dog or a tarpaulin, didn't you?' Pel said.

Jourdain nodded. 'Yes,' he agreed heavily. 'I knew.'

'Why didn't you report it?'

'I was scared.'

'So why did you in the end.'

'Because I was still scared. At first I thought I'd got away with it. Then Jean Amentaëz said something about a man being killed on the motorway near Mailly-les-Temps by a hit-and-run driver. He came into my office. He has the shop next door and goes up the motorway early in the morning to collect things. They were just clearing the scene, he said. There were cars and vans and things. He asked about it. His wife's brother's a cop and he'd heard about it. And then I knew what I'd done. In the end I couldn't stand it any longer and went along and saw his brother-in-law. He telephoned somebody and then these two young policemen of yours arrived. They were decent enough, I must say. And now you've come.'

They let him have his say, then they sat back and looked at him.

'Better tell us what you saw,' Pel said.

'I've told you.'

'Tell us again. With more detail.'

Jourdain went over it again. 'I was driving home,' he said. 'And then I saw this thing in the road and realized I'd been dropping asleep. I'm sorry about that and I expect I'll probably go to prison or get fined, at least. But he must have been as drunk as I was to be lying there.'

'How was he lying?' Pel asked.

'Well, he was just – well, lying.'

'How?'

'In the road.'

'On his back? On his side? On his face?'

'On his back. Feet to the road. I remember seeing his feet

sticking up. He couldn't have done that if he'd been lying on his face, could he? Not unless he was deformed.'

Jourdain gave a little snigger at his feeble joke but nobody smiled.

'What about the rest of him?'

'I didn't see his face. He seemed just to be lying on his back.'

'Feet apart?'

'They must have been because I felt two distinct bumps.'

'Arms?'

'I didn't notice. I was past and it was gone into the darkness behind too quickly.'

'You didn't stop at all?'

'I slowed down a bit, thinking I ought to stop, but then I changed my mind and went on. Lost my nerve, I suppose. What will they do to me?'

'They'll charge you,' Darcy said bluntly.

'What with?'

'They've got several choices. Manslaughter, for a start. Drunk in charge. Failing to report an accident. Failing to go to the assistance of a citizen in distress. That's under Section 63. What about your insurance? Is that in order, because if it isn't you're in trouble with that, too.'

'Holy Mother of God!'

'Take it easy,' Darcy said drily. 'They might think up one to cover blasphemy as well.'

While Jourdain was making a statement inside, they went out-side and examined his car. It was one of the big Citroëns, the sort of car a man would have who liked to be noticed. There were no marks on it.

'Anything underneath?'

'No, *patron*,' De Troq' said. 'I had it down to the garage along the street and they put it up on the lift. I could find nothing. Perhaps Forensic'll find something, but there's nothing obvious.'

Pel frowned. 'I don't suppose there would be, would there, if he simply ran over his legs. Besides, it's a streamlined car. Not the sort to cause the wounds Cham found. So he can't be

55

charged with manslaughter. Driving under the influence, failing to report an accident, all the rest, yes. But not with killing him. All he did was pass over his legs with his right wheels. Nothing else touched him. And, as Cham's suggested, the man must have been dead already.'

There was plenty to occupy them. Statements had been taken and reports had been written and everything had been passed to the *Procureur*. The next step was for the *juge d'instruction* he assigned to the case to join the party.

In his office, Pel picked up the paper. The bribery cases in Lyons had reached the front page. 'LYONS COPS ARRAIGNED' one of the headlines said. 'BRIBERY ACCUSATIONS MADE.'

Pel shrugged and tossed the paper aside. They'd all been expecting it. But nobody liked it. For a while, after such a case, everybody assumed that all cops were corrupt. He'd talked to the Chief about it and the Chief had been wary.

'That chap, Misset,' he said. 'Haven't you suspected him of this sort of thing?'

'I've suspected he's passed information to the newspapers,' Pel admitted. 'But I've never pinned it down.'

'He'd better be watched. We can't risk anything just now. After this, they'll be looking out for it. You'd better be nice to the Press for a change.'

Back in his office, Pel summoned the city newsmen in for a chat. They were Sarrazin, the freelance and the moving spirit among the press in the city; Henriot of *Le Bien Public*, the local rag; Fiabon, of *France Dimanche*. Ducrot, of *France Soir*, was down with flu. Between them, with linage, they represented almost every newspaper and agency in the country.

Pel indicated the line of chairs and beamed on them. It wasn't a great success as an exercise in sycophancy. Pel wasn't very good at stooping to the Press, and the smile he offered looked more like the smile of a tiger spotting a victim. When he offered brandy, they seemed to think something was wrong and looked quickly at each other. As they all tossed it back, however, they seemed to feel reassured.

Pel explained their dilemma. 'If anybody saw anything,' he said, 'we want him to come forward.'

'It's as good as done, *patron*,' Sarrazin said, and that meant the others would follow his example. 'There's just one thing.'

Pel knew what was coming. Sarrazin never gave anything away without a collateral.

'These hold-ups, Chief. The Tuaregs. There've been a lot of them. Eight to my reckoning.'

'None of them big,' Darcy said.

'No. None of them big. But they're using shotguns. When do you expect to nail them, Chief?'

'When do you expect a big scoop to appear?' Pel asked mildly.

'When one turns up.'

'That's when we expect to nail the Tuaregs. When what we're after turns up.'

'What are you hoping will turn up, Chief? We might be able to help.'

Pel considered. They were looking for a fawn-coloured Sierra 2000, number unknown, but perhaps now wasn't the time to make that information public property. Armed with it, the Tuaregs would know at once the car could lead to them and would promptly get rid of it.

'Nothing,' he said. 'Nothing special. We've got a good team on it, though. Nosjean and De Troquereau. You know them both. They'll turn something up. There's a lot of luck in police work just as there is in newspapers.'

They accepted the parallel and went away, satisfied, to make much of what they'd got. It would be in the columns the next day; with an updated description of the man on the motorway and an appeal for anyone who knew him to come forward.

As they left, Pel headed back to his own office, considering he was entitled to a surreptitious drag at a cigarette and a glance at the paper. As he passed her office, Claudie Darel looked up and grinned. 'You've got a visitor, *patron*,' she said.

Pel scowled. He didn't feel like visitors just then. He was hoping to enjoy a little peace and quiet in the comfort of his office – large, to go with his rank, comfortable chair, carpet colour of his choice, and a picture on the wall. He didn't like the picture and the only colours they had had to offer for the

57

carpet made him feel sick, but he had come to regard the place as a snug little bolt-hole to get away from people and do a little thinking.

It was Judge Brisard, he supposed, with his fat behind, big hips, smarmy manner and holier-than-thou attitude. The vendetta had been going on from the day when Brisard, new to the job, had first swum into Pel's firmament. Pel usually led on points because behind his sour-innocent expression there was a lot of experience and a measure of deep cunning that Brisard could only match with spite. Pel didn't bear him any ill will – only, perhaps, hoped he would drop dead – and he felt too tired and too riddled with what he was sure was influenza to be bothered with Brisard just then.

But it wasn't Brisard. It was a young woman. She was small and dark and had the sort of figure that went in and out in all the right places. She looked round as Pel appeared and rose to hold out her hand. Her smile dazzled Pel. He wasn't used to having attractive young women smiling at him.

'Ghislaine Castéou,' she said. 'I've just come over to introduce myself.'

For a moment, Pel was at a loss, then the penny dropped and he understood the meaning of Claudie Darel's grin. She knew who Ghislaine Castéou was, had probably been introduced to her by her boy friend, Bruno Lucas, from the Palais de Justice.

'You're Judge Polverari's relief,' he said.

'That's right.'

Pel was thrown into a panic. Beautiful young women weren't normally among the perks offered to ageing chief inspectors, and he was about to start roaring for Claudie to bring coffee when she appeared, with the coffee service they kept for special visitors. None of your thick mugs. She was doing her best to see the newcomer was impressed.

Pel flapped a little. 'Castéou,' he said. 'I know that name.'

'My husband, I expect,' she said. 'Armand Castéou. Ballistics.'

'Got him. Gunsmith. He pinned down that murder at St-Denis. I thought he'd given up.'

58

'He's set up as a consultant. He leaves the gunsmith work to a manager. He's so busy.'

'I got on well with Judge Polverari,' Pel said as he poured coffee. 'We were good friends.'

'I hope we will be, too,' Judge Castéou said. 'I know Judge Polverari well. He's my uncle, in fact. He helped me get the job. He's a great admirer of yours. He said there was nowhere better than here to learn the job. I was a junior in Marseilles, but there are so many there you get lost among them. I preferred somewhere I could take a bit of responsibility.'

'You've met Judge Brisard, I suppose?'

'Yes.' The reply was so short and unadorned Pel could only assume that she liked Judge Brisard no more than he did himself. It pleased him to think he might have an ally.

'I shan't get in your hair,' Judge Castéou said.

Pel didn't know whether to be pleased or not. He couldn't stand *juges d'instruction* sitting on his shoulder like vultures after carrion, but he felt Ghislaine Castéou could sit on his shoulder any time.

'I hope we can work together,' she went on. 'My uncle said you worked best left alone. I'll do what I'm supposed to do and leave the rest to you.'

He explained about the motorway case and she listened carefully, sitting close to him as he handed her the statements they'd prepared. Her perfume made him dizzy.

He was still bright-eyed when he arrived home. Yves Pasquier, aged twelve, from next door, was in the road when he drove up. His dog was with him and as usual Pel spoke to the wrong end. It was the original shaggy dog and it was hard to tell which end bit and which wagged.

'He's pleased to see you,' the boy encouraged. 'The evening paper says you're trying to identify a man hit by a car on the motorway.' He always took an interest in what Pel was doing because he had every intention of becoming a policeman himself. 'Was it going fast?'

'Not particularly.'

'Was there a lot of blood?'

For once Pel could answer honestly. 'Not this time.'

'They can always tell who did it, can't they? They search for

59

flakes of paint and match them up with the damaged part of the car.'

'Not in this case.'

'Why not?'

'There weren't any.'

'Oh! Was he a crook?'

It was a possibility, Pel felt, but he refused to commit himself.

'You never know, though, do you?' the boy said. 'I mean, look at the Count of Monte Cristo.'

'Who?'

'I'm reading this book. Monsieur Balanais – he teaches us literature – he says we ought to read French classics. So I found this book on the shelf. It's about a man who pretends to be something he isn't. He's actually a sailor and he's put in prison falsely. But he escapes and finds a lot of money, so he calls himself the Count of Monte Cristo and sets out to ruin his enemies. He does, too. You can never tell, can you? Your man might be a count.'

'He might,' Pel agreed. 'But I don't think he is. He's more likely just an old man who was sick and confused. He was lying on the motorway when he was hit.'

'Drunk?'

'It's possible.'

Satisfied with the daily report, the boy wandered off and Pel headed for the house. Madame Routy opened the door for him. It was as if she'd been waiting behind it ready to stab him.

'What have you spoiled for dinner tonight?' he asked.

'Nothing that you need to worry about,' she retorted, taking his briefcase and putting it down. 'You wouldn't know what good food tastes like.'

Pel nodded and she nodded back. It was another little daily ceremony taken care of. Pel and Madame Routy had been insulting each other from the day she had first turned up at his house as a new housekeeper. She had been found for him by his sister who was married to an outfitter in Chatillon. His sister had been worried that if he weren't looked after his clothes would eventually begin to smell as if they'd been boiled in the soup.

His wife had also just arrived home and was pouring aperitifs. As they sat down, she turned up the record player so they could hear a little Mahler while they drank and talked. It was very comfortable, Pel felt – except for Mahler.

'I hear Judge Polverari's relief's arrived,' Madame said.

He wondered how the hell she had found out. 'That's right,' he agreed.

'It's a woman, isn't it?'

'Yes, it is.'

'Is she nice?'

'I got on very well with her.'

'Pretty?'

'Not very.'

Madame laughed. 'Go on with you,' she said. 'She came into the salon this morning for a shampoo and set before she came to see you. She was nervous and wanted to look her best. Sylvie did it. She's gorgeous.'

As Pel settled down at home, Darcy was settling down in the Relais St-Armand. Opposite him was a girl.

That was usual enough for Darcy. But he was looking at this one thoughtfully. She was tall and slender and she was regarding him as though he were important. Darcy had known many girls. With a profile like a matinée idol and teeth that shone like jewels in a Disney cartoon, he had pretty well everything in his favour, so it wasn't difficult. Girls had a tendency to fall at his feet and there had been times when he had had to fight them off. This one, Angélique Courtoise, though, had been around a long time. He had met her first when he had been involved in a drugs investigation at the university and they had got on like a house on fire at once. There had been interruptions since, of course, but somehow Darcy always came back to her.

'Busy?' she asked.

'We're always busy.'

'Too busy to telephone?'

Darcy managed to look contrite. 'You'd be surprised what a rotten world it is.'

'It's the television,' she observed cheerfully. 'That and porn videos. Your time must be very full.'

Darcy frowned at the teasing. He was at the peak of his ability

61

but somehow he felt things weren't as right as they should be. He had always felt he knew how to manage his life and Pel didn't, but now that Pel had married he seemed to have settled down. He was as miserable as ever as a cop and just as relentless in his crusade against criminals, but there was a comfortable core to him these days that Darcy felt he ought to have, too – and didn't.

Nobody had given Pel much hope of success at the time he had first met his wife in the Relais St-Armand because he had always been regarded in the Hôtel de Police as a dead loss where women were concerned. But Darcy had seen the possibilities in the Widow Faivre-Perret and had put his oar in occasionally to help the affair along. It had been well worth it, too, because nowadays there were occasional days when Pel wasn't in a bad temper. He looked at Angélique Courtoise and wondered if she had chosen the Relais St-Armand because of what it had done for Pel.

'Why didn't you ever get married?' he asked.

She looked at him and smiled. 'I very nearly did,' she said. 'If you remember, when you first appeared on the scene I was about to be. At least I was engaged. You managed to persuade me my fiancé wasn't suitable.'

'You didn't argue much. Did you ever have anything in common with him?'

'Well, he wasn't a cop and I was working for Professor Foussier at the time, so I suppose I did a bit. I must have. After all, we got engaged.'

'It didn't last long.'

'Not after you turned up.' She looked shrewdly at him. 'Is something worrying you?'

'Probably.' Darcy paused. 'A type called Goriot.'

'Who's he?'

'A detective inspector. He was one of those who were injured in that explosion in the Impasse Tarien. He's recently been declared fit and he's back shoving his nose into things. He doesn't like me.'

'Does it worry you?'

'A bit.'

'I didn't think you worried about anything. Not even me.'

Darcy reached out and laid his hand on hers. She gave him a grateful look.

'That's why I keep turning up,' he explained. 'Because I *don't have to worry* about you.'

'You might have to one of these days,' she said seriously. 'I'm twenty-eight now. It's a nervous age for a girl. She begins to feel she might miss the bus. And buses keep coming past, you know. Good-looking buses with big cars and lots of money. *They* seem to need reassurance, too.'

5

Misset's enquiries hadn't progressed much. In fact, they had
stood quite still. Chiefly because Misset found the Bar de la
Petite Alsacienne of much more interest than Aloïs Ferry whom
his neighbour, Raymond Jouet, had accused of damaging his
garden.

The barmaid was watching two men playing billiards. She
kept looking sideways at Misset and he felt she was interested
in him. She'd been eyeing him sideways a lot lately. She was
wearing a yellow dress with a plunging neckline that gave him
a view down her front almost to her navel every time she bent
to pick up a glass, and she seemed to be aware that he'd
noticed.

He wondered what it would be like to be married to her.
There should be tests for marriage, he felt. You had to have a
test before you could drive a car; you ought to have one before
you got married. Misset had thought he was marrying a Deux
Chevaux and had found he'd married a tank.

Someone had put a coin in the juke box and it was clattering
away to the strains of what sounded like 'We go up the stairs.
We go up the stairs.' There should also, Misset thought sourly,
be a juke box where you could put in a coin and get five
minutes' silence.

The girl behind the bar looked up again. She had eyes like a
spaniel, big and brown and damp-looking. Her mouth looked
soft and warm – Madame Misset's mouth was like a rat trap –
and it intrigued him. Though not half as much as her bust.
Misset couldn't take his eyes off her bust and had even started

to fantasize about it. It was much more interesting than Jouet's garden.

He sighed and decided he'd better do something. Finishing his beer, he headed for Jouet's house. The same two cars he'd seen before – Councillor Lax's and Senator Forton's – were parked along the road. They were seeing a lot of each other lately, he decided. They must be up to some funny financial business or something.

Jouet's garden looked no better. If anything it looked worse. The brown patches Misset had noticed on the lawn seemed more numerous than before and appeared to be spreading into each other. Before long the lawn would be one large bare patch. The flowers didn't look very healthy either. But Misset could find nothing to connect to the damage that was being done, and Ferry had noticed him prowling around and was becoming hostile. He was doing something to the engine of the ancient blue Peugeot as Misset halted.

'What do you do for a living?' Misset asked as they met at his front gate.

Ferry looked round, peering through his thick spectacles. 'What's what I do for a living to do with atomic fall-out or whatever it is you're investigating?' he demanded.

Misset improvised rapidly. 'There's some theory that men can bring home noxious substances on their overalls,' he said. 'They pick them up at work and they get scattered as the man takes the overalls off.'

'I don't wear overalls.'

'Oh!'

Ferry gave Misset a long hard look full of suspicion. 'You're pretty nosy for a government inspector,' he said.

'Government inspectors *are* nosy,' Misset agreed. 'It's their job. You have to be.'

'Who's your boss?'

'Chief Inspec . . .' Misset stopped. 'Type called Pel,' he said. 'Evariste Pel.'

'Tells you what to do, does he?'

'Yes.'

'Runs the show? Responsible?'

'Yes.'

'Lives round here, does he?'

'Leu. Big house there. Married a woman with money. She runs that beauty parlour in the Rue de la Liberté. What sort of truck do you drive?'

Ferry shrugged. 'Usual sort. You know, four wheels – those round things – and a steering wheel.'

'Who for?'

'Trudis.'

Trudis was a large transport firm covering the whole of Eastern France and one of their main bases was in the city. Ferry gestured. 'They use everything from eight-wheelers with trailers to small vans for delivering light-weight packages.'

'Which sort do you drive?'

'One of the little ones.'

'Make much money at it?'

'Not these days.'

'Why not?'

'I've been stood off. Shortage of orders.'

In Pel's office they were taking another look at the dead man on the motorway. They still didn't know who he was but the fact that the case had been taken over by Judge Castéou confirmed that they no longer regarded him as just another item in the Chief's Missing Persons enquiry.

The number on the card found in his pocket had produced nothing. The police in Royan, as they had expected, had informed them that the Club Atlantique was nothing but a small affair operating from a hut on the beach, with a bar and a couple of showers, and that its members were usually holiday-makers in the town for the month of August.

'Geriatrics trying to get their bellies off,' they said. 'You know the types. They do an hour's gentle exercise, then leave the beach at lunchtime to fill up again with food and wine and go home at the end of the month weighing exactly the same as when they arrived but feeling they've done themselves good. The club used to close down for the winter but people have got into this callisthenics business in a big way lately, and it goes on these days with a few locals during the winter.'

'Telephone?'

'They haven't got one. They've just moved into a new place. It's an old barn, I think, and they're still putting the roof on and the windows in.'

'So,' Pel asked as Darcy put the telephone down and they sat back. 'Who is he?'

It was a good question. The man on the motorway hadn't come from Mailly-les-Temps or Ponchet and nobody had reported an abandoned car which could possibly have belonged to him. So where *had* he come from? And why had he such severe head wounds, in which glass splinters as if from headlights had been found, if – as Jourdain insisted – he'd been lying flat on the motorway when he'd been hit. According to Cham, the broken legs were explainable, the head wounds were not.

'I can only think,' Darcy said, 'that somehow he was hit by a car while he was stooping or on his knees – drunk – and that caused the head injuries. This spun him round and he landed flat on his back. Then, while he was lying there, our friend, Jourdain, ran over him.'

'In that case,' Pel asked, 'where's the blood? There was little on the road. And who hit him the first time? Jourdain can be charged with being drunk in charge and with failing to report an accident. But he can't be charged with manslaughter. In which case, who can? He obviously didn't do it himself. And who in God's name is he?'

'He wasn't young,' Cham said. 'But he was reasonably well preserved, though he had false teeth. They were still in his mouth, incidentally.' He frowned. 'Which also is odd,' he continued. 'I'd have expected if he'd been hit on the head by a car moving at speed they'd have been jerked out of his mouth. It's not hard to lose your dentures by accident. In fact, it's remarkably easy. I had an uncle who played a practical joke on a friend while boating on the lake at Evron and it was so successful and he laughed so hard his false teeth fell into the water.'

'I once saw a man at a symphony concert,' Darcy added, 'who was so bored and yawned so hard his dentures *jumped* out. Made a hell of a clatter when they hit the floor.'

'Which,' Cham said, smiling, 'is why I don't understand this

67

type's dentures still being in place. He was struck a blow on the side and back of the head, it seems by a car travelling at speed. That would be enough to knock anybody's dentures out.'

'Eyes, too, I reckon,' Nosjean murmured.

Pel was thoughtful. 'We have a lot of odd factors here,' he said. 'This business of the teeth. The absence of socks and underwear. The shirt buttoned up wrongly. The waistcoat inside out. Let's keep all these things to ourselves. Just in case. They're not to be included in anything that's handed out to the press. What else do we know of him?'

'I found an appendicitis scar and a kidney op. scar,' Cham pointed out. 'Numerous scars on his wrists.'

'Suicide attempts?'

'I'd say not. They seem to run the wrong way for attempts to slash a vein. There was one other thing. I noticed also he had flat feet.'

'I think I've got flat feet,' Pel said.

'The knuckles at the root of the big toes protruded,' Cham went on. 'A condition known as hallux valgus. There was only one shoe – the left – but I noticed the sole was built up slightly on the inside. That gave me a clue. It was an attempt to help him walk on the outside of the foot. There's probably a similar build-up on the missing right shoe. It indicates flat feet, which is a deformity in which the arches of the feet are impaired. It's caused generally by long periods of standing and is often found in policemen, waiters, domestic servants and hospital nurses. Come to that, so are varicose veins and piles.'

'They say Napoleon suffered from piles,' Darcy said.

'It was that long walk all the way back from Moscow.'

Cham grinned. 'It used to be much more common in the old days, due to the lack of proper diets, which affected the bones, but we've overcome that problem these days. It's also liable to occur after a fracture of the ankle and it causes pain along the under and inner part of the foot.'

'No wonder my feet ache,' Pomereu muttered.

'It should be treated early by massage and exercises. Patent supports are sometimes worn but they simply stretch the tendons and ligaments further.'

Pel was listening quietly to the exchanges. 'This built-up sole,' he said. 'It would have to be done by a shoe repairer, wouldn't it? Let's try a few, Daniel. One might have his address.'

Pel was right and Lagé was put on the job. He was growing fat but he was always a willing worker – so much so, Misset often got him to do *his* work. Lagé was easy-going and never complained, but he was patient and one of the best they had when it came to long-winded enquiries. As it happened, this one started off well. He found the shoe repairer who had built up the sole of the dead man's shoe late in the afternoon. His shop was in the St-Alban area of the city and he recognized the shoe at once.

'Yes,' he said. 'That's my work.'

'What was the name of the owner?' Lagé asked.

The shoe repairer dug out the book of stubs that went with the tickets he handed out as he took in work. 'Here it is. "Build sole up." Dupont's the name. I've got it here.'

'Address?'

'I don't ask the address. They've got the ticket for confirmation when they collect the shoes.'

'What about first name?'

'I don't ask that either. After all, we're only repairing shoes, not setting diamonds in platinum.'

The weather changed at last and the sun finally came out. The sun in that part of France had a special quality of gold in it and as Pel and Darcy left for Lyons it was shining as if it had God's blessing in it.

They stayed in Lyons all day. As he had been involved with the policemen charged with accepting bribes, Pel was questioned about them, and Darcy was a witness in an assault case. They had driven down in Darcy's car and, after his stint at the police headquarters, Pel joined Darcy in court where he'd been awaiting the verdict. The judges had only just left, together with many of the lawyers who had been watching from the well to see how their elders and betters put their case, and it was late as they set off home. They sank a quick beer and ate a hurried snack at a brasserie nearby before heading back up the motorway in the darkness of the evening towards Nadauld's booze-up at the Bar Transvaal.

The pale stones of the Palace of the Dukes, once a prestigious home for a family who had defied the kings of France, now only a headquarters for the local authority, glowed in the glare of the flood lights. As they entered the Hôtel de Police car park, they bumped into Lagé. He was just trudging from his car wondering if he'd got flat feet, too, and he passed on his information briskly to Pel.

'It'll be worth following up,' Pel agreed. 'In the meantime we'd better head for the Bar Transvaal.'

As they talked, they heard the wail of a police siren just starting up from the front of the building.

'Something's up in there,' Darcy said. 'There seems to be a lot of panic going on.'

'Later,' Pel suggested. 'We started at six this morning. I think first we'd better go along to the celebration and drink the health of Nadauld and Sergeant Gehrer.'

As it happened, there was no celebration and Nadauld's health had taken a distinct turn for the worse.

The Bar Transvaal was surprisingly empty for a celebration. There wasn't a single policeman there when they had been expecting a crowd.

'There was a telephone call from the Hôtel de Police,' the proprietor explained. 'And they all shot off.'

'What was it?'

'They didn't tell me. Nadauld said something about a bomb at the airport. I'd laid in extra stock for the party. What do I do with it?'

'Better try drinking it yourself, *mon vieux*,' Darcy suggested as they headed for the door.

In the Hôtel de Police the man on the front desk looked harassed and every telephone bell in the place seemed to be going. As they entered, they met Nosjean and De Troq' heading for their car. Nosjean enlightened them.

70

'Nadauld's been shot,' he said. 'They've rushed him to hospital. It looks bad. Gehrer and two others were hit, too – one of them Aimedieu.'

'Name of God,' Darcy said. 'What happened?'

'A bomb went off at the airport.'

'Another?'

'Yes. The airport staff thought we ought to know and Nadauld, Gehrer, Aimedieu, and Gehrer's successor, a type called Lotier, shot off in that VW open tourer of Gehrer's. The next we heard was a panic call saying they wanted reinforcements and that Nadauld had been wounded. I think he's in a bad way. All four were hit.'

'What did they do the shooting with? A machine-gun?'

'That's what it looks like. I'm on my way now. De Troq's heading for Marix-sur-Larne. The Tuaregs have struck again. They held up a coach-load of Dutch tourists and relieved them of their wallets, jewellery and passports.'

Pel frowned. The area seemed to have come to life with a vengeance. 'Who's in charge at the airport?'

'Goriot. He happened to be here when the call came. Forensic, Fingerprints and Photography have been alerted. Doc Minet's still down with flu so it's Doc Cham again. I was just heading after them and leaving De Troq' to handle the Tuaregs.'

Pel made up his mind quickly. 'You go with De Troq',' he suggested. 'It'll need more than one. They'll all have to be interviewed. I'll go to the airport.' He turned to Darcy. 'Get everybody out, Daniel. It seems we're going to need them. Then get somebody to sit on the telephone and follow me.'

As Nosjean, De Troq' and Darcy vanished, Pel headed for his office to stock up with cigarettes. His campaign to stop smoking seemed to have gone with the wind. As he left again, the Chief appeared, coming in like a bull wondering which china shop to ravage.

'What in God's name happened?' he said.

'I don't know yet,' Pel said. 'It seems the Tuaregs have struck again. At Marix-sur-Larne. Nosjean and De Troq' have gone out there. And there's been another bomb and a shooting at the airport. It sounds like someone with a machine-gun. Four men have been hit. Nadauld's in a bad way.'

There seemed to be men everywhere at the airport and lights blazed in every office and outbuilding. There was one Islander aircraft standing on the tarmac at the civil end of the field with a few privately owned small planes belonging to officers of the Armée de l'Air, whose heavy-shouldered grey Mirages stood at the other end of the tarmac in the official area of the field.

Goriot had deployed his men round the gate where the incident had taken place. Gehrer's car was jammed hard up against a pole that supported a sign indicating the way to the headquarters and administration block. It was already taped off and a photographer with a flash camera was taking pictures. There were holes in the hood.

To Pel's surprise, Sarrazin, the free-lance journalist, was there, too, trying to get past the guardroom. He was arguing with the orderly officer who had been called by the sergeant of the guard. The orderly officer was refusing Sarrazin permission to enter the field.

'I can go to the civilian half and get in that way,' Sarrazin was yelling. 'All I have to do then is walk across to here!'

'The civilian half of the airfield closes down at nine o'clock,' the officer pointed out patiently. 'And, should you try to get in here, I'll see you're arrested.'

'I have a press pass.'

'It's not a pass to enter a restricted military area.'

As Pel appeared, Goriot emerged from the darkness. 'Somebody seems to have sprayed the car with a sub-machine-gun,' he said. 'The Air Force have men looking for ejected cartridges.'

The colonel commanding the field, a man called Le Thiel, was in his office with another officer and the manager of the civil end of the field. He was in evening dress, having been called from an official dinner in the city. He shook hands briskly.

'The shooting,' he announced at once, 'was done by one of the sentries. He's admitted it. He's been put under arrest. Since the last bomb scare they've had orders not to let anyone on to the field without identification and, as far as I can make out, when the bomb went off the adjutant informed your headquarters as we arranged after the last explosion. A car load of policemen arrived and when the sentry challenged them, they failed to hear and didn't stop. The sentry opened fire.'

'What with?'

'His service rifle.'

'And wounded four men? Did he keep on firing?'

'He claims he fired once only.'

Cham appeared from nowhere. 'Four men have been wounded,' he said sharply. 'Nadauld seriously. The other three received only flesh wounds. But the same bullet couldn't have hit all four.'

'What about the bomb?' the Chief asked.

'It was placed near the gate,' the Colonel said. 'It was home-made again, we believe, but it was bigger than the last one. When it went off, the sergeant of the guard sounded the alarm, warned his men not to let anyone pass, and made a search. It was about this time that your men arrived and the sentry – a man called Girard – fired on them.'

'Four times?'

'He insists only once. So does the sergeant of the guard. I've seen Girard. He's a conscript and not a technician. He's a general duty entry. General duty men, if they aren't aircrew, are available for anything that crops up. And, since the technicians are involved with the aircraft and do their own watches at the hangars, guards are usually done by this class of man. Girard doesn't seem to be very bright and insists that he was only doing his duty. He claims he shouted twice at the car to stop and when it didn't he fired.'

'Four times?' The question came again.

The colonel frowned. 'Once,' he insisted. 'I've checked his rifle. Personally. It has certainly been fired but only one bullet from those issued to him is missing.'

'Are you quite sure of that?'

'It's a standard FN rifle,' Le Thiel said. 'As issued to all our forces. It has a magazine of 20 rounds and can be fired automatically or for single shots. It's a particularly good weapon for internal security. In view of terrorist activities and the recent bomb scare, the magazine's loaded for night guard duties. But only one shot's been fired.'

'Nobody else fired?'

'Nobody. We've checked.'

'But four men have been hurt! One seriously!' Pel turned to Cham. 'What's your view?'

'They were in Sergeant Gehrer's car. It's a tourer with a hood and a plastic rear window. The bullet went through the rear window and struck Nadauld on the chin. Gehrer was hit in the right eye. It's thought he might lose the sight of it. They're working on him and Nadauld now at the hospital. The car went out of control and hit an iron post supporting a sign giving directions about the camp and came to a stop. Everybody in it had been hit. Nadauld has a severe wound in the face and a fracture of the lower jaw. There appear to be a number of bullet marks on the car, two in the windscreen and one on the windscreen frame, together with other smaller marks. It looks as if it's been sprayed by a machine-gun.'

'Only one shot was fired,' Colonel Le Thiel insisted again.

'That's what Gehrer says,' Cham agreed. 'So do Aimedieu and Lotier who were the other two men in the car. They're not much hurt. They insist they only heard one shot.'

'Could the others have been fired by a gun with a silencer?'

'The man who fired had been drinking,' Colonel Le Thiel said. 'To be fair, he hadn't expected to be on sentry duty but when the bomb went off, everybody was turned out and general duty men were posted round the perimeter fence. Girard's post was at the gate. He will, of course, be charged with assault and culpable homicide and tried by the courts in the proper way. I think we'll find that, although subject to service discipline, he'll still be within the reach of the ordinary law of the land and will not be able to plead exemption by being in the service.'

The hood of Gehrer's old-fashioned VW was up. Gehrer had had the car for years because he was an open-air fiend and didn't like closed cars. It still stood, with its right headlight broken, jammed against the post supporting the sign indicating the headquarters and administrative block. It was surrounded by broken glass.

When Leguyader of Forensic arrived, with the aid of a torch they examined it as carefully as they could. There were two holes in the windscreen, each apparently made by a separate bullet. The hood had been pierced, and there were several other marks. On the upper part of the windscreen frame there was an oval dent about two centimetres long which appeared to have been made by a 7.62mm bullet. In and around the windscreen, on the frame of the front passenger seat, on the seat itself and on the hood, there appeared to be small pieces of lead and nickel and fragments of human tissue and bone, obviously from Nadauld's wound. On the back seat was a portion of a 7.62 bullet, consisting of the aluminium tip and the cupronickel jacket.

'It looks to me as if two or three bullets were fired,' Leguyader said. 'From the windscreen alone it seems more than one struck the car.'

Colonel Le Thiel frowned and shook his head. 'The sergeant and the other members of the guard insist only one was fired,' he said again. 'We've made a search for used cartridge cases. We found only one.'

'So, if only one bullet was fired by Girard,' Pel said, 'where did the others come from?'

6

The special conference called by the Chief for the following morning looked like being a gloomy affair. Nadauld's wound was appalling and he was in the intensive care unit.

When Pel appeared the Chief hadn't yet arrived but they all knew Nadauld was on the danger list and, from the report from the hospital, it looked very much as if Gehrer still might lose the sight of an eye.

'Fragment of glass,' Cham said. 'The bullet must have thrown it out from the windscreen. If it had been a bullet, it would have killed him.'

As Pel took his place, Darcy came up behind him quietly. 'Goriot's picked somebody up,' he said.

'Who? The bomber? The man who fired the shots?'

'He thinks they're the same man.'

'Anybody we know?'

'Not half. It's Philippe Duche.'

'What!'

'He was stopping all the traffic in the area and Duche happened to be there with one of his trucks. Goriot hauled him out. He's going to charge him.'

'What happened?'

'I told him not to be a damned fool.'

'How did he react to that?'

'He pulled rank.'

'He has the same rank as you.'

'He's had it a bit longer, *patron*.'

'And been out of action for a long time. You'd think he'd feel his way a bit.'

'I think being blown up changed him, *patron*. I used to think of him as being a bit solid between the ears and slow to act. He isn't now. Still solid between the ears but he's too busy for my liking.'

'Where's Duche now?'

'In the cells.'

'And Goriot?'

'Making out the charge.'

'Go and see him. Duche's to be allowed to go unless Goriot has a cast-iron case. Duche's no fool and he'll sue if he hasn't.'

Goriot was in his office sitting at the desk writing. He had a look that was almost ecstasy on his face.

'I hear you've picked up Philippe Duche for the affair at the airport,' Darcy said.

'Yes.'

'Why?'

'He was there.'

'Charged him?'

'No. Not yet.'

'Had he a gun?'

'He'd hidden it.'

'Where?'

'I expect he threw it in the ditch.'

'Searched the area?'

'We're doing it now.'

'You'd better find something,' Darcy warned. 'Where did you pick him up?'

'In traffic passing the airport gate.'

'Going to the airport or away?'

'Almost outside.'

'*Which way?*'

'*To* the airport.'

'So he couldn't have been there when the shots were fired. I think you'd better release him. Otherwise you'll make a fool of yourself.'

'Duche was known to possess a sub-machine-gun.'

'Eight years ago.'

'He must still have it. Four men have been hit. In quick succession. That indicates a machine pistol. Duche's brother was the only man known to have one. Duche must have it now.'

'Did he admit it?'

'He denied having anything to do with it. Or with the bomb.'

'Of course he did. He never went in for explosives and he's straight these days.'

'How do we know?'

'We know.'

'I don't,' Goriot retorted. 'And I never take for granted statements made by habitual criminals.'

'You heard what the Chief said. You're making a mistake.'

'I'm making an arrest!' Nevertheless, Goriot, his eyes blazing, began to screw up the form he had been writing on. Indifferent to his look of hatred, Darcy turned away and descended the stairs. Philippe Duche was sitting in the interview room, glowering at the wall, watched by one of Goriot's team. He didn't rise as Darcy entered.

'I haven't even got a gun,' he said at once.

'You had one.'

Duche managed a smile. 'More than one. But I handed them in. You know I did. I was even fined for possessing firearms without a licence. I thought it was worth it to have proof that I'd got rid of them. It all came out in court.'

'Well, you're free to leave.'

'Who says I am?'

'I do.'

'The other guy – Goriot – says he wants to question me.'

'He's changed his mind.'

Duche's expression changed at once. 'No strings?'

'No strings. Just one question. What happened to that FN you had?'

Duche gave the hint of a smile. 'I was once going to use it to kill your boss,' he said. 'I had it hidden. In my mother's home. But when I escaped from gaol I daren't go near it. Then you put me back in gaol. When I was finally discharged I smashed it. With a sledge hammer. I threw the pieces in the river.'

'That's what I heard. You'd better go before Goriot changes his mind.'

78

By the time Darcy returned to the conference, the Chief had arrived. He looked about as amenable as an atom bomb.

'Nadauld's in a bad way,' he announced. 'The hospital says it's touch and go. There's another point. I was telephoned by Sarrazin, the free-lance. Apparently he heard of the bomb as soon as I did.' He flourished a piece of paper. 'And this morning in the post I received a letter from Councillor Lax wanting to know why police aren't permanently on duty at the airport. Who informed Lax?'

'Sarrazin?' Pel offered mildly.

'I'll see Sarrazin,' the Chief said in a way that boded ill for the journalist.

'If he's available,' Pomereu observed. 'I heard he spent most of the night in the guardroom. He was warned not to try to get into the field via the civilian half, but he bribed a night watchman. He was arrested.'

'Good,' the Chief said.

Eventually the bad temper subsided and they got down to discussing the puzzle of the four bullet wounds but only one shot.

Darcy looked up. 'Perhaps there *weren't* four bullets,' he observed.

'That's nonsense,' Goriot said. 'Four men were hit. How would one bullet do that?'

'Bullets do some funny things,' Darcy pointed out. 'There was that case in Marseilles when that cop was hit. Rifle bullet from a distance of ten to fifteen yards. It passed through both legs. The guy died from loss of blood within an hour. The bullet went through the fleshy part of the right thigh. Clean-cut entrance wound, but the damage increased as it left the leg and the exit hole was six centimetres across. It then entered the left thigh. The entrance hole this time was a lacerated wound sixteen centimetres by seven. It struck the lower end of the left femur and smashed it to bits. Several fragments made their exit on the other side of the thigh. It was thought for a long time that two shots had been fired. One from the left. One from the right. They thought they were looking for a gang. It turned out to be a kid of seventeen.'

'That was different,' Goriot argued. 'Here there are *four* clear

79

wounds. Four! Four different men were hit. Not a bullet through both of one man's legs.'

'We require expert help,' Leguyader, of Forensic, said. 'I'm not competent to speak much on the subject.'

It was a tremendous admission for Leguyader to make because he liked people to think he was an expert at everything. He was even said to read the *Encyclopédie Larousse* every evening after dinner so he could blind people with science the next day.

'Ballistics is a specialized subject,' he went on. 'Gunshot wounds are not always as obvious as they look. There can be too many misleading signs. Distance, angle, type of weapon are all important. Where bone is close to the point of entry, anything can happen. It seems to have done so in poor Nadauld's case. We need someone expert in ballistics who can tell us what happened.'

'Try Judge Castéou,' Pel said.

'She's an expert?' Leguyader looked startled.

'Her husband is. He's Armand Castéou. He's the top man in his field.'

The latest report on the injured men arrived as they talked. It indicated that Aimedieu and Lotier had both been allowed to leave the hospital, that Gehrer's injury had been found to be less serious than at first thought, but that Nadauld's condition had deteriorated.

A guarded announcement had already been made to the press, giving away little detail on the understanding that the press would find that out for themselves. Most of them reacted cautiously but Fiabon, of *France Dimanche*, gave it the full treatment.

'BOMB AT AIRPORT', he announced. 'FOUR BADLY HURT.' The report made it sound as though the bomb had done the damage. Fiabon had let his imagination run away with him and claimed the police had got a good lead and were on the track of the bomber.

'It'll keep the bastard quiet for a bit, at least,' Darcy said. 'He'll not be planting any more bombs for a while.'

'Why did he plant them in the first place?' Pel asked.

'Why?' Darcy looked startled. 'Well, we've got the Free Burgundy Movement and the Friends of the Soil, who seem to

80

like blowing holes in it to prove their loyalty to it. There are Communists and Nihilists and Anarchists. We've even had trouble with the Free Brittany lot and the Basque Separatists, though what the hell they have to do with us I don't know.'

The talk moved to the Tuaregs' latest coup. Because of the newspapermen's concern with the bomb, they had only a sketchy version of the hold-up. But Nosjean was growing worried. He and De Troq' had spent all the previous evening with the Dutch tourists, forty of them, in their hotel, all indignant at being robbed, with their holiday ruined. As usual, none of them was able to help much with descriptions. Some claimed the men who had robbed them had worn stocking masks, some said they hadn't. Some said they'd been threatening, others said they'd been polite. Some said they were tall and thin, others short and fat, or dark, or fair. One man claimed he had struggled with them and tried to show a bruise, but apparently he was known to the others as a tall story type and he was shouted down.

It hadn't been easy because the tourists didn't speak French. Fortunately De Troq', who seemed to be able to speak every language under the sun from Eskimo to Swahili, could speak German, and the Dutch were able to understand that. He gave the Chief the version he'd picked up.

'Two pistol-carrying men appeared as the tourist bus stopped near Marix,' he said. 'It drew into a lay-by for a rest period and they appeared from the trees. They'd followed it in. The tourists were robbed of every valuable they possessed. The women had their necklaces, earrings and rings removed, and the men had to throw their watches, money, travellers' cheques and passports into carrier bags that were held out.'

'Any descriptions?'

'They were so shocked they could only give the vaguest descriptions. We've issued them to the press, of course.'

There was just one clue. One of the tourists had noticed that the carrier bag into which he had tossed his money had been marked with red lettering and it had the name 'Talant' on it.

'It was obviously one of those they used when they robbed the supermarket there,' Nosjean said. 'It doesn't prove much, though, beyond that they were the same gang and that they've turned their attention to other means of earning their living.'

'Is that all?' the Chief asked.

'Not quite. There was a bit of a scuffle. One of the women tried to resist and her glasses were knocked off. One of the Tuaregs trod on them. By accident. He picked them up and handed them to her. Trying to do a Claude Duval highwayman act. Bags of politeness, chivalry and apologies for damaging them. They were bent and the right lens was broken. I've passed them to Prélat in case there are fingerprints on them because the fingerprint from the till at Talant was no good. Too smudged. We might just get one from the glasses.'

'Any theories?'

'I still believe they're first-timers who've found an exciting way of making money. In all their hold-ups they've used stolen cars – more than one – and switched from one to another until they picked up their own, which we now think might be a fawn Sierra 2000. But we've noticed that in all their earlier hold-ups, the cars they used were stolen from places like Lyons, Amiens, Auxerre, Strasbourg. The last three times they've been lifted here in the city. Two in the University district. They're probably growing over-confident – or just lazy. I'd like to have someone watch the area.'

'University's a big district,' the Chief said.

'We could have someone prowling round. They might spot some youngster in a fawn Ford Sierra.'

'What have you in mind?'

'Claudie Darel. With another woman detective to alternate with her.'

The Chief looked at Pel.

'It could work,' Pel said. It had worked before. There was the famous case of the young cop who had arrested a driver for not wearing a seat belt and been startled to discover he'd picked up one of the most wanted men in the country.

'Very well,' the Chief said. 'We'll give it a try. Set it up. I'll ask for a uniformed policewoman to help out.'

Nosjean and De Troq' were chiefly intrigued by the fact that in their hold-up of the Dutch tourists, the Tuaregs had carried the loot in a plastic carrier bag from the supermarket at Talant.

'That supermarket has the strange ability to be involved with us about once every other month,' Nosjean said. 'If it isn't a break-in or a fire or a fight, it's a carrier bag containing loot and bearing its name. Let's go and have another word with that girl who got the gun stuffed up her nose.'

Janine Ducassis seemed to have recovered well from her ordeal, particularly as the manager, also recovering, had praised her and made her a till supervisor. Her job was no longer to sit at a till and take money, but to collect notes when the tills became too full and convey them to the office accounts department.

They found her sitting at a desk counting money and she beamed at them as they appeared. Carefully – the manager had obviously chosen well – she finished the counting, put the money in the safe and motioned them to a couple of unoccupied chairs.

As they sat down, the manager's secretary, Pascal Dubois, entered with a cup of coffee. She seemed surprised to see Nosjean and De Troq' but Janine Ducassis gestured.

'I think we can run to two more cups, Pascal,' she said. 'Decent ones. Not from the machine.'

By the time the coffee came and Pascal Dubois had left again, they had been through all the rules and regulations governing the giving away of plastic carrier bags.

'Except,' Janine said, 'that I didn't give him one. They're free with fifty francs' worth of goods. Below that you have to pay for them. Twenty centimes.'

'I don't suppose he paid, did he?' De Troq' asked.

'No,' she said. 'He just reached under the counter and helped himself to several. From the other side.'

'So he knew where they were?'

'He must have done. He didn't fiddle around searching for them. He didn't even look.'

'Have you ever seen him before? I mean, could he have made a point of coming in to case the joint? I expect he did at some point – or someone did – but had you ever noticed anyone of that sort?'

Janine Ducassis hadn't. Nor had she ever before noticed anyone in the store wearing Canadiennes such as the robbers had used.

'And I didn't see their faces,' she said. 'They had these scarves over them. Tied tightly. Like motor cyclists. And dark glasses. Did you get any fingerprints?'

'One,' Nosjean said. 'Not a very good one. What about the girl who left her key in the till? Did she get the sack?'

'Yes.' Janine Ducassis nodded. 'Monique Vachonnière. It's against the rules to leave the key in the till. You have to collect it at the office and sign for it and even if you leave your till for a minute, you take it with you. But I'd seen Monique do it before. More than once.'

'What's her address?'

'She lives on the housing estate at Talant. Rue Marcel-Sembatte. I don't know the number, but it's only a short street. You could find her at the Supermarket Sport at Chenove. She got a job there. Filling shelves.'

The Supermarket Sport at Chenove was smaller than the one at Talant and they found Monique Vachonnière, who was plump and spectacled and nervous, busy stacking packets of washing powder on the shelves from a huge trolley. The manager had to be approached and he was wary.

'Police?' he asked. 'Why do you want to see her? Has she a record?'

'She hasn't a record,' Nosjean said. 'But she was at the supermarket at Talant when it was robbed and we'd like to speak to her.'

'Was she involved? You have to be very careful whom you employ these days.'

Well, Nosjean thought, in a way she *was* involved, but it seemed it was carelessness rather than criminal intent.

In the end the manager gave his permission for them to talk to the girl and she took them to a store room, where they leaned against the cartons of washing powder to interview her.

'I wouldn't have left the damned till,' she said, her eyes filling with tears. 'But Pascal Dubois once told me it was all right for

84

a few seconds. I had to. I'd had a cup of coffee and – well, you know. The tills can't be opened in a second. But that man opened it straight away so he must have known how to. I was just coming back and I saw him. I was paralysed and started screaming when Janine started. I told the manager what Pascal had said but she said she didn't and, of course, he believed her rather than me. She's better looking. It cost me my job. Filling shelves isn't as good as handling cash.'

It didn't lead them very far but they still had the Ford Sierra that the old man had seen left at Morbihaux which appeared to have been swopped for the car used in the hold-up. Claudie had managed to see a similar car briefly heading past the Faculty of Science in the area of the University, containing a man and a girl. They were a handsome couple and not at all what they were looking for, but it seemed worth while keeping a look-out for them. It was late in the evening and the girl just might have been Janine Ducassis.

7

The weather continued to improve. The heat mounted until it seemed like midsummer and the city glowed with the glory of the Lord. Pel's cold seemed a little better and it only needed a miracle to put him right.

As he drove to work through the ancient villages, he drew a deep breath because he loved the uplands outside the city, rich and golden in the summer, bleak in the winter. In the same way he loved the busy streets of the city itself, the magnificent buildings, the varnished roofs. Even the quiet cafés on the outskirts where, in an atmosphere of red wine and Gauloises, old men played dominoes or a slow game of boules, the players solemnly measuring the spheres with stalks of grass, watched by children or women resting their legs after shopping.

His buoyant mood didn't last long after he entered the Hôtel de Police. Darcy was on the telephone to the Missing Persons Bureau and he remembered they were still struggling to establish the identity of the man on the motorway.

'It seems to me,' he said, 'that there has to be a reason for all this modesty. Here we have a man whom nobody knows found dead on the motorway. Why is it so hard to come up with his name? We've tried Fingerprints but he's obviously not a criminal because his dabs aren't on record.' He paused. 'If nothing else, he's one of the Chief's Missing Persons. We don't know who he is and neither, it seems, does anybody else, so he must be. And if someone who's missing is found dead, the relatives should know, though it isn't our job to inform them. That's the duty of the Bureau of Missing Persons. But *this* might be murder and that makes it different.'

Lagé's discovery from the shoe repairer at St-Alban had led inevitably to the city doctors.

'If his feet were bad enough to have his shoes built up,' Darcy suggested, 'it seems to indicate he'd seen a doctor about them. He might, of course, have made the decision on his own but it seems to *suggest* medical advice. I've got Lagé going through all the doctors in the area now to find if any of them made the recommendation.'

Meanwhile Nosjean and De Troq' were trying their new angle and Claudie Darel was following Janine Ducasssis wherever she went. It was easy to see the tills of the Talant supermarket from outside through the glass doors. A prowl around the place would give the Tuaregs the layout and they could easily have waited for the correct moment to strike by watching from a car. Unless – and it was a possibility – some sort of signal had been given from inside. The wave of a coloured handkerchief could have indicated the absence of officials or customers from the area of the tills and check-out desks, and they had begun to suspect by this time that this was exactly what had happened because it seemed more than fortuitous that Monique Vachonnière had been away from her till at the time of the raid.

Janine Ducassis drove a tiny Fiat Panda and Claudie and the policewoman lent by Uniformed Branch, looking like two housewives returning from shopping, followed her home in an unmarked car. She lived with her parents in an unpretentious house near the Arsenal, down a dusty street where the male inhabitants seemed always to be playing boules as she arrived and had to pause to allow her to pass. She seemed to be all she claimed to be – a hard-working till supervisor with a responsibility.

Then, as Nosjean checked through his files late in the evening, the man at the front desk rang through to say there was a man to see him.

'Name of Philibert,' he said.

Nosjean looked puzzled. 'Philibert? Who's he?'

He turned out to be the owner of the bar at Morbihaux who had reported the presence of the fawn Ford Sierra that had been parked near the church on the day of the hold-up at Talant. There had been so much arguing going on in the bar

about the car, its colour, its make and its number, Nosjean had
concentrated chiefly on the old man who'd first noticed it and
had barely noticed the man behind the bar.

'We've remembered about it,' Philibert said. 'We've been
arguing about it ever since. It came from Garages Europe Automobile.'

'Here? In the city?'

'Well, it might have been Garages Europe Automobile in
Paris. They're a big group. But somebody remembered there
was this sticker on the rear window. You know how garages
stick them on when they sell a car. I always make them take
them off mine when I buy one. I tell them if I want to advertise
anything on my car I'll advertise my own bar.'

'Go on,' Nosjean encouraged before he got carried away.

'Well, one or two saw the car and everybody thought different. Even about the colour. Was it grey or fawn or brown? In
the end we decided it was fawn. Nobody could remember what
the sticker said either, but then another car with the same
sticker parked outside the bar yesterday – two sales representatives from Metaux de Dijon – and everybody remembered. It
was Garages Europe Automobile.'

It was as good as having the number of the car and it didn't
take them long to establish from Garages Europe Automobile
the names of everyone who in the last three years had bought
a Ford Sierra 2000 from them. The colour reduced it further,
and, finally, they pinned the car down to a Jean-Philippe de
Rille. His address was given simply as Montagny.

'Where in Montagny?'

The directories solved the problem.

'Fancy address,' De Troq' commented. 'The Manoir. That's
all. Sounds expensive.'

'Some crooks have expensive ideas,' Nosjean said drily.

When Pel arrived in the Hôtel de Police next morning there
seemed to be a lot of loud voices in the sergeants' room. The
loudest belonged to Aimedieu who had planted himself in the
middle of the floor as if he were defying anyone to try to shift
him. 'I'm back,' he was saying defiantly.

88

'Did Goriot send you?' Darcy asked.

'I sent myself.'

'You haven't had orders to report back here?'

Aimedieu's face was that of an angelic choirboy and at the moment it was a very stubborn and angry choirboy. 'No,' he said.

'Then you'd better return to Inspector Goriot, hadn't you?'

Aimedieu scowled. 'I'll resign first,' he announced. 'That damned man doesn't know how to treat his subordinates. I'm on the Old Man's team.'

'The Old Man's temper's not exactly a thing of beauty and a joy for ever.'

'The Old Man's all right,' Aimedieu said stoutly.

'Not long ago you couldn't stand him.'

'Well, now I can. He doesn't nag. And you know what he's up to.'

'Do you?' Darcy said. 'I never do.'

'All the same, either I work with someone else or I quit.' Aimedieu's stubborn expression crumbled as he stared at Darcy. 'For God's sake, sir, have a word with the Old Man for me.'

Pel listened quietly to Darcy.

'I'll see the Chief,' he said.

'And Aimedieu?'

'Tell him he's back on my squad.'

'Who takes his place with Goriot?'

'He can have Lacocq. Last in, first out. That's how the unions think. Besides, Lacocq's a placid type and not likely to complain much. He also isn't as smart as Aimedieu. Point out, of course, that like Aimedieu, it's only temporary. If Goriot wants a team, he has to pick them himself. I'll arrange it with the Chief.'

Pel was still thinking about Aimedieu when word arrived that one of the city doctors had turned up the mysterious 'Dupont' whose name they'd acquired from the shoe repairer. A doctor called Billetottes claimed to know him.

'I've got a Dupont with flat feet on my books,' he said.

Because things were quiet, Darcy decided to look up Doctor Billetóttes himself. It gave him the opportunity to drive about the city. Darcy regarded the city as his back garden and he liked to know what was going on in it. He often drove round it after midnight when the streets were deserted and everything was silent. Every now and then he liked to stop and wait as if he were listening to it breathing. He never knew what made him stop and why he chose the places he did, but he liked to watch the bars closing and keep an eye on the people going home. He never got involved – that was the job of the men in uniform – but he liked to get the feel of the place.

Doctor Billetottes was an enormously fat man who refused to consider talking until they both had a drink in their fists.

'Jean Dupont,' he said. 'That's his name. He's one of my patients. I saw him about two months ago.'

'Address?'

'I haven't got one. Not a proper one.'

Darcy frowned. 'That's unusual, isn't it?'

'I suppose it is. But he's a bit of a mystery man.'

'That's our impression. How come you haven't an address?'

'He gave me the address of the Hôtel Central. Said he was staying there.'

'Right. I'll get it from there. Did he come often?'

'No.'

'Know anything about him?'

'He's a widower. That's all I know. He came on my books about five years ago.'

'How old is he?'

'Seventy-eight.'

'We were told between sixty-five and seventy.'

'He's in pretty good shape.'

'Not now, he isn't,' Darcy said.

'Why not? Has something happened to him?'

'Yes. He died.'

There was a long silence. 'Well,' Doctor Billetottes said, 'I must say that's a surprise. I'd have given him another ten to fifteen years. Last time I saw him he seemed fit enough.'

'Well, he's not now. What did you see him about?'

'His feet. They were flat. So flat they were curling up at the ends. He took to sitting down a lot.'

Darcy seemed to have found their man. 'I expect he developed good sitting bones instead,' he said.

Doctor Billetottes laughed. 'He didn't just sit down for the sake of sitting down. He played cards. He loved cards.'

'Who did he play with?'

'God knows. Neighbours, I suppose. Women. He liked women.'

'How do you know?'

'Things he said. He said he was here to see a woman. That was why he was staying at the Hôtel Central. He'd done it before, he said. I got the impression that he'd been in the habit of following them about. What happened to him? Heart attack? I wouldn't have expected it. He had a heart like a trip hammer.'

'It wasn't his heart,' Darcy said. 'At least, only in so far as it stopped. He was found dead on the motorway.'

'What was he doing there? He didn't drive.'

'He wasn't driving. He seems to have been drunk and staggering about and was hit by a car.'

'It doesn't sound like him. Sure you've got the right man?'

'Appendicitis scar? Kidney operation scar left side?'

'That's him, all right.'

'Did he suffer from depression?'

'*Mon Dieu*, no! Why?'

'I wondered if getting himself hit by a car was a new way of doing himself in, and whether the whisky he'd drunk was to help him screw up his courage. After all there were lots of scars on his wrists as if he'd tried to open veins.'

Doctor Billetottes laughed again. 'They weren't suicide attempts. They were accidents. I asked him about them. He told me he once had a property in the hills. Lots of trees along one border. He felt they needed lopping to let in some light and decided to do it himself. But he wasn't very good at it and a bow saw's not an easy thing to handle when you're up a ladder. It's a wonder he didn't cut his hand off.'

'Did he hit the bottle much?'

'He liked a few drinks. Who doesn't? But I don't think he overdid it.'

'He seems to have done this time,' Darcy said.

8

The following day they heard Nadauld had died.

'Septicaemia and shock,' the Chief said. 'His jaw was shattered. They must have been using explosive bullets.'

He was grim-faced and wearing a dark suit, obviously on his way to see Nadauld's widow. Within an hour the hat was going round. Nobody argued and everybody offered something because they knew it might easily be their own turn next.

The Hôtel de Police was gloomy all morning. Nadauld had been an easy-going friendly man and the fact that he had died on the eve of his daughter's wedding had made the tragedy worse. In addition, they were making no headway into the mystery of his wounding, or for that matter, the identity of the man on the motorway.

The Hôtel Central was the biggest hotel in the city and stuck faithfully to the law demanding that guests should fill in a *fiche d'hôtel*, the little card indicating who they were, where they came from, what their nationality was, where they were born and why. What was more, it was unlike some of the smaller hotels in that passports or identity cards were demanded there so that details could be checked. It was part of the law of France but it was a law that was inclined to be forgotten when a hotel was busy.

The manager was a tall portly man who didn't like having the police making enquiries on his premises in case their presence got the place a bad name, but he always tried to help. It paid. This time, however, he could offer nothing. The books and files were extensive and they had them for ten years back, but though they'd had plenty of Jean Duponts passing through, they hadn't one who fitted the description the police had. Jean Dupont, it seemed, had not been eager to be recognized.

Then, with Pel scowling at a report on his desk from Colonel le Thiel at the airport, unexpectedly they got the break they were waiting for.

Doctor Billetottes telephoned. 'Have you found the address of that chap, Jean Dupont, yet?' he asked.

'No.' Darcy's answer was short. He had a feeling that Doctor Billetottes – and a few others too – had not been doing their job properly.

'Well, I've just remembered something. I have a bit of a problem with prescriptions from time to time. I have arthritis in my fingers and the chemists complain they can't read my writing. Nobody expects to read a doctor's writing at the best of times, anyway, but arthritis makes it worse, and there was a query a few weeks back from the dispenser at the chemist's in St-Alban. It was for a prescription for sleeping tablets. He couldn't read the quantity and was checking up.'

'And?'

'I've just remembered. He gave me the name on the prescription so I could check with my records. It was Jean Dupont. It was for the type you're looking for.'

Well, it wasn't much, but it was another pointer, this time to the St-Alban district.

The chemist didn't know Jean Dupont but he remembered him once turning up for his prescription when it wasn't ready. Dupont had pointed out his age – seventy-eight, he said – and complained it was difficult to get into town since he no longer drove a car. The dispenser had asked where he lived and had volunteered to drop the prescription in on his way home.

'And you did?' Darcy asked.

'Yes.'

'And the house?'

'Name of "Vauregard". Rue Poincaré. You can't miss it.'

Darcy made no comment because he'd missed many a place he'd been told he couldn't miss. Being told he couldn't miss somewhere was the best way he knew of making it disappear from sight for ever.

'Where is it exactly?'

'On the Beaucelles-St-Julien crossroads. It's a red-brick place.'

The house at the crossroads had a short drive dropping from the main road to a sunken garage beneath it. There appeared to be nobody at home. Since Dupont was a widower and was dead, Darcy didn't really expect much in the way of family, but he had thought there might be a puzzled-looking gardener or a housekeeper, at least a daily help, wondering where the owner was. He tried the house on the opposite side of the crossroads. It was a much older house, built some time just after the First World War. It had peeling paint, an overgrown garden, and net curtains at the front window that twitched as he climbed from his car. When he knocked on the door, it was opened a fraction and a long nose was poked out.

'I'm enquiring about Monsieur Dupont,' he said.

'He doesn't live here,' the owner of the nose pointed out. 'My name's Mallard. Madame Mallard. Elise Mallard. That's his house. Across the road.'

'Yes, I'm aware of that,' Darcy said. 'I want to find out something about him.'

The woman behind the door looked the sort who'd make sure she knew everything and Darcy suspected the net curtains had often twitched as Dupont left or returned home.

'What do you want to know?'

What Darcy wanted to know was how Dupont had met his death, but he suspected Madame Mallard couldn't supply the answer to that.

'Were you a friend of his, Madame?'

'No.'

'Speak to him much?'

'Never.'

'Know what he did with himself?'

'He came and went.'

'What does that mean?'

'He didn't live here all the time. He had another house somewhere, I think.'

'Know where?'

'No.'

'What else did he do?'

'He played cards.'

Darcy glanced through the window. Dupont's house was a good distance away. 'You could see?' he asked.

'I've got good eyesight.'

More than likely a good pair of binoculars, too, Darcy thought. 'Whom did he play with?'

'There was Maninko. He's the butcher from the village. He's a Pole. And Georges Serral, who keeps the stationer's. There were others. Rollin, the undertaker from St-Saôn, was one.'

'You knew him?'

'I saw his car. It has his name on the side. In small letters. What's happened to him?'

'He's dead,' Darcy explained. 'He was found dead on the motorway.'

'Shot?'

'Why should he be shot, Madame?'

'That's what happens, isn't it? Gangsters throw bodies out of cars.'

'Was he a gangster?'

'I shouldn't think so. But he knew a few. Maninko told me.'

'Did any doubtful characters ever visit him?'

'None I ever saw.'

'So why should he be thrown out of a car on the motorway?'

'I didn't say he was. I asked, that's all. He didn't drive himself. He always took a taxi. He was well off.'

'Which taxi?'

'It was always a different one. I think he didn't want people to know what he got up to.'

'What *did* he get up to?'

'Something, I bet. Or what was he doing on the motorway?'

That was what was bothering Darcy. 'Had he any relatives round here?'

'I think he had a daughter.'

'Know her name?'

'No.'

'So how do you know about her?'

'Everybody knows.'

95

'Did he tell people?'

'Only the people he drank with and played cards with at the bar.'

'So how do *you* know?'

'It gets around. I heard it at the grocer's.'

'Does she know her father's dead?'

'How do I know?'

'Well, have you seen her around?'

'No. He didn't have visitors. Except his card-playing friends.'

It took some time to identify the daughter. Darcy went to see Dupont's 'card-playing friends', but they knew remarkably little about him. He was, it seemed, a tight-mouthed man who never talked about himself and it did nothing but add to the mystery.

All Rollin, the undertaker, knew was that Dupont had a daughter. He thought her name was Zoë, but he wasn't sure.

'What about her surname?'

'Don't know it. He always just called her Zoë. Serral, who runs the stationer's, might know.'

Serral *didn't* know but he added a little more. 'I think she married a man who runs a big ironmonger's in Dôle.'

It was another step forward and Maninko, the Pole, supplied the last link. 'I think it's in the Main Street,' he said.

A telephone call to the Dôle police provided the answer.

'Chappe,' they said. 'Thomas Chappe. It's the biggest ironmonger's in the town.'

'Home address?'

'Hang on.' There was the sound of rustling pages and murmuring voices, then, finally, the answer. 'Thomas Chappe, 7, Rue Pasteur.'

It seemed to indicate a visit to Dôle.

'Not Dupont,' Madame Chappe said. 'Not Jean Dupont. His name was Achille-Jean Quelereil-Dupont.'

'Ah!'

It was quite a mouthful and it suddenly wasn't hard to see why they had not been able to find out much about the dead man.

Madame Chappe didn't seem surprised at her father's death.

She was small and fat and was alone, because her husband was working late with his staff stock-taking at his shop.

'It could have happened any time,' she explained. 'He was old.'

'He didn't die of natural causes, Madame,' Darcy explained. 'He died of injuries he received on the motorway.'

She looked puzzled. 'He didn't drive.'

'He wasn't driving. He seems to have been walking.'

'But he hated walking!'

He told her what they knew and watched her expression change to bewilderment. 'Why would he be wandering about on the motorway?' she asked.

'Did he make a habit of drinking?'

'Not really.'

'He *had* been drinking. There was a high level of alcohol in his blood. He'd been drinking whisky.'

'Well, he liked a whisky. But he didn't drink much.'

'We've checked the villages along the motorway in the area where he was found. Did he know people in Mailly-les-Temps or Ponchet?'

'I don't think so. He had a house at St-Alban, which isn't far away, and, apart from holidays, he didn't travel much. He liked to go to the bar to play cards or dominoes. Sometimes two or three friends came in to play. As far as I know, that's it.'

'Could he have been visiting somebody?'

'I can't imagine whom.'

'Would you have a key to his house?'

'I insisted on having one in case something ever happened to him. It seems now that something has.'

'Do you think you could accompany me to St-Alban to check the house?'

'It's late.'

'It ought to be done. We'll make sure you're brought safely home.'

Madame Chappe looked dubious. 'Oh, well, all right. I suppose I'd better. Could we call at the shop on the way and warn my husband where I'm going?'

97

For a woman who had just lost her father, Madame Chappe didn't seem much moved. She showed no signs of grief and it puzzled Darcy, who used the drive from Dôle to get to know more about the nebulous Archille-Jean Quelereil-Dupont. He wasn't helped by the fact that Madame Chappe let out information only in small driblets.

'Had he always lived at St-Alban?' Darcy asked.

'No,' she said. 'That house at St-Alban wasn't his only house.'

'So I've heard.'

'He had another. In Dôle. A bigger one. He bought the one at St-Alban a long time ago and went to live there for a time.'

'Why did he do that? Family problems?'

'He felt it was safer.'

'Safer than what?'

'Being at his house in the city where everybody knew him.'

'He was hiding?'

'Sort of.'

'Why?'

'He was afraid.'

'What of?'

'A man.' Madame Chappe drew a deep breath. 'A man he prosecuted. He was sent to prison for twenty years.'

Darcy stared at her. 'Your father was a barrister?'

'Yes.'

Well, at least they'd finally managed to find out who 'Jean Dupont' was.

It was dark when they reached St-Alban, bitterly cold and raining, the roads reflecting the reds, greens and yellows of the neons which sparkled in a dazzling display of jewels as the windscreen wipers swept the water away in waves.

Pel, whom Darcy had telephoned, was waiting for them, sitting in a car, looking frozen under his knitted carapace of woollen garments. The car was driven by Claudie Darel who'd been brought along to help if Madame Chappe became at all upset.

The house looked typical of an old man's home. It was shabby through the indifference of someone unconcerned with the looks of the place and Madame Chappe seemed to feel she ought to apologize.

'I was always going on at him to get new furniture and curtains,' she said. 'He bought it furnished and he said it wasn't worth changing things at his age, that they'd last his lifetime and, besides, it was too comfortable and he was too old to bother. Anyway, what are you looking for?'

'Something that might explain why he was on the motorway at midnight,' Darcy said.

She pushed her key into the lock, opened the door and switched on a light. Pel and Darcy were about to step inside after her but she didn't move. Glancing past her, Pel saw the drawer of the hall stand was on the floor.

Madame Chappe turned and stared at them, her eyes wide and shocked. 'I think someone's been in here,' she said.

'I suggest,' Pel said to Madame Chappe, 'that you stand quite still and don't touch a thing.'

There was a small salon just off the hall and the door was open.

'Anything missing that you can notice at first glance, Madame?'

'No.'

Darcy pushed past her. The room, which looked over a secluded overgrown garden, had clearly been turned over by an intruder. Papers were scattered on the floor and drawers had been pulled out of a chest near the door.

Madame Chappe stared at it all for a moment, then her hand went to her mouth. 'My God,' she said. 'The porcelain!'

Darcy closed the door. 'What porcelain, Madame?'

But Madame Chappe was heading for the stairs as she spoke. Quelereil-Dupont's bedroom looked much like the dining-room. Drawers stood open and a cupboard was agape.

'Oh, my God!' Madame Chappe was almost in tears. 'They've gone!'

'What have gone, Madame?'

'He had two pieces of porcelain. He said they weren't worth

anything. But they were. I know they were.' She gestured at the cupboard. 'That's where he always kept them.'

'Did he know they were valuable?'

'Of course. He pretended they were worthless but I knew they weren't. I looked them up. They were Meissen and they dated back to 1739. They were made by Johann Kandler and I think they were worth a lot of money.'

Her hands went out to move things for a better look but Pel stopped her.

'Please stand still, Madame,' he said. 'Don't touch anything.' He turned to Claudie Darel who was waiting at the bottom of the stairs. 'Get on the radio, Claudie. Get Fingerprints and Forensic out here.'

As Claudie vanished, he turned again to Madame Chappe who was still staring at the wreckage in the bedroom. 'Now, Madame! These pieces of porcelain. Can you describe them?'

'They were Chinese in style,' she said. 'And they *looked* Chinese. They were supposed to be court jesters and they had big laughing mouths. They were in bright colours.'

'And they were worth a lot of money?'

'Five hundred thousand francs, I was told.'

'Who by?'

'I got an expert to come and look at them.'

'Who was he?'

'His name's Vincent. Paul Vincent. He runs an antique shop in Dôle. He's a friend of ours.'

'Is he trustworthy?'

'Of course he is.'

'Why did you get him to give you a valuation?'

'Because I felt they should be somewhere safer than in that cupboard. In the bank, for instance.'

'Were you hoping to have them eventually?'

'Naturally.'

'Do you collect porcelain?'

She shrugged. 'I'd have sold them as soon as they came into my possession.'

'No feeling of them being a family heirloom?'

Madame Chappe sniffed. 'No.'

100

'Who else knew about these pieces of porcelain? Apart from this Paul Vincent. Anybody?'

'I doubt it. I knew about them because I was his daughter.'

'Your husband? Did he know about them?'

'Of course.'

'Could he – or you – have mentioned them to anybody?'

'I certainly didn't. I was hoping they'd be mine when my father died and I kept quiet about them because there's a cousin in Strasbourg with a reputation for being a bit quick off the mark and I was afraid that if he learned about them they might disappear.'

'You mean he'd steal them?'

She looked shocked. 'No. Not that exactly. But you know what happens when people die. Relatives turn up. Small things vanish. My mother had a gold necklace she promised me over and over again. I never found it after the funeral.'

Downstairs in the salon, while Prélat and the Forensic boys were going through the house, Pel got Claudie to make coffee and tried to question Quelereil-Dupont's daughter.

'I'd like to know more about your father,' he said quietly. 'It might help us clear up a lot of things. If his name was Achille-Jean Quelereil-Dupont, why did he call himself simply Dupont?'

She was silent for a moment and her mouth tightened. 'That was later. He preferred it that way.'

'Did he once use his full name?'

'Yes. His mother was one of the Quelereils. They own a lot of land in the Auvergne. They were very important and when she married – a Frederic Dupont, who was a lawyer in Périgueux – she felt it right to retain her old family name. Everybody approved. Including my father, who was their son. He used to feel it gave him class.'

'And he was a barrister?'

'Yes. He became quite well known. Perhaps you've heard of him? He wasn't on the bench. He prosecuted for a while. I still have his red robe. Then he decided he could do better in defence and changed it for a black one. When my mother died he bought this house.'

'Because he was afraid of someone?'

'A man called Lévêque. Georges Lévêque. He was charged with murder and my father was the prosecuting counsel. It was in Marseilles. Lévêque went to prison. There were relatives of his in court and they shouted that they'd kill my father. I think he bought this house because he thought they might try.'

'Did they?'

'No. Not as far as I know. But he was well known. Surely you've heard of the Marival-Midi swindle.'

'I've heard of it, Madame,' Pel said. 'Though it was a bit before my time.'

'Five financiers went to prison. He prosecuted in that case, too. Then he changed sides to defend a man who was accused of murdering the Countess de Perrenet. He got him acquitted.'

'He must have been quite famous.'

'I suppose so. It didn't last long, though. He got involved in politics.' Madame Chappe spoke unhappily. 'He was wonderful at first. He was even thought brilliant. He earned a lot of money. But he gambled. He chased women. Then something happened. I don't know what it was. I was quite young and I never really learned. Something to do with his clients, I discovered. But that was all. People didn't come to him any more. He went down and down and seemed to have no money at all. But recently he seemed quite well off again.'

Pel had got their man clear now. Quelereil-Dupont's career had gone up like a rocket and, like a rocket, having reached its peak, had descended as quickly. Pel had seen him in court as a young cop and admired his skill. But he also remembered seeing him defending a Lyons gangster accused of a particularly ugly murder. He had got him off on a technicality and had undoubtedly made a lot of money from it, but Pel had noticed that the other advocates had avoided him like the plague, as though contact with him soiled them.

Instinctively he reasoned it had something to do with his being dead on the motorway.

As Yves Pasquier had said of the Count of Monte Cristo, you never knew with people.

9

'It produces a new angle, *patron*,' Darcy said.

'Not for being on the motorway,' Pel said.

'For being dead.'

They had discovered that, in addition to the pieces of porcelain, a silver candlestick and other pieces of valuable silver were also missing, to say nothing of bearer bonds to the value of many thousands of francs, and possibly several thousand francs in cash. Because Dupont didn't drive, he had been in the habit of going to the bank and extracting large sums of money, on which he drew when he needed cash. He had drawn out 50,000 francs the week before he had been found dead but there was no sign of it. They had also checked on the Meissen pieces. Not with the Museum of Fine Arts, which was closed, but with Nosjean's girl-friend, Mijo Lehmann, who knew all about antiques. She confirmed what Madame Chappe had said.

'At least five hundred thousand francs,' she claimed. 'Possibly almost a million if they're in good condition.'

Nothing of moment had been found by Prélat's fingerprint boys, beyond an immediate intimation that whoever had gone through the house had worn gloves. 'There are smudges everywhere,' Prélat said. 'Somebody's done a good job of ransacking the place and been into everything. Otherwise the only prints are Dupont's, confirmed by prints off his razor, toothbrush, and so on, and a few which seem to belong to his daughter, confirmed by those on the coffee cup Claudie gave her. Nothing else. It looks as though the place's been gone through by someone who knew what he was looking for.'

Dupont's other house in Dôle seemed to have been

untouched. There was no sign of a break-in there and no sign of a search. Madame Chappe, who had made a point of visiting it regularly, could see nothing out of place. There were even valuable artefacts about that had remained untouched.

'Why did he have the Meissen figurines at St-Alban?' Pel asked.

'He must have liked to have a few things there with him.'

'It still doesn't explain how he came to be dead on the motorway,' Darcy said. 'With head injuries and two broken legs. We know about the broken legs but the head injuries seem a bit odd and, beyond that, why was he there at all?'

'The break-in could be sheer coincidence,' Pel said. 'Somebody noticed the house was empty and decided to do it. It's a habit people have these days. On the other hand, it might have been done by someone who *knew* he was dead. And that seems to suggest they might even have had a hand in getting him drunk and *putting* him on the motorway. Someone who wanted him out of the way so they could remove the porcelain. Do you reckon his daughter could have taken it?'

'She had a key, *patron*, and there was no sign of a break-in.'

'Perhaps she needs money.'

'She seems to have plenty, Patron.'

'People always want more. She certainly had her eye on the porcelain. What about her husband?'

'He seems an indifferent sort of chap.'

'Where money's concerned nobody's indifferent.'

'No. There's also this cousin she mentioned. Name of Jean-Jacques Richter. Comes from Strasbourg. Works on and off for a bookmaker. She suspects him of stealing other things. He liked to visit Dupont, who was his uncle, and she thinks he helped himself to things while he was there. He played the horses and was always short of money.'

'Would you say she and her husband were the type to dump Dupont on the motorway?'

'No, Patron,' Darcy admitted. 'But you never know.'

As Yves Pasquier had said, you never did.

Pel frowned. 'This money he had,' he went on. 'He made a lot when he was young, then gambled it all away. But now he seems to have been in the money again. Let's find out where he got it. It might explain why he was on the motorway. I'll see his daughter again. You stay here and keep Goriot from making a fool of himself. I want to know more about this Achille-Jean Quelereil-Dupont. After all, for a while he was one of the Chief's Missing Persons and if we find out what happened to him, that's one off his list.'

Madame Chappe claimed to know no more than before about how her father had come to be on the motorway.

'What were his interests?' Pel asked. 'What did he do with himself?'

'He used to say that when you get to seventy-eight, you were too busy just living to do anything else.'

'He must have had some interests.'

'He liked his food.'

'He must have done something else besides eat. Did he collect things of value?'

'Not really. Just the porcelain. But he didn't really collect that even. It was given to him in settlement of fees, I believe. Somebody who ran out of cash, or borrowed from him. It's increased enormously in value, of course, since he acquired it.'

'What about the pieces of silver? The candlestick and the other things?'

'The same, I think. People he'd defended gave them to him. I never knew who they were.'

'So if he didn't fill in his time collecting, what else? I believe he played cards.'

'He loved cards,' she said. 'He used to say piquet was the aristocrat of card games for two. But he liked people round him so he played more bridge than piquet.'

'Regularly?'

'Yes. With the man from the garage at St-Alban. And the undertaker, I think.'

'*And* the stationer, we heard.'

'I think that's right. I expect Madame Mallard from the house opposite told you. She seems to know everything.'

'It doesn't seem a very esoteric way of entertaining himself

105

for a man who, apart from his feet, appeared to be in pretty good shape and had had such an interesting life.'

She hesitated, then blushed. 'He used to like to go to health spas and health farms.'

'Was he ill?'

'No, he went for a holiday.'

'A holiday? At a health farm?' A holiday in a health farm to Pel would have been a step nearer the grave. He was terrified of such places, convinced that if all the ills he was sure he was assailed with didn't develop there into galloping campaigns and finish him off, he would contract some sort of dreaded disease from another patient which would have the same effect.

'Well,' Madame Chappe said. 'They weren't holidays exactly. He liked to take a week or two off now and then and have everything done for him.'

'At a health farm?'

'They'll accept you if you can pay. You don't have to be ill or unfit. He seemed to like to go and just be looked after for a while.'

'Wouldn't he have preferred to come to you? To his daughter's?'

Madame Chappe's face stiffened. 'He didn't seem to,' she said.

Pel's eyes narrowed. 'Did you get on all right?'

'In a way.'

'In a way?'

'He could be difficult.'

'What about your husband? Did he get on with him?'

'Of course. But my father didn't like Dôle. It's a small town and he'd been used to bigger cities. He couldn't walk very well. He preferred to sit around and that could be boring. And he had no friends here and we're occupied all the time with the business. We have no children. But we didn't quarrel. My husband wouldn't permit it.' Madame Chappe frowned. 'Besides, I didn't see him often enough for that. I offered him a home when Maman died but he insisted he was best on his own. I went to see him occasionally, but never without telephoning first. He had his reasons.'

'What were they?'

'I don't know. That's just what he always said.'

'But you always had a key to his house – to both his houses?'

'In case of emergency, that's all.'

'Did he often go to a health farm for a holiday?'

She blushed. 'Yes.'

'But he wasn't ill?'

'He had no problems, apart from the trouble with his feet which he'd had ever since he was a child.'

'With flat feet he could hardly run about much,' Pel said drily. 'Was it to slim?'

She drew a deep breath, her face pink. 'I think chiefly he liked to see women – young women – in shorts and vests. He liked women. My mother had a lot of trouble with him. When I was young, I had to warn him when she came from shopping. He was sometimes in one of the bedrooms with the maid. I was too young at the time to know what was going on. When I grew older, I refused to have anything to do with it. But it didn't stop.'

'So he went to these health farms to see the young girls?'

'Some weren't all that young. I found once he'd been dating one of the instructresses – a girl of twenty-two. But I also found he'd been going round with a woman called Bapt whose family owned a string of grocery stores. He was an oversexed old man.' Tears came to Madame Chappe's eyes. 'My mother used to call him a randy old swine and she was right.'

For a while Pel sat in silence waiting for Madame Chappe to collect herself.

She sighed. 'I was a bit ashamed of him,' she said eventually. 'There was a time when he made a lot of money from the law. But then he seemed to go downhill. He sold the house in Dôle and bought the one at St-Alban because it was smaller. But then he seemed to start making money again and when the house in Dôle came on the market again he bought it back again.'

'How did he start making money again?'

'I don't know. There was some scandal. I told you. Not a public one. It was kept very quiet and I never found out what it was. He gave up law and he didn't appear to have two

107

centimes to rub together. But then he was suddenly in the money again. I never knew where I was with him.'

'You've no idea what this something – this scandal – might have been?'

'No.' The word was bitten off and it was Pel's impression that she did know but was not prepared to dredge it up again.

'Were you by any chance afraid your father would remarry?'

'Yes.'

'Because of his money?'

'Of course. We've always hoped that when he died there'd be a little for us.'

'He could have lived a long time.'

'I know. We often thought we'd be old ourselves before he went.'

'Who'll get his money? You?'

'There's nobody else. Unless' – tears came to her eyes – 'unless he's left it to one of these old women he chased. He might well have.'

'Was there a lot?'

'I think so. He'd started to boast about it. But I don't really know. I never saw his bank statements. He kept them to himself.'

'A lot of money is sometimes a good reason for getting rid of someone.'

'Yes.' She nodded, then looked up, startled. 'Surely you don't think – '

Pel did think. Certainly the thought had crossed his mind. Madame Chappe appeared to be distressed by all that had happened, but Pel had been in the game long enough not to be surprised. The sweetest old women managed to poison their husbands or contrive accidents. Madame Chappe could well have done so too.

'Of course not,' he lied. 'But there seem to have been other women in his life. Women he'd also boasted to about how much he was worth.'

She nodded again and he went on quickly.

'Could he have met someone at one of these places he went to who would wish him dead?' he asked.

Madame Chappe sighed. '*I* sometimes did,' she said.

108

Darcy's worries didn't go away, and Angélique Courtoise wasn't slow to notice.

'You're thinking about that Goriot again, aren't you?' she said.

Darcy nodded. 'Yes,' he admitted. 'He's taken it badly that I've got Aimedieu back on my team.' He paused, frowning. 'I heard some funny things today. I think someone's after me.'

'Goriot?'

'Someone.' He managed a smile. 'It's a rotten world.' He looked at her warmly. 'Not you. If anybody isn't rotten, it's you.'

She looked startled. 'That's unexpected.'

Darcy grinned. 'I'm getting sentimental. It's a habit of men at my age. It must be the change of life.'

As he studied her, she looked steadily back at him. 'When we first met,' she said, 'you convinced me getting engaged was dangerous.'

'It was to that chap.'

'You said that, married, I'd be certain to need a lover. Someone to fill in the time when my husband was dozing in front of the television after a hard day's work. You said I'd be pulsating with desire and reeking of perfume and my husband wouldn't even notice, and that to avoid being completely frustrated I'd need to get out and meet someone else – you, I seem to remember.'

'Well, you would, wouldn't you?'

'Would you feel the same way about the situation if you were the husband?'

Darcy laughed. 'Not if I were *your* husband.'

'You've changed your tune a bit.'

'I think I must be growing old. It's a Pel syndrome. It must be infectious.' Darcy paused. 'All the same, my pad does seem emptier than it did.'

'You need someone to support you when you wilt.'

Darcy shrugged. 'There are a few people I can fall back on.'

'You can fall back on me.' Angélique's expression was just a shade wistful. 'You've been falling back on me a long time, in fact. Goriot can't harm you.' She paused and looked anxiously at him. 'Can he?'

109

'There are a lot of things than can happen to a cop that he doesn't expect,' Darcy admitted. 'One of them is people setting him up. A cop's not only got to keep his nose clean, he has to be seen to be keeping it clean. And if someone suggests he isn't doing so, it's surprising how quickly people begin to believe it.'

The following day Darcy approached Pel.

'I think we ought to check on that Club Atlantique in Royan,' he said. 'It seems to be linked to our friend, Dupont.'

'More than we thought, I suspect,' Pel agreed. 'He seemed to like health clubs.'

'They might be able to come up with a reason why he's dead. But it hasn't a telephone number, so it'll mean a visit.'

'Who're you suggesting?' Pel asked.

'Me, Patron. It's a long way for – ' Darcy nearly said 'an old man like you' but managed to change it at the last moment to 'someone who's as busy as you are. After all, it's about as far as you can go in France from east to west. It'll take two days. Perhaps three.'

Pel eyed him curiously, far from fooled. 'You have an interest in Royan perhaps?'

Darcy grinned. 'If nothing else,' he said, 'it'll take me a long way from Goriot. But otherwise no, *patron*. I have no interest in Royan.'

He hadn't either. He proposed to take his interest with him. He put it to Angélique Courtoise that evening as they ate. 'Three days. On the coast. It's not much of a place. All concrete because the Americans bombed it by mistake during the war. They did their best to put things right, though, and even the church's concrete. There's a good hotel I know near St-Georges de Didonne next door. Fancy it?'

She smiled. 'What do you think?'

It proved to be a good break and they both enjoyed it. The beach club was closed, of course, because it was winter and you could hardly expect elderly ladies and gentlemen to try to touch their toes on the beach in a screaming wind off the

110

Atlantic. But for the off-season months, for the local custom the Club Atlantique had been transferred to the basement of an old church at Bernon. It was a huge room, with a restored floor of sprung pine, and blazing with lights. Three dozen men and women, all past middle age and all corpulent, were gently swaying to the pounding beat of pop music from a set of amplifiers.

'Up – and down – and up – and down.'

A woman in her twenties, with 'Maybelle' stencilled on her T-shirt across a splendid bosom, was shouting instructions at them and demonstrating how to do it without even panting or growing pink.

'Press your knees together! It reduces the thighs. Clasp your hands and pull. It increases the muscles. Don't forget we're fighting the flab. Right, again: up – and down – and up – and down – '

It seemed ideal for coronaries.

Receiving Darcy's message, 'Maybelle' halted the class and told them to carry on in their own way. They slackened off immediately she took her beady eye off them.

'Dupont?' she said. 'That's a pretty common name. And over seventy? He sounds a bit old. Most people of that age have the sense to stop this lark. You'd better have a word with Abd-el-Krim. He ran the class on the beach in the summer.'

Abd-el-Krim's real name was Jean-Jacques Rabot and he undoubtedly got his sobriquet from the neat black beard and moustache he wore. He was young and as dark-skinned as an Arab – he probably even *was* an Arab – but he didn't recall Dupont. However, the number 579 on the card they'd found took them a step forward. Rabot looked it up.

'Last year,' he said. 'Name, Jean Dupont. I've got him now. He was a bit old for us and I don't think he was really interested. He was on holiday and he liked to see Maybelle jumping up and down. I often caught him watching. I even caught him once round the back where the showers are. She was inside. He was a dirty old sod.'

'Did he make any arrangements with any woman who might have had a husband?'

'Well, there was a woman called Massières. She had a hus-

111

band somewhere. She also had a shop in St-Georges. When she left, he left. Perhaps he followed her.'

They found the address of the woman, Helene Massières, who ran an expensive boutique in the main street. She was a blonde and a youthful fifty, with a good figure and no superfluous fat, and looked as though she spent all the time when she wasn't selling clothes doing exercises or concentrating on slimming. In addition to looking younger than she was, she was also a super saleswoman, and before they knew where they were she had sold Angélique Courtoise a skirt and blouse. Darcy managed to project a question through a chink in the sales talk.

It stopped her dead and she answered shortly. 'He was a nuisance,' she said abruptly.

'In what way?'

She seemed reluctant to talk. 'In what way *is* a man a nuisance to a woman? He followed me the whole day.'

'Was he in love with you or something?'

She gave Darcy a cold look.

'But he stopped in the end?'

'Yes.'

'Why?'

She hesitated again before speaking. 'He met a woman from Dijon and transferred his attentions to her.'

Well, Dijon was nearer home and there didn't seem to be much point in hanging around so they went to the hotel Darcy knew. It was old-fashioned and, as there was a gale blowing off the sea, had a huge fire roaring in the grate. There were extensive grounds so they wrapped up well to walk round them. Angélique had a red scarf round her neck and her hair blew in the wind. Her nose was pink but so were her cheeks and she looked bright and cheerful.

'Happy?' Darcy asked.

'Of course.'

'Let's go to the cinema when we've eaten.'

They took tea in front of the fire, then drove into town to a restaurant Darcy knew where they ate *tripes à la mode de Caen* with a local wine. Afterwards they went to the cinema. They didn't even bother to enquire what was showing and sat in the

112

back row, Darcy with his arm round the girl. Afterwards, they returned to the hotel and drank coffee and brandy.

'Do you go out at nights much when you're home?' Darcy asked.

'Only with you.'

'What do you do when I'm not there?'

'Wait until you are.'

'Isn't there anyone else?'

'No.'

'Why not?'

She looked gently at him. 'The others pale into insignificance.'

'Don't you ever cheat a bit?'

'No.'

Darcy paused, 'I'm glad you came,' he said.

'So am I.' She paused. 'Unfortunately, I don't think it will get me very far.'

'Why do you think that?'

'Because I know you.'

'I'm not so sure,' Darcy said slowly, 'that these days you do. I'm not so sure I know myself.'

'Is Goriot worrying you?'

'A bit. But it's not Goriot. It's the effect that worrying about Goriot's having on me that's worrying me.'

She didn't understand what he was getting at. For that matter, Darcy wasn't sure he did himself. He saw her eyes were moist.

'What's the matter?' he asked.

'I'm the matter.'

'How?'

'I know it will all come to nothing and I ought to back away from you. But I don't want to. Life's rotten, isn't it? There's no future, Daniel.'

Darcy felt guilty.

'There are other men around,' she went on. 'Plenty. But no bells ring. Not even a little tinkle, and I'm used to hearing great resounding peals when I'm with you. I really ought to have been more careful.'

113

They climbed into the car next morning, not quite looking at each other and half-imagining that the other guests were watching them. Dropping Angélique outside the Faculty of Medicine at the University, where she worked, Darcy moved on alone, trotting round the aerobics and callisthenics clubs in search of Achille-Jean Quelereil-Dupont, better known simply as Jean Dupont. His quarry couldn't have chosen a more anonymous alias because Jean Dupont must have been the commonest name in France.

He found him again at the Palais des Sports at Mirabeau. It was less a palace than a set of barns converted into a luxury complex. One of them was a huge hangar-like shed behind the central building, and from it he could hear the thudding of the beat music that always seemed to accompany physical exercise. People in track suits or satin shorts and T-shirts were moving about the entrance hall, heading down a corridor marked 'Showers and Changing Rooms'. Among them was a blond young man with bulging muscles and teeth that flashed almost as brightly as Darcy's own.

'Come on,' he was saying. 'Hurry up! It's the run next! Change your shoes and be back here!'

'Okay, Tony.' The man who answered was surreptitiously biting a bar of chocolate.

On Darcy's right was an office and he was met at the door by a woman whose age he guessed to be around sixty. She was slim, expensively dressed and had once been beautiful. She had peroxided hair and a heavily made up face.

'I'm Alicia Coty,' she said. 'Madame Coty. Do you wish to enrol for our courses?'

Darcy shook his head, put on his best smile and produced his identity card with its red, white and blue strip. Her smile vanished abruptly.

'Police?' she said sharply. 'What do you want? We've nothing here of interest to you.'

'I think I'd better decide that, Madame.' Darcy didn't like being dismissed before he had even opened his mouth.

'We have no criminals here. People come here to get fit or to become more attractive to the opposite sex. They pay a lot of money for it.'

114

'So I imagine. I'm looking for information on a man called Jean Dupont. He was keen on your sort of activity and he might well have attended your classes.'

She tempered her manner to wariness and listened as he described what he knew about the man he was seeking.

'Well,' she said, 'we have health and beauty – that's for women, of course. I run that.'

'You're an expert?'

She managed a stiff smile. 'I should hope so. I own this place. We also have computerized fitness, nutrition analysis, rejuvenation and longevity training. He might have been interested in those if he was getting on in years. We have stretch and tone isometrics, therapy massage, tension-reducing aerobics – '

'Is that the one where they jump up and down?'

'Well, yes, a little. They also do toe-touching and torso swinging – to reduce the hips.'

'Who conducts this class?'

'Annie Albert. She's a fully qualified instructor – '

'Young?'

'Yes.'

'I think you'd better check the names in that class. That's probably where he was.'

Madame Coty stared at him hostilely, then she spoke slowly. 'Why do you want this Dupont?'

'I don't want him, Madame. I just want to know about him. I want to know why he was found dead on the motorway on the 14th of last month.'

Her face went pink. 'He's dead?'

'He is, Madame. You seem concerned.'

'No! No!' She suddenly seemed a great deal less hostile. 'I know the man you want. He came here. But he was asked to leave the class.'

'Ah! Why?'

'Annie said he was a nuisance.'

'I'd like to have a word with Annie.'

Annie Albert was an attractive woman in her late twenties, with a good figure and a surprising bust for a gym instructress.

'He didn't bother with the exercises,' she said. 'I don't think he was interested in them at all. When he came into the class

115

he just stood at the back moving his arms and bending his
knees a little and nothing else. Everybody else was giving it all
they'd got. You have to if you wish to make progress.'

'Why was he here then, do you think?'

'Well, he came with a woman called Guignard. Jeanette Guignard. She came from somewhere in the city. But she left. I think
she objected to his attentions.'

'Old? Young?'

'Fiftyish.'

'Well preserved?'

'Not particularly. She hadn't paid attention to herself. She
was overweight.'

'When she left, what did Dupont do?'

'He joined the aerobics class. As I say, he didn't do anything.
Just watched me.'

'You, of course, were doing the exercises?'

'I led the class.'

'Jump up and down a bit? That sort of thing?'

'Of course.'

'Why do you think he watched you?'

'Because he was a dirty old man. I'm engaged. To Tony
Sarcino. He looks after the male classes.'

'The one who looks like a Greek God?'

Her serious face cracked in a smile. 'He does a bit, doesn't
he?' she said.

By this time she had clearly decided that Darcy wasn't bad-
looking himself and was much more friendly. She invited him
into a room labelled 'Instructors' and offered him a coffee.

'Have you been doing this work long?' he asked.

'No. But it's not hard to learn. We've got cardio-fitness tests,
sun lamps, therapists, nutritionists, steam baths, inhalation
rooms, active mud.' She grinned. 'It's all balls, of course. It
does make you fitter, but a normal person who doesn't overeat
doesn't need it – *or* grapefruit juice and brewer's yeast. You
don't really need to wear yourself out keeping fit.'

'Did Dupont try to molest you?' Darcy asked.

'He once put an arm round my shoulder. I told him pupils
weren't allowed contact with instructors – any sort of contact.

116

It's not true, of course. Some of the pupils are just friendly and it does no harm. He was different.'

'What happened?'

'He left. I told him of a place at Yon.'

'What place is that?'

'The Reggio Hall of Health.'

'Same sort of place as this?'

'Not as good.'

'Why did you send him there?'

'I heard one of the instructors goes in for the sort of thing he wanted. Barbara Valendon. She was here for a while. She tried to get her mitts on Tony. She got the push.'

Darcy wondered if Annie Albert had arranged it.

10

By this time, Sergeant Gehrer's car was in the yard at the back of the Hôtel de Police, watched by the curious from windows and by a group of uniformed men who had just brought in one of the patrol cars.

Leaning inside was a tall man wearing spectacles. He was examining the damage to the windscreen with a magnifying glass. Watched by the Chief, Leguyader from Forensic, and Pel, he stretched a tape measure from one of the holes in the hood to the front seat. He was Judge Castéou's husband and Madame Pel had done her stuff by inviting him and his wife to supper. To Pel's surprise they had got on quite well together. It was always a surprise to him when people got on with him. He didn't expect anyone to get on with him, and most of the time he was right.

Castéou had arrived promptly and had insisted on examining both the car and the body, and had spent two whole days with Cham and Leguyader.

Nadauld had then been buried with the ceremony to which his rank entitled him and all the precise cadences of the Latin responses of the Mass. There had been the usual sad-faced relatives, including his wife, his daughter and her new husband, and the inevitable group of grim-faced policemen – the Chief, huge and sombre; Pel, small and grey-faced; Darcy; Nadauld's sergeant, Gehrer, with a huge bandage over his eye; Nadauld's successor, Inspector Turgot. The slow funeral ceremonies had followed like a sad pavane with the women wearing black veils, then the *Dies Irae*, part of the mass for the dead, and finally the dismissal, as the congregation got ready to depart.

Castéou removed his head from inside the car and straightened up. 'It will take a few days,' he said. 'I have a few ideas, a few suspicions, but I can't be sure yet. I take it we have the bullets and the fragments of bullet that have been found.'

'I have them,' Leguyader said. 'They don't amount to much. We didn't find more than one. Perhaps the others are in the upholstery of the car. Or on the grass near the guardroom. We've searched but we've produced nothing yet.' He frowned. 'But four men were hit so there must be something somewhere.'

Castéou nodded. 'I think we'll find the answer,' he said. 'It'll take time but we'll get there.'

With Darcy away, it seemed a good idea to see Madame Chappe's husband. Pel had a feeling that Madame Chappe had been telling the truth about her interest in the porcelain jesters but her husband was another matter.

As it happened, Edmond Chappe seemed to be all she claimed for him. He was an earnest-faced man, stooping, with a moustache and thick spectacles, and he explained that he didn't get on very well with his father-in-law.

'He came here occasionally,' he said. 'But he never wanted to stay. I don't honestly think we wanted him to, either.'

'Did you know the value of the porcelain figures he had?'

'Of course. My wife always hoped they'd come to her. He said they were to be hers but he liked to keep them and she was satisfied with that.'

'They were worth a lot of money.'

Chappe smiled. 'We'd have converted them into money straight away. Things like that belong in collections and I was always terrified one of them would be broken. That would have meant the loss of thousands of francs straight away. They were a pair and, while individually they were worth around four hundred thousand each, together they were worth a lot more.'

Vincent, the expert, had a small antiques shop further along the street. It wasn't open but a telephone call from Chappe enabled Pel to meet Vincent on the premises.

'Of course I knew the value of the porcelain,' he said. 'I never get to handle things like that these days. Antiques have become big business with too many whizz kids in the game. But I knew their value. It's in all the books.' He produced a thick volume and indicated a picture of the porcelain jesters. 'Identical pair,' he said. 'Meissen. Made by Handler. This gives them a value of three hundred thousand each five years ago. Five hundred thousand each would be nearer the mark now.'

'The Chappes say they'd have sold them if they'd been theirs. Would you have done the selling for them?'

'I don't suppose so. I'm not important enough. But I'd be on hand with advice to make sure they weren't done.'

'What would you get out of it?'

'I told them I didn't want anything but Zoë said I'd have to take a commission. There would be plenty over, of course, even if I did. We had a working arrangement but, of course, that was a long way in the future. Her father seemed a fit old man and nobody expected him to die.'

Unless, Pel thought, he had been helped on his way.

On his way back to headquarters, he passed the house at St-Alban. There was a car outside. It was a flashy-looking Honda and there was a man at the door. Pel's interest was caught at once, especially as the man looked as flashy as the car. He was dressed like an Englishman, with fawn trousers, a blazer with brass buttons, a blue shirt and a red-spotted cravat, and a skimmer cap as flat as a plate. Pel halted his car but the man at the door failed to notice him until he was standing alongside.

'You live here?' Pel said.

'Yes.' The man started at his voice and turned. For a moment he looked disconcerted, but he recovered quickly. 'Yes, this is my home.'

'And you are?'

'Jean-Jacques Richter.'

'Profession?'

'Haven't got one. Just "gentleman". I have money.'

Pel smiled. It looked like the one on the face of the tiger. 'How come,' he asked, 'if this is your home and you're Jean-Jacques Richter, that this house is registered in the name of Jean Dupont?'

Richter looked disconcerted. 'Oh! Is it?'

'According to the law. According also to his daughter, Madame Chappe. She was here yesterday with a key to let me in.'

Richter frowned. 'Who the devil are you?'

Pel showed his identity card. 'Chief Inspector Pel,' he said. 'Brigade Criminelle of the Police Judiciaire.'

'Oh!' Richter looked taken aback. 'What are you doing here?'

'I'm more interested in what *you*'re doing here. You were trying to get in, weren't you?'

'No. I was just calling.'

'You have a banker's card in your hand. Made of plastic. It's a method criminals use to force doors.'

'I wasn't doing that. I just happened to take it out.'

'Why?'

'I'm going down to the bank now. Monsieur Dupont's my uncle. I came to see him. His real name's – '

'I know what his name is. I also know yours. You're Madame Chappe's cousin from Strasbourg.'

Richter smiled. 'You've heard of me?'

'Yes. It's a good job, isn't it, that you hadn't actually got inside the house. I would have had to arrest you. What were you after?'

'To see if the old boy had left me anything,' Richter admitted. 'He once promised me one or two things.'

'Such as what?'

'Well, he had a nice bit of porcelain I liked.'

'Two, in fact?'

'Well, yes. Two.'

'Meissen?'

'Yes, Meissen. He said I could have them.'

'I'm sorry to inform you that they've disappeared.'

Richter's face fell. 'Disappeared!' he yelped. 'Has that bitch, Zoë Chappe, got them?'

Pel smiled. 'No, she hasn't. As a matter of fact, she's been wondering if *you* have.'

Although Jean-Jacques Richter had seemed very likely to have

121

been involved in the death of Jean Dupont, there was nothing much they could pin on him. He seemed to be nothing more than a *demi-sel*, – a cheap crook picking up a living from minor frauds.

It seemed a case of 'Back to square one', back to the same old question: what was a faded ex-barrister with a past, and, judging by the fact that he was in the money again, a future, doing on the motorway near Mailly-les-Temps when his home (both homes, for that matter) was miles away?

It was well into the evening and Nosjean and De Troq' had been on their feet all day. Nosjean was anxious to get back to the flat he shared with Mijo Lehmann, the expert on antiques and painting, and De Troq' was expected for dinner at the flat of one of the secretaries from the Palais de Justice whose family also had a title. Not an old one like De Troq's, just a Second Empire one that impressed nobody much. To a man of De Troq's background, however, it was better than nothing.

The Manoir at Montagny was an imposing edifice. Not large but large enough, with slated turrets and wide steps up to the front door. It was set in extensive grounds and they were met at the door by a butler. Nosjean and De Troq' glanced at each other. By mutual consent, it was De Troq' who spoke. De Troq's accent – his whole manner even – spoke of breeding and appealed to the snobbery in wealthy people, and it was always left to him to ask the questions when they were involved with the self-important or the aristocratic.

'Baron de Troquereau,' he announced himself. 'And my colleague, Jean-Luc Nosjean. We'd like to have a word with Monsieur Jean-Philippe de Rille.'

'Which Monsieur Jean-Philippe de Rille would that be?' the butler asked.

'There's more than one?'

'There's Monsieur and his son. They have the same names.'

'Are they both at home?'

'No, monsieur. Only Monsieur de Rille, the Father.'

'Not the son?' Or the Holy Ghost, De Troq' felt like saying.

'No, monsieur.'

122

'Then we'd better see Monsieur de Rille, the Father.'

Monsieur de Rille, the Father, might well have been God. He was tall and thin, with an aristocratic nose and a cold manner. It didn't put De Troq' off: De Troq' had been handling people like Jean-Philippe de Rille, the Father, ever since he could walk. They ended up sitting down and being offered brandy.

'A Ford Sierra?' De Rille said.

'Exactly, monsieur. Number 1091-AR–41.'

'That sounds like my son's.'

'When will your son be home?'

De Rille managed a wry smile. 'I couldn't tell you. He comes home only occasionally. He has a flat in the city.'

'He has a job there?'

'If you could call it that. He calls himself a car salesman but he has no showroom and no premises. Not even an office.' De Rille shrugged. 'But he *does* sell cars. Always expensive ones. By contacts, through people he knows. He knows a lot of people. He doesn't *have* to work, of course. He was left a great deal of money five years ago by his grandfather, my wife's father, because he was his only grandson. I believe he's got through a lot of it, but, on the other hand, he does seem to make money from time to time. He only uses this place to tinker with the cars he buys and sells. Judging by the noise of engines by the stables, I suspect he invites his friends to use it, too.'

'And this flat of his, monsieur? You have the address, of course?'

De Rille gave another of his wry smiles. 'No. As a matter of fact, I haven't. But I have a telephone number.'

It didn't take long to get the address from the Telecommunications office.

'Flat 4, 17, Rue Barnabas,' Nosjean said. 'We'll see him in the morning. It's late now and he sounds like a type who spends his nights out on the town – this one or some other town. Come to that it might well be St-Trop'.'

'He sounds interesting,' De Troq' agreed. 'A man who likes spending and makes a lot of money occasionally. Drives a big car. No fixed job. Might be worth looking into.'

123

Seventeen, Rue Barnabas, turned out to be a new block of flats and, arriving early the following day, they fully expected Jean-Philippe de Rille, the Son, to be still in bed. He wasn't, but he opened the door to them clad in a dressing-gown. He was tall and good-looking but at that moment unshaven, his hair tousled, and holding a mug of coffee.

'Had a late night,' he explained. 'Took a long time waking up.'

They explained why they were there and he looked indignant.

'What is all this?' he demanded. 'Where did you get hold of my name?'

'You own a fawn Ford Sierra, number 1091-AR–41?'

'Yes. Why not?'

'No reason why not. Bought from Garages Europe Automobile?'

'Yes.'

'It was left near a bar in Morbihaux on the twelfth and remained there most of the day. Some time during the night it vanished. In its place was a Citroën 19, number 714-CS–13, belonging to an estate agent from Marseilles by the name of Paul Lebriand, who had lost it while visiting the city on business.'

'So?'

'The Citroën had been used in a hold-up. At Talant.'

'And you think I did it?' De Rille laughed. 'I don't need to hold up supermarkets – '

'I didn't say it *was* a supermarket.'

'Sorry, I thought you did.'

'No.'

'I must have read it in the paper.' De Rille smiled. It was a charming smile – a good salesman's smile – that Nosjean suspected was practised in front of a mirror. 'But I've no need to go in for crime. My grandfather left me a small fortune.'

'Have you still got it?'

'What do you mean?'

'He died five years ago. Have you spent it yet?'

De Rille's smile came again. 'Quite a bit of it. But not the lot by any means.'

'How come the Citroën turned up at the bar at Morbihaux in

place of your Sierra which had been parked there for a matter of several hours?'

De Rille smiled. 'Well, I don't know about the other car but I left *my* car there because I had been visiting the area with a girl friend.'

'Name, sir?'

'Tassigny de Bré. Dominique Tassigny de Bré. I don't suppose you'll know the family.'

Nosjean smiled as De Troq' bridled. 'I might,' De Troq' said shortly. 'My name's de Troquereau de Tournay-Turenne. Baron de Troquereau.'

De Rille pulled a face. 'Sorry, old boy. One doesn't expect to find the aristocracy among the Fuzz.'

'Where can we find this Mademoiselle Tassigny de Bré?' Nosjean asked.

'Bellecroix. Big house as you enter. Faces the square. It hasn't an address. It's simply Tassigny de Bré, Bellecroix.'

Another of them, Nosjean thought, while De Troq' was assessing lineage and breeding and coming to the conclusion that the Tassigny de Brés, like the De Rilles, were jumped-up parvenus from Napoleon III's gimcrack Second Empire.

Whatever the background, they couldn't let the thing go and Nosjean asked if De Rille possessed a gun.

'Several,' he admitted. 'I grew up with guns. I had a rat gun when I was still a small boy and started using shot guns and two-twos when I was around thirteen.'

'I'm thinking of twelve bores.'

'Yes. Those, too. I shoot clay pigeons. I belong to the Montagny Shooting Club. I also help keep vermin down on my father's land. Rabbits, magpies, foxes. That sort of thing. We go out regularly. Arthur Tassigny – ' De Rille smiled, 'he's the brother of Dominique Tassigny – comes now and then. He was at school with me.'

'I'd like to see your guns if I may,' Nosjean said politely.

De Rille produced two twelve-bores, one a splendid Purdy, and a German Mannlicher 303.

Nosjean indicated the Mannlicher. 'What do you use this one for, monsieur?'

'Boar. There are a lot in the forest round Montagny. There's another gun at my father's house. They're all licensed.'

They were, too – all legitimate and above board – and there was no ammunition.

'I keep it at my father's place,' De Rille explained. 'For safety. Mademoiselle Tassigny will confirm my statement about the car.'

'What is she to you, monsieur?'

'Girl friend.' De Rille smiled enigmatically.

'Tell me about her, monsieur.'

'Twenty-one and very beautiful. Bit of an artist. But she doesn't work at it. Prefers cars. Unfortunately she can't afford them so she picks boy friends who can.'

'Such as you?'

De Rille smiled modestly. 'Such as me. She once had a Lotus.'

'What did she run it on?'

'Petrol, of course.'

'Money, I mean.'

'Oh! No, not money. Debts. She's crazy about cars. Never misses Le Mans. Potters about in the pits there. She had a boy friend once – Emilio Almoranti, the racing driver. He let her have a go in his Ferrari. She put up a surprisingly good show.'

Nosjean paused. 'What would you have been doing all the time your car was parked near the bar at Morbihaux? It was there a long time.'

The question came abruptly but De Rille only smiled. 'Well, some of the time we rowed a boat.'

'Hired?'

'No. We just found it by the bank. It had oars. We helped ourselves.'

'And the owner?'

'Well, no one objected so I imagine he was occupied in doing something of his own.'

'That surely didn't occupy the whole period the car was parked near the bar?'

'No. The rest of the time we were occupied in – ' De Rille smiled. 'Well, Dominique is young and very attractive. What *would* we be engaged in doing?'

'She'll confirm this?'

'Of course. Unless it was just a beautiful dream. It might have been.'

Dominique Tassigny did indeed confirm De Rille's claim. She was an exquisite little creature with ash-blond hair, as De Rille had said, and enormous eyes. She gave them a rhapsodic account of their time on the river and in the woods, the only discordant note about the interview being the presence throughout it of her brother, Arthur Tassigny. He was a smooth-faced young man with a high aristocratic nose and the same confident manner as De Rille.

'I'd like to be present while you talk to my sister,' he said.

'Oh?' De Troq' said coldly. 'Why?'

'She has no father or mother. They died a few years ago, and I'm her sole surviving relative. And I don't trust the *flics*. You could frame her.'

Though they resented the implication that they were in the business of corruption, they said nothing. Nevertheless, they both noted with interest young Tassigny's use of the word '*flics*'. It wasn't really the sort of expression someone would use who was at ease with the police.

De Troq' gave the boy another icy look and turned to his sister. 'Sorry to be so personal,' he said. 'And to demand such details. But what were you doing all the time you were with Monsieur de Rille?'

She gave him a cool look and smiled. 'Well, we ate a bit and drank a bit and then – well, what do young people usually do when they're together?'

'If I remember rightly, it was a cold day. Where did you do this thing that young people do together?'

She beamed. 'Here.'

'Monsieur de Rille's car was at Morbihaux. This place is twenty kilometres from the river. How did you get here?'

'We had my car as well.'

'Which is?'

'Only a small one. A Peugeot 205. We don't have the sort of money Jean-Philippe has. We've had to keep ourselves ever

127

since Arthur was eighteen. I was fourteen. My parents were killed in a car crash.'

'It tends to inhibit your spending,' her brother put in. 'That's why we let most of this place off as flats. I have an apartment in town. Dominique stays here as a sort of caretaker. I drive a Renault. A small one. When the oldies were alive we had a Mercedes. A big one.'

The girl beamed. 'And we went back later for the Sierra,' she said.

De Troq' and Nosjean reviewed what they had discovered. They had made further enquiries and come up with some answers. But by no means all of them.

On the way back to the city, they had even been to the river and found the boat just as De Rille had described. The owner, a farmer called Brienne, admitted that the oars would be aboard, tucked under the thwarts, because he always left them there.

'People borrow it,' he agreed. 'A lot of people know about it. But who's going to steal it? It's too big to take away. You'd need a truck. And anyway, there's nowhere to go with it except further up the river.'

'Doesn't it *ever* get stolen?' De Troq' asked.

'It has been but it always comes back and, as I don't use it much myself, it doesn't inconvenience me.

Nosjean studied his notes as they parted. 'I don't like them,' he said.

'Neither do I,' De Troq' admitted. 'But we've nothing on them and we've got to have plenty. They've got too much money behind them. Jean-Philippe de Rille, the father, controls Produits Chimiques de Bourgogne. It's one of the biggest chemical combines in the country. I've looked him up.' He gestured. 'I've looked them all up, in fact. They're just what they seem. De Rille's a *fils de papa* – a spoiled son of a rich father. Occasionally he sells cars. Big cars. Garages Europe Automobile use him from time to time. Know why? It's a subsidiary of Produits Chimiques de Bourgogne. He's a sort of unofficial salesman.

He introduces wealthy young men he knows and draws a commission. Never does any proper work. Bit of a lady killer. Goes around with the Tassigny girl. Her brother seems to be another of the same sort. The girl – ' De Troq' shrugged. 'She's just a girl. Never seems to have done anything. She's actually quite a clever artist – I managed to see some of her drawings – but she doesn't work at it. As he said, she prefers fast cars. She never misses Le Mans.'

11

Pel was also on his way home. But as he reached for his jacket and picked up the keys of his car, the sous-brigadier from the substation at Ponchet, a man called Chevraux, brought in a shoe. He had it in a plastic bag and held it as if it might explode.

'I thought you'd want to see it, sir,' he said. 'It doesn't look as if it's been thrown away because it's been worn out. It's pretty new, in fact.'

'Where did it come from?'

'Near the motorway.'

'Where the body was found?'

'No, sir. Two kilometres further on. Outside Lugny. One of my boys found it when he was out walking with his dog. The dog turned it up. Could it belong to the old boy on the motorway, sir?'

Pel examined the shoe. The inside of the sole had been built up so that it was almost a centimetre thicker than on the outer edge.

'I'd say,' he said carefully, 'that it *did* belong to the old boy on the motorway.'

The discovery of the shoe delayed Pel's departure home. He had it sent along to Forensic with a note to see that it was passed on to Doc Cham, and this led to a round of telephone calls and a talk with the Chief about a new press hand-out. When he reached home, he found his wife had taken a day off from her businesses and was enjoying working in the garden. Someone had cut the grass – something Pel was always promising to do and never did – and she was busy watering.

'I'd like to make it an English garden,' she said. 'They have such lovely gardens in England.'

'That's because they have such dreadful weather,' Pel observed. 'It's green because it's always raining.'

'They work hard in their gardens, too,' Madame pointed out reproachfully.

Pel pretended to be deaf – it was a habit he'd picked up from the Chief – and his wife tactfully changed the subject.

'I bought an antique warming pan today,' she said. 'From that old place near St-Seine l'Abbaye. The old woman who kept it died and it's been taken over by somebody new and they're trying to clear away the junk. It was cheap and it's really very good.'

'Perhaps it's the one they used to smuggle the Man in the Iron Mask out of the queen's bedroom,' Pel said. 'As a baby,' he added. 'You remember, he was the king's twin brother. That's why they put him in the Iron Mask. Young Yves next door's been telling me about it. About the Count of Monte Cristo, too. He's been reading a lot of Dumas just lately.'

Madame smiled. 'Madame Routy and I will get to work on it,' she said. 'It's in a terrible state but a bit of good polishing will bring it back to life. It'll take a few days but it will be worth it. Oh, by the way, Daniel telephoned.'

'He's back?'

'He wanted to know if you'd be in tomorrow. He wants to talk to you.'

'What about? The man on the motorway?'

'No, it's personal, I think.'

Darcy was as brisk and confident as ever when he appeared next morning, his teeth shining, his profile in top gear. Pel guessed why he had chosen to go to Royan and wondered who it was this time. It was time Darcy married, he thought. It was Darcy who had pushed Pel into marriage when he hadn't had the gumption to go ahead himself. Perhaps it was now Darcy's turn to need a shove or two.

'I've traced him all over the country,' he was saying. 'From one health and beauty centre to another. He seems to have been a randy old bastard. He wasn't interested in the health, just the beauty. He liked women. The last place was here, in this city. Chasing a woman called Jeanette Guignard. I've tried to trace her but she seems to have left the area. It seems he became a bit of a nuisance in these places.'

'So why does he come to be dead on the motorway between Mailly-les-Temps and Ponchet? Is there anything of that sort there?'

'Nothing, *patron*. I've checked.'

Pel frowned. 'Somehow, somewhere,' he said, 'there has to be a motive in all this. A randy old man who liked women, but too old to be much of a danger any more. But he seems to have had money and he seems to have chased women because he went to health spas.' Pel's frown deepened. 'But not to get fit. Just to look at girls jumping up and down in shorts and vests? Would he do that? He could do it on a beach in summer. What puzzles me is where he obtained his money. We know there was a period when he was broke but he seems to have been in funds again when he died, although he was seventy-eight and had been retired a long time. Where does a man of that age obtain large sums of money?'

Pel tossed the file on to his desk, rubbed his nose, lit a cigarette, had a coughing bout that made him feel better, and looked up. 'You wanted to see me? Geneviève said you seemed worried.'

Darcy admitted it. He *was* worried and that was unusual because Darcy didn't normally worry much. His attitude to police work was cool. He was never quite as much committed as Pel but he was a good cop and took his work seriously. He hesitated a moment, then fished in his briefcase and produced a newspaper. It was *La Torche*, a virulent minor publication known to live off scandal. Darcy's finger pointed. 'There. That's what I found when I got back. It's a reference to that bribery case in Lyons. They're suggesting now that we're hiding something *here*. Something on the bomb case. They've linked the two cases together. "Have we got it nearer home?", they're asking. Sarrazin wrote it. I recognize the style.'

'Have you *asked* him if it's his?'

132

'He swears it isn't. He says it came from Paris – news agency stuff. Their own investigative journalists.'

'Investigative journalists should be cut into strips and fed to the pigs. They do nothing but harm.' Not for nothing was Pel the founder, president, secretary and only member of the Bigots' Association.

'I don't believe him, of course,' Darcy said. 'He wrote it because he's heard something, but he's afraid to say so out loud.' Darcy frowned. 'And when I got back I found people looking at me, *patron*. As if I had two heads or something. People I talk to here at headquarters don't hang about. They go away. Even Pomereu.'

'Pomereu's a fool. He always was.'

'And that girl who works in the typing pool. Danielle Delaporte. She came here from Beaune. She's – well, you know her, *patron* – she's – ' Darcy made vague shapes with his hands.

'I know her,' Pel said.

'I took her around for a while. It finished a long time ago but we stayed good friends. Whenever I go near her now she gets up and walks away. What's wrong with me, I thought. Do I smell? Then I bumped into Brochard. He was with Louis Leblanc. Louis the Limp. You know the guy. He works at Garages Blaine and produces information for Brochard. He was saying someone's going to knock off a bank.'

'Which?'

'He didn't know.'

'And when?'

'He didn't know that either.'

'Has Brochard informed Nosjean? It might be the Tuaregs.'

'Nosjean's been told. But Louis also heard Jacquot Hugo talking. You remember Hugo. He was sent down for burglary and he said something that bothers me. He said, "If Duche can get away with it, why can't I? How much do I have to pay?" '

'Was he accusing someone of taking bribes over Duche?'

'I went to see him, *patron*. At number 72. He was accusing me.'

Pel said nothing and Darcy went on angrily. 'No wonder people don't stop to talk to me any more. It doesn't pay to be associated with doubtful characters.' Darcy's face reddened. 'Where did a rat like Hugo get that, *patron*?'

'Did he say it to you?'

'To Brochard. Brochard passed it on.' Darcy passed a hand over his face. 'I've always got on all right with Brochard.'

'Has *he* heard something?'

'Rumours. That's all. Name of God, *patron*, I think he actually thought there might be some truth in it. On the principle that there's no smoke without fire.'

'Who do *you* think's behind it?'

'Aimedieu's heard it, too. He was in Goriot's team and all Goriot's lot are talking about it. They're saying I was slow getting to the airfield when Nadauld was shot. *Patron*, I was just behind you.'

'Is Aimedieu just trying to do for Goriot? He doesn't like him.'

'Aimedieu's not like that.'

'No, he's not. Neither is Brochard. What about Misset? He's the one who spends more time than anybody else talking. Has he heard anything?'

'I've not asked him, *patron*. And I'm not going to. You don't go up to a guy and say "Somebody's spreading tales about me", do you? That makes him begin to wonder, "What tales?" And then he listens harder. And he hears them, too, because, having been warned, he reads into things suggestions that aren't there. Is it Goriot?'

'Why should Goriot be after you?'

'That business over Duche. I as good as told him he was a damned fool. He doesn't like it. He also doesn't like the fact that, in spite of being senior to me in service, he's junior in fact. Also, *patron*,' Darcy paused, '– he doesn't like *you*. You got the job he hoped to get and you got his team – or what was left of it: Aimedieu.'

'He's not got Aimedieu any longer.'

'He won't like that either.'

Pel reached across the desk and helped himself to a cigarette from Darcy's packet, then sat back in his chair. Office politics were always part of any job. For every man doing a decent day's work, there were two who were wheeling and dealing.

It was the same with police work as with any other profession. There were always men who made it their aim in life to be near the people who mattered, to be noticed, who always talked louder about things than better men, because that way they came to the notice of the people at the top. When there was a job going, they were the ones who got it. Pel didn't like it, but everybody had to live with it in some form or other.

He wasn't personally worried because he knew his career was safe. It was expected he'd get the Chief's job when the Chief retired and, if it had anything to do with the Chief, he would. But there were plenty of other men with influence who might come up on the rails at the last moment. With Pel, it didn't matter much because he preferred being out in the field. Darcy was more vulnerable, however. It was Pel's hope that when the time came for him to move up or move out, Darcy would take his place. Darcy was the best fitted for it. Nosjean was cleverer and probably so was De Troq', but Nosjean lacked Darcy's drive, and he suspected De Troq', who enjoyed being known as the titled cop, wasn't really interested.

It was worrying, and Goriot and his problems were taking up far too much of Pel's time. In addition they seemed to be getting nowhere with their enquiries.

But then, the shoe Sous-Brigadier Chevraux had brought in seemed to start things moving again.

'Patron,' Lagé said, appearing in Pel's office, 'I might have a lead on our friend, Dupont. That shoe's his, all right. It matches the other and I wondered why was it found where it was. So I took a look at the map. There's another village about five kilometres away. Lugny. I wondered if there were any connection – if he had a woman there, for instance. If he didn't, how come the shoe was there?'

Pel listened gravely and Lagé smiled. 'So I tried his bank and they let me see his statement. He was getting a regular income from somewhere, *patron*. There's a monthly figure of ten thousand francs and another of five thousand. They don't know where it comes from because it comes via a Swiss bank. They said there were others as well but one by one most of them

135

stopped. I also noticed there were several payments over the last year to a place called the Hospice de Lugny. I wondered what the Hospice de Lugny was. I thought it might be a health and beauty clinic but it turned out to be a nursing home. It's no more than two kilometres from where he was found. I wondered if he'd been spending time there.'

Pel reached for his cigarettes. 'Only one way to find out,' he said. 'Come on, Daniel.'

The Hospice de Lugny was an old-fashioned house of grey stone, ugly because it belonged to the era when, with blossoming business at the end of the last century, industrialists without much taste had tried with their homes, carriages and clothes to make themselves look more important than they were. It had turrets and a short flight of steps to the front door.

As they stopped the car a bulky young man was working outside, repairing the steps with new stones. He tossed down the square bricklayer's hammer he was using, and rose and studied them for a moment, his expression blank.

'You booked in for a stay here?' he asked.

'No,' Pel snorted. 'We're not. Who's in charge?'

'I am.'

'You own the place?'

The young man frowned. 'Well, no.'

'You the Matron?'

'No.'

'Then you aren't in charge.'

'I am when the others are busy.'

'There are others?'

'Yes.'

'Then you'd better go and find them. Tell them the police wish to speak to them.'

The young man studied them for a moment or two longer, then he turned sulkily and vanished, leaving the door open for them to enter. They followed him inside. There was no reception desk but in the hall there was a room which appeared to be an office, in as much as it had a desk, a telephone and a few files. Across the hall was a dining-room of sorts. It had

136

four or five small square tables, each set for two people. On each one was a small glass vase with a single wilting flower in it. A woman in an apron was arranging them. She was youngish and well built and she stared at the door with contempt.

'No manners,' she said.

'Who?' Darcy asked.

'That boy. Throws his weight about. Not quite right in the head. Measles as a child. Behaves as if he owns the place.'

'Who *does* own it?'

'Madame Weill.'

'He's gone to fetch her?'

'He'll have to go a long way.'

'Oh? Why?'

'She's away on holiday. She's gone to see her daughter. She lives in St-Trop'.'

'You part of the staff?'

'I'm most of it. I'm the cook. We could do with more help. They're always making alterations. Taking up floors. Painting windows. Digging up the grounds.'

'Why are they digging up the grounds?'

'They say they're looking for a well. They say there's an underground spring here and they're trying to find it. They had maps and books out of the library on it. They say spring water's good for the residents. Pure. Good for the kidneys. They even talking of selling it. They'll never find it. I don't think there is one.'

'Did you know a Monsieur Dupont?'

'Him!'

'You *do* know him?'

'Of course I did. He tried to get me in corners.'

Pel stared about him. 'What is this place?' he asked.

'What do you mean, what is it?'

'A health farm?'

'This?' She looked startled. 'It's a rest home for geriatrics.'

As she collected her tray and shuffled off, they looked round in bewilderment. They had half expected bouncing young gym instructresses in tight T-shirts and satin shorts.

A moment later they heard feet clattering and a woman appeared. She was good-looking in a beefy sort of way, tall

with a bosom like a frigate under full sail, her hair blond but
going grey. Pel had a feeling he'd met her before but he couldn't
place where.

She was breathless and shook hands hurriedly. 'Sully,' she
said. 'Marianne Sully. I'm sorry to keep you waiting, but we've
got some alterations going on in the laundry. This is an old
building. We're putting in a new floor and the concrete mixer's
going. My husband also works here. I'm running the place at
the moment. My son said you were the police and wanted to
see me.'

'You'll be the Matron?'

'Deputy Matron, actually. Madame Weill, the owner, is the
Matron.'

As they talked, a man appeared. He was tall, dark and good-
looking. Madame Sully introduced him. 'This is my husband,
René,' she said. 'We only have a small staff because most of
the people who come here come just for a rest and a little quiet.
To convalesce. To get over a death. Because they're just tired.
Because their children who look after them need a break. We
concentrate just on looking after them and feeding them well.
We have a good kitchen staff and a few odds and ends but the
responsibilities lie between us and the Matron.'

'Do you know a man by the name of Jean Dupont?'

Madame Sully's hand went to her mouth. 'Name of God,'
she said. 'You've found him?'

'We seem to have, madame.'

'Is he all right?'

'I'm afraid he's dead, madame.'

'Was it his heart?'

'No, madame, it wasn't his heart. It was a motor car. He
was found on the motorway near Mailly-les-Temps with head
injuries. Was he a resident here?'

Madame Sully sat down heavily. 'Yes,' she said. 'He was.
But he disappeared. I thought he'd gone home.'

'Why would he do that?'

'He quarrelled with the last place he went to.'

'Which place was that?'

'I don't know. It's what he said. Apparently he often quar-

138

relled. I thought that was what must have happened. Something had upset him.'

'Didn't you know he was dead?'

'No.'

'Didn't you see it in the newspapers?'

'We don't have them. We find they upset some of the residents. They read the death and *in memoriam* notices and start thinking how old they are.'

'The television then? The radio?'

'We must have missed it. I wanted to telephone his home, but he was a widower and we hadn't got a number.'

'Why not?'

'He refused to give one. He said there'd be nobody there, anyway. He liked to keep to himself. He said he had his reasons.'

It was a phrase Madame Chappe had said he used.

'He had a daughter,' Madame Sully offered, almost as though she could read Pel's thoughts. 'I know, because he spoke of her. I thought perhaps he'd gone to her.'

'Did you know her?'

'No. So I couldn't telephone her.'

'Why didn't you report he was missing?'

'Why should we? He wasn't ill or deranged. Apart from having bad feet, he was perfectly fit – almost too fit at times. He paid to come here for a rest – more than once – and he was free to leave if he wished.'

'When did he come this time?'

'A month ago.'

'What did he do here?'

'He liked to play cards. We played with him.'

'Who did?' Darcy asked.

'I did. And my husband. We also usually raked in Bernard. That's Bernard Ruffel, who's my son by my first husband. He's quite good even though he's not clever. He didn't want to play. He'd been repairing the kitchen floor. It's one of those flagged ones and he's good at that sort of thing. He brought his tools because he'd been busy and he has difficulty changing direction when he's concentrating. He's – well – subnormal, but he's a good boy. He put his tools in the hearth.'

139

'What tools would those be?'

'Chisel. Trowel. That sort of thing.'

'So the three of you played cards with the old man?'

'Yes. After the kitchen staff and the daily workers go home, we're the only ones here. We don't do a night duty. Because we don't take in sick people. Just old people and people needing a rest. We demand a medical certificate to indicate they won't go on the rampage or anything like that. They're mostly people who want peace and quiet and we make it clear we can't accept responsibility for anyone who's sick. If they become ill, they have to go to hospital.'

Pel frowned. Something was at the back of his mind that he felt he ought to have clear but he wasn't certain what it was. 'Are you a qualified nurse?' he asked.

'Yes. So is my husband. But we haven't the facilities here to look after the chronically sick and, with old people, it's usually chronic. Obviously we treat minor ailments. But that's all.'

'How did this Monsieur Dupont come to disappear?'

Madame Sully looked at her husband. 'He must have been confused and just walked out. He got confused at times. Old, you see.'

'Was he ever difficult?'

The Sullys exchanged glances. 'Yes,' Madame said. 'The night he disappeared he knocked over a tray of glasses and a bottle of red wine. We'll have to get the carpet changed.'

'When Monsieur Dupont was found, it was discovered he'd been drinking whisky. Did he drink it here?'

She shrugged. 'He liked a drink and he had his own bottle.' She indicated an almost full litre bottle of Johnny Walker on a side table, with glasses, a water jug and a decanter of sherry. 'That's it. So he might have. He might have had another in his room, though I've never seen one. But on the whole he didn't drink much. Except occasionally when he took too much. Then he drank a lot. We had to put him to bed from time to time.'

'When did you last see him?'

'The night he disappeared. He just went. We played cards. My husband and I had dined out. My son did the sitting in. We always have someone on duty in case of emergency and always leave a telephone number where we can be contacted.

140

When we got back he said he'd like a game of cards. So we played.'

'For money?'

'Of course. But for small stakes.'

'Who won?'

'He did. He usually did. He was good at cards. But the stakes were so small it didn't matter, and he always left a good present for us all when he went home, so it made no difference really.'

'So you played cards and he went to bed?'

'He'd got ready to go to bed and watch television in his room but then he said we'd play cards.'

'So you did?'

'We played bridge.'

Madame Sully's husband interrupted. 'But *Dallas* was on. They say you can get *Dallas* in Russia now. We thought we'd watch it.'

'That's right,' Madame Sully agreed. 'We wanted to watch it, so we decided to stop the game for an hour. I decided to go and find some food for us all and Bernard decided to do his rounds. It's his job to check the boiler and lock all downstairs windows and doors.'

'Against burglars?'

'Against the residents. Sometimes they get out and just wander off. Some are a little confused. When I came back with the tray Monsieur Dupont had gone.'

'How?'

'Well, we were playing in the small salon and that has french windows. But they were secured from the inside still, so he couldn't have gone that way. We decided he'd suddenly felt tired – he sometimes did – and had gone to bed. We ate the food and then I went round to check the rooms of all the residents, as I always do, and that's when we discovered he'd gone. He must have slipped out through the hall before Bernard locked the front door.'

'Could he have gone out and then not been able to get back in?'

'There's a bell. And a knocker and that would wake the dead.'

'So what took him to the motorway?'

The Sullys looked at each other and shrugged.

Pel shifted his position. 'I'd like to speak to your son,' he said. 'May we have him in, please?'

The youth appeared, staring about him with the painful intensity of someone whose brain didn't function as swiftly as normal. He seemed as bewildered as his parents.

'He must have been a bit nippy,' he said slowly. 'I locked the front door about ten minutes after we stopped playing cards. He couldn't have wasted much time.'

'Perhaps he went out for some fresh air,' Sully said. 'And he went further than he thought.'

'Why would he do that?'

'Some of the dirty socks we have do funny things,' the boy said.

Pel didn't miss the sharp angry glance he received from his mother.

'Dirty socks?' he asked mildly.

'It's Bernard's name for the old people,' Madame Sully said quickly. 'It's a slang expression the young use. They call old people geriatrics, wrinklies or dirty socks. I forbid its use here. But it slips out occasionally. You must forgive my son. He had a bad illness as a child.'

Pel gestured dismissively. 'You keep records of all residents, of course?'

'Of course.'

But the records weren't very helpful and, indeed, didn't seem very extensive.

'We don't need much beyond their age and address,' Madame Sully explained. 'Perhaps his name's not Dupont.'

'In fact it is. Do you check?'

'Not really. Why should we? Just age and address. We ask for payment ahead, you see. Madame Weill insists on that. We also find out what medicaments they need, but, as I say, this isn't a hospital. It's really just a rest home for old people. We had one old man who was here three years.'

'What happened to him?'

'He died.'

'In hospital?'

'No. Here. There was no point in sending him to hospital. He was just old and worn out. It was quick.'

142

Pel often considered *he* was worn out, with rusty joints and clogged up veins and things.

'When will the Matron be back?'

Madame Sully shrugged. 'I can't tell you. She said she was going to visit her daughter in Toulouse. She said she might make a good holiday of it.'

'Have you informed her?'

'I'm afraid we can't. She didn't leave an address.'

'That's odd, isn't it?'

'Not with Madame Weill. She's getting on a bit, too, these days.'

'I wasn't thinking of the Matron. I was thinking of you. I'd have thought you'd have insisted on a telephone number at least.'

Madame Sully shrugged. 'Perhaps I should have. But why? Her daughter's changed her address recently and Madame Weill's been away for long periods before. I've often run the place on my own.'

'Did she know Monsieur Dupont at all?'

'No better than the rest of us. Perhaps not as well. She doesn't have a lot to do with things these days.'

'Do you have drugs here?'

'Just the ones we need. Laxatives. Diarrhoea tablets. Tablets for rheumatism. Pain-killers. Anti-inflammatory pills. That sort of thing. Nothing very powerful. Madame Weill orders them.'

Pel nodded. 'We'd better talk to some of the other residents. But first perhaps we'd better see Monsieur Dupont's room.'

The room appeared to be like all the others in the hospice, comfortable but not luxurious. There were a chest of drawers, a wardrobe, a wash-basin, a bed and an armchair facing a small television set.

'They're all the same,' Madame Sully said. 'They differ in size, of course, and the people who stay longer have the bigger rooms.'

Pel began to go through the drawers. 'Three sets of underwear,' he noted aloud. 'I wonder why he wasn't wearing any when he was found. And why no socks?' He looked up. 'There's only one pair of pyjamas here.'

'Some people manage with one.'

143

'How long had he booked in for?'

'Six weeks.'

'With one pair of pyjamas? And these haven't been used. What happened to the ones he wore the night he disappeared?'

Madame Sully looked puzzled. 'I've not seen them. I thought he must be still wearing them – under his clothes or something. It was a cold night and a suit had gone.'

Pel frowned and rubbed his nose. 'What do the people do here with their time in the evenings?'

'They can stay in their rooms or come downstairs. Just as they wish. Monsieur Dupont liked company and came down. Most prefer to watch television. But it varies. If there are one or two who prefer to come down, then sometimes it's quite lively. If they're mostly television watchers, they stay in their rooms because they all have their own preferences about programmes. Then it's quiet downstairs.'

There were several old ladies and one old man sitting in the communal sitting-room. They all looked decrepit and it worried Pel that this was how he was due to end up. But they all seemed comfortable and none of them could add anything to the mystery of Dupont's disappearance.

'He liked a joke,' one of the old women said.

'He used to talk of going for a swim in the river,' another said. 'Joking, of course. Have you dragged it?'

'There's no need, madame,' Pel explained. 'He's already been found.'

'In the river?' she asked. 'Floating, I expect. They get caught in the reeds. I had a brother who drowned himself. But that was in a dam near Clermont Ferrand. He was a solicitor. They said he'd helped himself to clients' money. I expect he had. I didn't like him much.'

12

The following day brought a new angle they hadn't expected. Enquiries revealed that Achille-Jean Quelereil-Dupont had been seen in the village of Lugny – alone, and not accompanied by anyone from the hospice, apparently on the look-out for something. He was known there simply as Dupont, the name he used at the hospice.

Enquiries at the hospice revealed that Dupont had indeed made a habit of going to the village from time to time.

'Well, he was quite entitled to go where he pleased,' Madame Sully said. 'He was only here to sleep and eat and, if he wished it, to rest. Some of our inmates never move out of the place. Others go for walks, for drinks. One or two take taxis in the evening and go to the cinema. They can do as they please.'

The local police hadn't noticed the old man wandering about the village but an old man answering to his description had been seen disappearing into the Bar du Moulin, a dark uninviting little place that seemed full of old men playing cards and dominoes. Outside, on the dusty verge of the road, more old men were playing boules between the parked cars. Among them they noticed an expensive-looking Datsun.

The owner of the bar managed to identify Dupont. 'Sure,' he said. 'He came in here. An old type who walked badly. He seemed to enjoy it and came again and again.'

'When did he first appear?'

'A year ago? About that. Then he vanished. Then he turned up again. He was usually around for about a fortnight, then he disappeared. But he kept reappearing and, because he seemed to have money, I decided he came from Dijon or Lyons or

Paris and had a week-end house here somewhere. He was old enough to be retired so it was possible. He played cards with that lot over there.'

'That lot over there' knew him, but only as Jean Dupont. They were all over seventy and preoccupied with their cards, so that Darcy was forced to threaten to bundle the lot of them into the police van and take them down into the city to question them. That stopped them dead and they put down their cards and began to listen.

They gave their names unwillingly, as if they were afraid of being arrested. Cardier, Jean-Philippe. Espagne, Georges. Siméon, Adenne.

There weren't many in the bar and Darcy eyed them speculatively.

'Whose is the car outside?' he asked.

'Which one?'

'The expensive one.'

The landlord nodded at Siméon.

'Go in for expensive cars?' Darcy asked.

Siméon glared at him. 'I like cars.'

'Got an expensive house as well?'

'It's not bad,' the proprietor observed.

Siméon swung round. 'People who run bars should mind their own damn' business,' he snapped. 'The things they should never talk about are politics, religion and the affairs of their customers.'

Darcy looked round him at the shabby bar, the adverts for drink on the walls, the photograph of the local football team, the cups they'd won, the two or three tables with checked cloths where it was possible to have a meal. It wasn't the sort of place he'd have expected a man with Dupont's background to have sought out.

'Why did he come in here?' he asked.

'Why do people usually come in a bar?' the proprietor asked. 'He came in for a drink.'

'He made up a four at cards,' Siméon said.

'When he wasn't busy,' Cardier added.

'Busy doing what?'

'I don't know. He didn't tell me. But I reckon he was up to

146

something. He always seemed different. As if he'd been someone and come down in the world. He liked to boast about
money.'

Espagne gave a little cackle. '*And* women,' he said.

Pel looked up quickly. 'What women?'

'All men have women. They go together.'

'Names?'

They pretended they didn't understand, then Siméon
grinned. 'Well, where do men go when they want a bit of fun
and games?' he asked.

'Inform me,' Pel said.

'Well, there are one or two about.'

'In the village?'

'The women don't like it. They don't talk to them.'

'But the men do?'

'Everybody knows about them.'

'All except me,' Pel snapped. 'So let's have some names.'

He got them in the end. 'Madeleine Bas Jaunes,' Siméon said.

'Madeleine Yellow Stockings?'

'She wears them. Her real name's Madeleine Reine. There's
also Isolde Dusoin.'

'What's *her* nickname?'

'The Brown Hen.'

'Why?'

'She looks like one.'

'There used to be three of them,' Siméon said. 'But Miranda
Moriou went to Grenoble. Said she could do better there.'

'So we're left with Madeleine Reine and Isolde Dusoin,' Darcy
said. 'Tarts, are they?'

The old men cackled and grinned.

'Did you visit them?'

They looked indignant but he knew they'd paid their visits
in their time.

'And Dupont visited them, too?'

'Only one.'

'Which one?'

'Bas Jaunes.'

They gave directions. Madeleine Bas Jaunes lived on the outskirts of the village in a small bungalow surrounded by high

147

hedges. It looked a discreet sort of place, a place she had obviously chosen to be away from the prying eyes of the village matrons.

They studied it from the car. 'Well,' Pel said. 'Let's go and get it over with.'

Madeleine Bas Jaunes was in her forties but she was well preserved, plump, over-made-up, with orange hair that had come from a bottle. She was different from the women of the streets in the city. There was no attempt at sophistication beyond the crude make-up, the ghastly yellow legs and a skirt that was far too tight across her behind. She was broad in the beam and they found her at the back of her bungalow feeding a few scrawny hens with a pernod in her hand. Her heels were so high she walked with her toes turned in like a pouter pigeon.

She eyed them with interest as though she considered them new clients. 'Well?' she asked.

Darcy didn't explain; he just showed his identity card with its red, white and blue stripe.

'Police?' she said. 'I've done nothing.'

'Nobody's saying you have. We're not interested. We want to know if you know a man called Achille-Jean Quelereil-Dupont.'

'Who?'

Pel repeated the name. She still looked blank.

'How about Jean Dupont?'

'Oh, *him*!'

'You know him?'

'Of course. Is that his name? Achille-Jean – whatever it was.'

'It *was* his name.'

'Well, I thought he must be somebody more than just Jean Dupont. He had a way with him. As if he'd been someone once.'

'How well did you know him?'

'How well do you think? He came here often.'

'How far did it go?'

'What's that mean?'

'You say you were friendly with him.'

'Yes, I was.'

'How far did the friendship go. As far as bed?'

'Of course.'

'At seventy-eight?'

'Was he *that* old?' She shrugged. 'Well, some men stay virile. He went to health classes.'

'Not for exercise.'

'Why do you want to know all this? I've done nothing. If one of those dirty old bastards in the bar says I have, you ought to ask them about themselves. They talk a lot, but they're no innocents. I've known them a long time. They were after me when I was only fifteen, and they've been after me ever since.'

'Do their wives know?'

'I expect so but they've got no proof. The old bastards were always cunning. I expect they learned it from Siméon.'

'Why Siméon?'

'Well, he's been in prison, hasn't he?'

'Has he? What for?'

'Robbery with violence, they say.' Madeleine Bas Jaunes shook her head. 'Mind, it was a long time ago now, but people don't change, do they? They just get more so.'

'And the others?'

'Espagne was once up for fraud. Fiddled the books at that forge he ran.'

'And Cardier? Don't tell us he's done time, too.'

'No. He just got a fat lip from Auguste Assas at the Hentelet Farm for pinching one of his lambs.'

'They're all dubious characters?'

'I wouldn't trust them.'

'What about Dupont?'

'He wasn't like them. He was different. He came out here about a year ago and stayed at the hospice. One night he came into the village and played cards. Those old ratbags couldn't keep their tongues still and the next night I found him on my doorstep. After that he came regularly. He used to tell them at the hospice he was going for a walk, but he went to the bar, played cards for a bit to find out if I was at home and, if the coast was clear, then he came here.'

'Then went back to the hospice?'

'Unless he went to Isolde Dusoin.'

'Did he pay you?'

Madeleine Reine looked at Pel as though he were stupid. 'You don't think I went on this game just for love, do you? Are you going to arrest me or something?'

'We're not the vice squad. He's been found dead.'

'I read about a Jean Dupont. I wondered if it was him. I've been a bit scared.'

'Why?'

'I wondered if I was involved somehow. I don't think I am.'

'Except that you might just have been the last to see him alive,' Darcy pointed out. '*Did* he see you on the night of the twelfth?'

'No. But he came the night before.'

'Was he drunk?'

'Not when he came here. He wasn't sober – you know what I mean – but he knew what he was doing. Name of God, he did. I'll say that about him. He knew more about it than some of the young ones who come.'

'Was he generous?'

'He paid well and he always left a good tip. He always seemed to have plenty of money on him.'

'Did he talk much? About himself?'

'He said he had a daughter and was going to leave his money to her. He said he had some. A lot, he said. And a few nice little things about the house that were worth a bit. Pottery, he said.'

'Did he always carry money?'

'He seemed to. I warned him once or twice about it. I told him he ought to put it in the bank, not carry it around with him. I was thinking of that lot in the bar. He just laughed. But his wallet was always bulging. I think he was worth a bit.'

Pel nodded. 'I think so, too, madame.'

They came away with Pel still feeling he had missed something somewhere. He had stumbled on some item that had slipped his mind when he ought to have noted it and forced it to stick.

'He seemed to like women all right,' he mused, his mind churning.

150

'Making love's one of the few sports you can go in for with flat feet,' Darcy said.

Pel wasn't satisfied. The thing at the back of his mind that he felt he ought to know about and didn't still nagged at his consciousness and failed to improve his temper, which was roused to irritation by Darcy's flippant remark.

'The night he was found dead,' he said slowly, 'he was in pyjamas. So before he left the hospice he must have put his clothes on. If so, why did he put them on the way he did? Was he *that* drunk? And why did he forget his underclothes? And why was there nothing in his pockets and where are the pyjamas he wore? Those we saw hadn't been worn. Finally, if he were trying to go home, why didn't he take his keys with him?'

Madeleine Bas Jaunes' information about the three old men proved correct. Cardier had been accused of stealing lambs, Espagne had been before the courts for fraud but had been found not guilty – a note in the file suggested that the case had been bungled by the police – and Siméon had not *one* mark against his name for robbery with violence but *two*. He had been picked up in Dijon some years before, while in his forties, after a break-in, and there was another mark against him for an incident in Paris ten years before that for hitting the owner of a bar with a bottle.

'Just the sort to do for Dupont,' Pel commented.

'They could have waited for him as he left Madeleine Yellow Stockings. What's *her* background?'

Enquiries revealed that Madeleine Yellow Stockings was an artist's daughter. She had had a good education and had worked in Paris as a model. Though she didn't have a record, she had had more than one boy-friend who had.

'She seems to like that sort,' Darcy said. 'She could have put the old bastards up to it.'

Pel pulled a face. 'Why did he go to that place at Lugny, anyway?' he asked. 'There were no young women jumping up and down there. No girls. Just old people on their way out.' He pushed papers around and picked one out of the pile. 'I've been checking with the health department. They know the place. They investigated it a few years back. They considered

Madame Weill was too old to have a licence and insisted she hired somebody younger to run the place. She took on a woman called François, but she didn't stay long, and when she left the woman who took her place was Madame Sully, the present one. The François woman went to a nursing home in Lyons. She might be worth talking to. She might even be able to supply Madame Weill's address. It seems to me we ought to know it. I think we ought to find her. And I think we ought to know a bit more about Dupont. Not the man on the motorway. Not the man who played cards at Lugny and went to Madeleine Bas Jaunes'. The one he used to be.'

They seemed to have covered every possibility, so, sitting in his office, smoking himself cross-eyed, Pel began to go over again the things they had already looked at. He was a great believer in chasing the details round the reports that landed on his desk. Still bothered by the nebulous something at the back of his mind that just wouldn't come to the front, he had a feeling that the masses of words might just throw it up.

They didn't, and in the end, he decided that the house in Dôle that Dupont had owned might suggest something. They had already been through it once but nothing had appeared to have been disturbed and they hadn't lingered. It might just be worth a second visit.

Madame Chappe agreed to give them the key and they stood in the silent hall and stared about them. The house was a much more imposing place than the one at St-Alban and looked as though Dupont had kept it as a prestige home, uncared for, with dust sheets over the furniture. There were a few pictures – 'Quelereils', Madame Chappe had pointed out, 'not Duponts' – and a few valuable items, but nothing that seemed to be of the same sort of value as the missing porcelain.

There was a safe but it was locked and suddenly it seemed necessary to see inside. Madame Chappe hadn't a key so they got in touch with the manufacturers in Lyons and during the afternoon one of their representatives arrived with a bunch of keys.

There seemed to be nothing of value inside – no money, no

jewels, no more valuable Meissen ware – nothing but dusty brown paper parcels containing packets of folded paper tied with string and pink tape.

Pel took one of them out and studied it. 'Briefs?' he said. 'Legal briefs?'

'I'd have thought his firm would have insisted on keeping those,' Darcy said.

The name of the firm Dupont had worked with was written on the bottom of the briefs in old-fashioned script. It was a lawyers' office, Boissard, Lacroix and Adéo. There seemed to be little else in the safe but the dozen or so briefs, which were clearly a hangover from the days when Dupont had been an advocate.

Pel spread them out on the table like a hand of cards. They had been typed on thick paper almost like parchment and had been folded for so long they were difficult to open. They appeared to concern cases in which Dupont had appeared.

'Why did he keep them here?' Pel said.

Darcy was already on the telephone. As he slammed the instrument down, he turned. 'There's no Boissard and no Lacroix,' he said. 'Just a Julien Adéo, who was a junior partner at the time when Dupont was at his peak. They say the briefs should be in their office archives and they want them back.'

'Eventually,' Pel said. 'When we've looked at them.'

There were thirteen of the briefs and one of them, they noticed at once, concerned the murder of the Comtesse de Perrenet. Attached to it were letters and notes.

'Get Claudie to look up the files,' Pel said. 'It would be interesting to see how they compare with the brief.' He flipped a packet of papers with his thumb. 'These are love letters from the Countess to a man called Louville.'

Struggling with the stiff paper, they opened another of the briefs.

'*Patron*,' Darcy said at once. 'That's the Marival-Midi brief. That was the case where all those financiers went to gaol.'

He picked up a letter and saw that it was signed 'Henri Massières.' There were other letters attached to the brief and one of them, he noticed, was addressed to a Madame Emilienne Coty.

153

'*Patron*,' he said. 'Coty! Massières! Those are the names of two of the women I met when I was chasing this blasted Dupont type round the country. Was he chasing them because he was fond of them? Or was it because he'd been involved with them during the time when he was practising law?'

Pel shrugged. 'Perhaps both,' he said.

Julien Adéo, the only surviving partner of the original firm of Boissard, Lacroix and Adéo, was a plump, pink man of sixty with iron grey hair and a cheerful manner. Darcy managed to see him at the Law Courts and arrange for him to meet them. He was just about to re-enter the court to hear a verdict and was adjusting his black gown as the red-robed judges filed in.

'This evening,' he said briskly. 'My chambers. Must go now. I'm involved in this.'

As they sat down opposite him that evening, he was quite blunt about Dupont.

'Didn't like him,' he said. 'Didn't trust him. He was brilliant – no doubt about that – but there was something shifty about him.'

As Pel spread the brown packages across the top of the wide desk he occupied, he eyed them indignantly.

'He must have stolen them,' he said. 'After his own premises were burned down in 1971. I suppose the fire destroyed all *his* records so he lifted ours. By rights they should be in our archives, though "archives" is rather a grand title for a set of shelves in the cellar filled with brown paper packages containing old deeds, documents, briefs, letters and what have you. Normally, they lie about anyhow in the office like dead bodies on a battlefield and nobody knows where anything is, but when they're finished with and they've been sorted out, they're like soldiers on parade, indexed and cross-indexed under the name of the client and the lawyer handling them, and kept in the strong room which is our name for a cellar with a thick door and a good lock. That's where these should be.'

He offered to glance through the briefs and the papers that were attached to them and give his opinion on them.

'But it'll take time,' he admitted. 'In the meantime, I suggest you see his old clerk. That's his writing on the bottom. I'm only playing detective – and good fun it seems to be, too! – but it might be worth your while to see this old boy. Name of Aristide Guérin, now retired and living with his daughter in Saumur. Clerks know more about their masters as a rule than their partners in practice and I suspect he will, too.'

Aristide Guérin's daughter had an apartment close to the Cavalry School and they found Guérin sitting in a sunny window looking out over the school's exercise area.

'I always sit here,' he said. 'I can see the horses when they bring them out. I served in the cavalry once. I love the horses.'

He had many of his diaries from the office where he had worked for Dupont.

'All that nonsense about someone threatening his life,' he said. 'There was nothing to it. There never is. It often happens when a man gets sent to prison.'

'He went to the trouble of buying a second house at St-Alban all the same,' Darcy pointed out.

The old man smiled. 'To get away from his wife,' he said. 'He couldn't stand her. She was a De Sassenzac. Very old family. It was a prestige marriage, to help him in his profession. They said, in fact, that he got her by lending her father money when he was in financial difficulties. She was stuffy – and he was always inventing excuses to avoid being with her. The house at St-Alban was one. She was in the way, you see. He liked women.'

'He seems to have liked cards, too.'

The old clerk smiled sadly. 'Yes, he liked cards. That's what finished him really. He started with bridge but he played all games. Piquet. Poker. I often had to fetch him out of a card game to appear in court. He was his own worst enemy.'

'Have you a list of the cases he was involved in?'

'No. But I can remember most of them. There was the Marival-Midi Finance thing. That made his name. Then he defended in the Comtesse de Perrenet murder. And the Gauchat murder. He did well. It didn't last long, though. To use an old expression, he couldn't carry corn. It went to his head. He had

155

women. He played the horses. We once had to fetch him from Longchamps when the races were on. Finally, things got too much for him and the big briefs stopped coming. Then the Christian Democrats adopted him as a candidate.'

'Was he elected?'

'Oh, yes. Impeccable background. Nothing was known of his gambling and his women, of course. It came out later when he resigned. The usual problem. He had other affairs more pressing than politics.'

'Women again?'

'And cards.'

'But he wasn't without money?'

'Oh, no! He made a lot of money. He continued to appear in small cases.'

'What happened?'

'He grew lazy and started manufacturing evidence. Nothing was proved but it got around. It finished him. He disappeared. Such a pity. He was clever. But he just couldn't handle fame or wealth.'

'Or women.'

'Or women.'

'But he still had money. Right up to the end. Plenty apparently. He started acquiring it again. Where from?'

The old man smiled. 'I have a strong suspicion that he might have been using information obtained during his cases.'

'He was extracting money from former clients?'

'He'd gone a long way down.'

'Know who they were?'

'No, monsieur, I don't. But he'd have plenty of choice. He always encouraged his clients to tell him everything, so he could defend them more ably. Especially women. Doubtless one or two talked too much.'

'Was there anyone else involved?'

'There was, monsieur. One of the clerks. A junior. An unpleasant young man called Degré. I think he mixed with criminals. In our line, one had to at times – over briefs, you know – and I think my master used the information he picked up. Together they must have been a formidable team.'

156

When Julien Adéo appeared, he had looked through the briefs. 'With increasing interest as I read,' he admitted. 'We were involved in all of them. They all seem to have been successful – Dupont was a good advocate – but it seems to me, reading the notes and letters attached to the briefs, that he wasn't a very honest advocate.'

'What does that mean?'

'It seems to me that more than once he suppressed evidence which by law should have been produced and even occasionally bribed witnesses.'

'Perhaps it's a good job he's dead.'

'Perhaps it is. And not just for that reason. The Law Society would have been after him for that, but there were other things that would be more likely to be of concern to the police.'

'Such as what?'

'Well, you have perjury for a start, conspiracy, and a few other things connected with the presentation of the cases. But they were a long time ago and perhaps the police wouldn't be prepared to pursue them. On the other hand, there was one aspect that, if he'd still been alive, they would certainly have been anxious to pursue.'

'What's that?'

'Blackmail.'

'You mean he was blackmailing former clients?'

Adéo shrugged. 'Well, I'm not a policeman but I am a lawyer and that's what it looks like.'

He tapped one of the brown paper packages laid out on Pel's desk. 'Comtesse de Perrenet,' he said. 'She was found dead and a man called Louville was accused. He was twenty-one and wealthy and he had been her lover. Dupont got him off, and judging by what's in there, he did it by bribing a gamekeeper to say they were together.'

'Doing what?'

'That isn't clear. But there's a suggestion that homosexuality was involved. Someone must have been paid handsomely to admit a thing like that. Dupont seems to have hung on to the knowledge. I think he blackmailed Louville. The boy's dead now.'

Pel sat back. He wasn't often surprised but every day threw up a new and unusual story.

Adéo was tapping another of the parcels now. 'The Marival-Midi case,' he said. 'This is an earlier one where he prosecuted. Five financiers went to jail. But it seems there were another five who should have and didn't. Names: Muller, St-Minde. Coty. Thoresse. Massières. Three of them are dead now. Only Coty and Massières are still alive. They must be pretty ancient now.'

'And supported by their wives who are business women,' Darcy said.

'You know them?'

'I've met them. Was he blackmailing them, too?'

'I suspect so. There are other names. A Madame Bapt. A Madame Guignard. I suspect they'd been having affairs and Dupont found out about them. Perhaps they went to him for advice and he gave it. But he remembered their names and used them later. They even seemed to have stopped paying him; but that, I suspected, was because their husbands died, so that it didn't matter any more. I checked the records and there they were all right – dead. Edouard Bapt. Maxime Guignard. They're in the city records.'

'I don't think our friend, Dupont, will be missed,' Pel said.

Adéo smiled. 'There are another one or two. Gustave Bloomfelt. Richard Roche. Mean anything to you?' Adéo tapped the other parcels. 'And these others?' he said cheerfully. 'I think they're all finished now. Dead, like Messieurs Bapt and Guignard. They'd have no more value. Only Gilles Massières and Maxine Guignard are still alive. I checked that, too.' He beamed. 'In this firm we are noted for our thoroughness.'

13

They had finally turned up something that seemed to be of value, a motive that might account for Dupont's appearance dead on the motorway. He'd been a mystery man like Yves Pasquier's vengeful Count of Monte Cristo. He hadn't been a count, but he'd made people pay for their misdeeds. He'd probably done it for mischief and spite as well as for money, and the Meissen figurines had more than likely been payment to keep quiet about what he knew rather than fees from someone he had defended.

And if he'd sunk to the blackmail of former clients, one of them might easily have turned on him in a fury of desperation and got rid of him. It seemed necessary to know more about the cases he had handled. The cases from his days as a prosecutor didn't seem to have much bearing on what they were after, but the cases where he had defended, where facts and details might have been kept back, could be a mine of information.

A study of the *Liste des Avocats et Juristes Français* gave Dupont's background. Born at Clermont-Ferrand, educated there and at the Sorbonne, he had obviously shown promise at an early age and shot to the top of his profession. His better-known cases were listed – the defence of Louville in the Comtesse de Perrenet murder, the Marival-Midi financial scandal, and several others.

As they'd half-suspected, neither Madame Massières nor Madame Coty was willing to talk. They admitted their husbands were alive but were far from being willing to admit they had ever been involved in any scandal.

'My husband,' Madame Massières said, 'is an old man and very sick and I'm not having him worried.'

A check on the two women indicated that both of them made a habit of going in for health and beauty treatment – how else did they keep their looks and their figures? Madame Coty even made money from it, and it seemed more than likely that one or two other women Dupont had been interested in had been the same.

'Was he blackmailing them *all*?' Pel asked. 'When he dodged about the country visiting these health and beauty centres, was he just looking for his victims? He'd know about them, of course. Without doubt they'd bared their souls to him at some point during the cases involving their husbands. Was his technique to pretend to be interested in them and then produce his demands?'

Going to the Palais de Justice, they dragooned Claudie Darel's boy-friend, Bruno Lucas, into producing for them a complete list of Dupont's cases. Every single one of them. He must have been through all the Law Society's records and all the records of the courts, but there it was, right from the beginning of his career. As they began to peruse it slowly, Darcy sat bolt upright. 'Siméon,' he yelped. 'What's this? Adenne Siméon!'

They persuaded Lucas to dig a little deeper and he came up with a dusty file. 'Robbery with violence,' he said. '1959. It was a wages snatch.'

'Siméon?' Pel said frowning. 'Is *he* involved too? It's too much of a coincidence.'

They went to see Adéo again in search of the young man, Degré, who had worked with Dupont in his under-the-counter activities. Adéo knew exactly where he was.

'He's in gaol,' he said. 'For fraud. I handled the case. It was a great pleasure. He once got away with a lot of our clients' money.'

Going to 72, Rue d'Auxonne, they found Degré to be a smooth, smiling man who obviously hadn't much of a conscience.

'Sure,' he said. 'I remember the case. Siméon had Emile Dustrenau to defend him but Dupont wiped the floor with him. One of their witnesses, who was a security guard, had a record and I found it. Dupont produced it. It threw doubt on his evidence and demolished Dustrenau's case completely. Siméon finally pleaded guilty to conspiracy and got away with three years.'

'Where was this wages snatch?'

'Marseilles. Bit before your time, I reckon.'

Marseilles police pushed them a few steps further.

'There were three of them,' they said. 'This Siméon was one of them. Two of them disappeared. We heard they'd gone to South America. Only one – this Siméon – was picked up. But all we could pin on him was conspiracy and he got away with a short sentence. He claimed the other two had swindled him out of his share.'

'Was the loot recovered?'

'No. It disappeared.'

'I suspect we might have found some of it.'

Faced with the facts, Siméon was silent for a while. 'Where did you get all this?' he asked eventually.

'The records,' Pel said. 'It's all there. It always is. Odd, isn't it, that your defence counsel should appear here and start playing cards with you?'

Siméon shrugged. 'He was good at cards.'

'Did he know you?'

'Not at first. Later.'

'Was he blackmailing you?'

'He tried. But I didn't do for him. I'm too old these days even to tweak anybody's nose.'

'Where were you the night he disappeared from the hospice?'

'Here.'

'Playing cards?'

'Yes.'

'With Dupont?'

'He didn't come that night.'

'He left the hospice at 11 p.m. Where were you at that time? Still here?'

'No. I'd left.'

'Anybody confirm that?'

Siméon indicated the man behind the bar. 'He will.'

'Where did you go?'

'Home.'

'Witnesses?'

'There aren't any. My wife left me years ago.'

Pel looked at the others. Guilt was written all over Cardier's face.

'I was in the woods,' he said.

'Doing what?'

'I had a gun.'

'Why?'

'There are pheasants there.'

'Not yours, I take it.'

'They belong to a guy called De Belloguet. He comes from Paris. He doesn't live here.'

'I thought he might not.' Pel turned to Espagne. 'And you?'

Espagne gestured at Cardier. 'I was with him.'

'No other witnesses?'

'No, just the two of us.'

'Get anything, did you?'

'No.' Cardier's answer was sullen. 'This silly con fell over a root and his gun went off. We had to leave in a hurry.'

Pel turned back to Siméon. 'I'm surprised Dupont didn't recognize you at once. After all, he defended you over that wages job. And when he did, he guessed you still had the money, didn't he?'

Siméon sighed. 'What are you going to do?'

Pel lit a cigarette. 'Take you in,' he said. 'All of you.'

They brought the old men to Judge Castéou's office for questioning.

'We have to hold them,' she decided. 'The case against them's too strong. Especially Siméon. Do you think they could all have been involved?'

'It would require more than just Siméon to carry Dupont so far from Lugny.'

'In that case, the others must have known of Siméon's part in the wages snatch. Could they be the other two in it?'

'The names are different.'

'They could have changed them. They obviously know Siméon's part in it. Do you think we ought to have Madeleine Bas Jaunes in as well?'

It was decided to leave Madeleine Bas Jaunes alone for the time being but the local cops were told to keep an eye on her movements and for the moment the three old men were their best bet yet.

'Three of them,' Darcy said. 'Regular partners at cards with Dupont. All with records – two official, one unofficial. And they knew who he was and why he was there. They also knew about his money and the porcelain figures because, before he realized who Siméon was, he'd boasted about them. A few more enquiries might show they were with Siméon in Marseilles.'

When they returned to the Hôtel de Police, Goriot was laying down the law about the explosion at the airport and the death of Nadauld.

'It was an attempt to capture the gate,' he was insisting. 'It must have been. Why else was there more than one man?'

'*Was* there more than one man?' Pel asked from the doorway.

'If there wasn't – ' Goriot whirled angrily ' – who fired the shots? The one that killed Nadauld and three others that wounded Lotier, Gehrer and Aimedieu. It must have been an attempt to take over the guardroom.'

'Why in God's name would they want to take over the guardroom?' Pel snapped. 'When I did my military service, the guardroom contained cells, a rack for rifles, beds for the guard to sleep on between shifts and fire buckets for army wrongdoers to scrape and paint and, when the paint was dry, to scrape again prior to painting again.'

Pel remembered those buckets only too well. He had not distinguished himself as a soldier and he had seen all too much of the interior of the guardroom. 'I'd have thought the armoury would have been their objective,' he observed. 'Or one of the

163

aircraft. And terrorists are a bit more sophisticated these days. They'd have used semtex, not a home-made bomb.'

'I still think we should bring in Philippe Duche,' Goriot insisted. 'If it wasn't an attempt by a gang, it was done by one man with a weapon capable of firing four shots in rapid succession. And there's only one man I know of round here who had access to a machine-gun of some sort: Philippe Duche. His brother was known to have one. Doubtless he had one as well.'

Goriot's constant obsession with the belief that Philippe Duche was involved in the attempt on the airfield worried Pel. He seemed to have gone completely over the top and he had a feeling he ought to see the Chief about what was happening, because Goriot was unsettling everybody. Nerves were on edge and there was a lot of bad temper.

Yves Pasquier was playing boules on his own at the edge of Pel's drive when he arrived home.

'Caught the Tuaregs yet?' he asked as Pel climbed from his car.

'Not yet.'

'*Somebody* knows who they are.'

'Yes,' Pel agreed. 'I'm sure somebody does.'

'But they're not telling, are they?' Yves Pasquier looked grave and determined. 'I'd tell. I'd always tell. I'm going to be a cop when I grow up so I'd always try to help.'

'You, *mon brave*,' Pel advised soberly, 'would be much wiser if anything happens to keep your head down in case you get hurt.'

It was nice to know that someone supported the police, all the same. The general view was that, in between taking bribes, they were there just for protesting students to pelt with stones.

Pel's worry showed so much through Mahler and the aperitifs that his wife expressed her concern.

'Something on my mind,' Pel admitted.

'Work?'

'Goriot chiefly.'

Finally deciding to do something about it, he made up his

mind to see the Chief, but when he arrived at the Hôtel de Police the following day, they had what seemed to be another murder on their hands.

'Mother of God,' he said furiously. 'Why can't they come one at a time? Who is it? Anyone we know?'

'I doubt it, *patron*,' Claudie said. 'He's English. Or to be exact, since he was born in Edinburgh, he's a Scot.'

'Kilts and everything?'

Claudie smiled. 'No, *patron*. Yachting gear. He arrived in the Barge Port last night. Name: Duff Forbes Mackay. Aged thirty-two. Bachelor. Address in Edinburgh. Teacher of maths at a school there. Found stabbed.'

'How does a Scottish teacher of maths come to be stabbed *here*?' Pel asked. 'Inform me.'

'Lagé took the call,' Claudie said.

'Let's have him in.'

Lagé was engaged in typing out the report, bashing the typewriter with two fingers as if he hated it. He probably did, because it was one of the machines that had grown so old the girls in the typing pool refused any longer to use them, so that they were considered just the job for the ham-fisted, two-fingered typists of the sergeants' room. Lagé was wearing his fingers down to the elbows with the details.

'One of the tourist barges, *patron*,' he pointed out. 'Barges Touristiques Bourgignonnes. You know them. Tour the canals. French cooking every evening. Burgundy with every meal. Visits to vineyards. It's quite a thing these days. They fly here and take the barge to the south of Châlons, and fly home from Lyons. Another lot fly to Lyons and join the barge there to bring it back here. They fly home from here. They're run by a crew of three or four who double up as waiters, cooks, barmen and bargees.'

'Right,' Pel said. 'We've set the scene. What happened?'

'They had a party. Some time during the night–' Lagé glanced at his notebook,' one a.m. to be exact – one of the people on board by the name of Alex Aloff, who's the manager and captain of the barge, telephoned for a doctor. One of the group – there are usually fifteen or twenty – had been found unconscious in his bunk, surrounded by blood. Doctor Duvain

165

attended, but by the time he arrived at the barge port, which was where the barge was moored for the night for the change-over tomorrow, the man Duff Forbes Mackay was dead. The doctor examined him. As he was a bachelor he was in a single cabin. Doctor Duvain found a stab wound to the left groin and decided he'd been the victim of an attack. He might have been. The barge port's not exactly in the best part of the city. He telephoned the police. I went along and found there had been a bit of trouble between this Mackay and another man – by the name of James Duart – over one of the girls in the crew.'

'Do they mix?'

'They all go out together at night. The crew set up visits to bars and night clubs and the girls tend to dance with the single men. It's quite obvious they get a bit of a percentage from the places they go to for taking the tourists there, but I think that's normal enough. The party last night consisted of seven couples, two bachelors and two single girls, and in addition there were two men and two girls from the barge crew. It was their last night and the tourists were due to fly home today. The next group have just arrived to take their places and the barge's due to head south immediately they're aboard.' Lagé smiled grimly. 'They won't be going,' he ended.

Pel listened carefully.

'They're pretty boozy dos,' Lagé went on. 'With a lot of arranged wine tastings and visits to places like Clos Vougeot. This one was a particularly noisy affair and a few words were exchanged over the girl, Marie-Claude Darc. Fists were swung. Nobody was hurt but there was a bit of yelling and the man who runs the affair, this Alex Aloff, decided it was time to get them all back to the barge. But tempers cooled and they started drinking again and the tiff was forgotten. Mackay disappeared and they all apparently went to their bunks.'

Lagé had found it very difficult getting the facts because none of the tourists spoke much French. One of them claimed to and offered to act as interpreter but his French turned out to be as bad as Lagé's English, while the French crew of the barge were saying as little as possible in case they were blamed for the fracas. It was their duty, it seemed, to keep the week light and airy and avoid difficulties, but Marie-Claude Darc had allowed herself to be caught emotionally between the two young Scots. She was saying nothing and the others were trying to back her up.

'I found,' Lagé said, 'that one of the men, this James Duart, the one involved in the quarrel, saw the victim shortly before he disappeared but he's now locked himself in his cabin and refuses to come out. He doesn't appear to trust French police. I also found a bloodstain on the adjoining cabin door – Mackay's – and decided it might be murder.'

'And now?'

'The barge's been impounded. Brochard's watching things. The group have been moved to a hotel until they can be questioned, and the new group, which has just arrived, are also in a hotel and are not allowed to proceed with their holiday.'

'Where's the body at this moment?'

'Still aboard the barge, *patron.*'

'We'd better go and see them. Will we need to bring in De Troq'? He speaks English.'

'I doubt if he speaks English like these people do, *patron.* They're all Scots.'

De Troq' was brought in, nevertheless. The interpreting wasn't as easy as it usually was, but De Troq', who usually had the answer to everything, went about it slowly and carefully, and between them all they managed to make some sense of what they heard.

The barge was empty apart from two policemen and the crew who had to live aboard, but ashore all hell was breaking loose. There was one group of tourists, the dead man's, yelling that they wanted to go home, and another, which had just arrived, yelling that they wanted the holiday they had paid for. In addition, the crew were loudly demanding their wages and there were three travel agents, one French, two English, all wanting to know what the blazes was going on.

There was a crowd watching from the quay. There would have been a crowd there if the body had been in outer space. Some of them were women still in their nightclothes with dressing-gowns over them, their hair still in curlers, who had appeared from the houses around. There were a few men, too, and the smell of Gauloises lay on the scented morning air. Inevitably it drove Pel to light one and he coughed for a while with a noise like a blocked sink. A shutter in one of the nearby shops went up with a roar. A dog lifted its leg against a bollard. It couldn't have been more normal.

Leguyader's men from the lab had finished going through Mackay's possessions and the photographers had completed their work. The mortuary van was waiting on the quayside for the body and Prélat's Fingerprint boys were still going over the cabin for fingerprints.

'Duart's fingerprints are there,' Prélat announced. 'But then, so are everybody else's.

It wasn't difficult to explain why. The tourists had visited each other's cabins, to lend books, to borrow books. The women had become friendly and visited each other when the men were in the bar. There had been no visiting after dark, however. Everybody seemed certain of that.

Doctor Cham was also on the barge. 'It's a funny one, *patron*,' he said. 'The wound's in the man's groin and that seems a funny place to stab someone. Unless his assailant was going for the stomach and missed his aim. It's also not a particularly deep one but it was enough for him to bleed to death.'

'Has the weapon been found?'

'Not yet. Perhaps he chucked it in the canal.'

Brochard had all the names, but only two seemed important – those of Duff Forbes Mackay, who was dead, and James Duart, who had probably killed him.

Mackay was in his cabin, lying on blood-soaked sheets, the front of his clothes red with blood. His hands were also red and there were red hand-prints and fingerprints on the door and bulkhead of the cabin, and spots on the deck outside.

'The blood spots are circular,' Leguyader pointed out. 'With the usual crenellated marks on the edges. There are only two that look like exclamation marks. He must have been moving at the time so that *they* hit the deck at an angle. It seems to me that when he was stabbed, the circular spots of blood fell while he was standing still and upright, probably shocked, but the others came as he tried to make his way into his cabin where he fell on his bunk and there died.'

'From loss of blood,' Cham said. 'The bunk's saturated and so is the mattress and the sheets. He must have been drunk and didn't realize he'd been stabbed.'

Judge Brisard was handling the case. He had a yacht on one of the lakes in the Jura and made a lot of fuss about using the correct nautical terms. He seemed to be in a hurry to get away and Pel eyed him coldly. Brisard, he decided, was growing fatter and fussier. It would be nice, he thought idly, if he could fall over the side and drown.

Nobody seemed anxious to talk and Pel formed the impression that the party that had been held to celebrate the culmination of a week's cruise had got a little out of hand. It had started simply with wine at dinner but afterwards, after they'd all had brandies, since the passengers were all Scots someone had foolishly introduced whisky, and the staff of the boat, who were supposed to keep order, had got involved.

The staff were waiting now in the cabin of the boat's manager, Aloff. They were all smoking and within two minutes so was Pel.

'I suppose this is the end for me,' Aloff said. 'We've been warned about getting implicated in any way with the passengers. Staying sober. Making sure trouble doesn't start. Well, there *was* trouble and we got involved. All of us.'

'Did you see any trouble between Duart and Mackay?' Pel asked.

Aloff sighed. 'A bit of bad temper. It was just jealousy. Mackay had been making eyes at Marie-Claude all week. Then Duart started. He spent the first few days of the trip drinking, then he seemed to spot Marie-Claude and he was a bit more polished than Mackay. I think Mackay went round in one of those skirt things in Scotland and he hadn't the technique Duart had. He put on his kilt one night to show off but it was too hot and he had to change it for a pair of linen trousers. He had a knife in his stocking.'

'He had a knife?'

'They always have them, *patron*,' De Troq' explained. De Troq' always knew everything. 'It's part of the Highland dress.'

169

'What do they use them for?'

'I think they used them originally for cutting up the deer they'd killed. Perhaps even for cutting up rivals. Nowadays they're just for show. Perhaps they use them for sharpening pencils or peeling apples. I don't think these days they're big enough for much else.'

'Get it, Lagé.'

Lagé produced the knife but Cham shook his head. 'I'll check it, of course, but there's been no blood on it.'

Marie-Claude Darc was suffering from a hangover and wasn't very willing to talk, but they eventually got out of her what had happened. She was pretty and it wasn't hard to imagine two young men coming to blows over her.

'They'd been following me around all week,' she insisted, holding her head. 'I didn't think much of it at first, but then I realized they'd both fallen rather badly.'

'Which did you prefer?'

'Duff Mackay. He was tall and good-looking. But it was only for the holiday, you understand. There was no funny business. I have a boy-friend already. He's a bank manager in Lyons.'

'And the other one, Duart?'

'He's divorced. He had some important position in London. In finance, which was how we started talking. I told him my boy-friend was in banking. He boasted a lot and I didn't like him very much. He was fat and tried to paw me. When we went to the night club, he suggested that when we got to the boat again I should go to his cabin. I told him not to be silly and pushed him away. He got angry and suddenly there was Duff Mackay between us. I think he had old-fashioned ideas about gallantry.'

'They seemed to have got him killed.'

She nodded miserably. 'They pushed at each other for a while, then Alex Aloff got between them and pushed them apart. He made them shake hands and after that it seemed to be all right, and when we got back to the boat, they were talking again. Unfortunately Alex allowed the bar to be opened again. Everything seemed all right, but then Duart produced a bottle of whisky. He said all Scots drank whisky and they started drinking again. When I went to my cabin, there were four of them still in the saloon – Duart, Duff Mackay and a married couple called Jenkins. The next I heard was shouting and I thought the fighting had started again. But Alex said Duff had been stabbed.'

The story was confirmed by the two Jenkinses but both had left the saloon before Mackay and Duart. It seemed to leave only Duart, who was demanding a British lawyer and refusing to open his mouth until he got one.

They persuaded him to appear in the end. He was a flabby man and was suffering from a monumental hangover so that his memory of the evening was far from clear. He was wearing a freshly laundered shirt and when they asked him about it, he said he'd just changed it.

'What about the shirt you were wearing?'

'It was dirty.'

'What sort of dirty?'

'Greasy. Wine stains.'

'Bloodstains?'

'No! No!'

'Find it, Lagé.'

The shirt had smears of blood on the front and round the cuffs.

Duart frowned. 'I'm saying nothing.'

'You can surely say how it got there.'

Duart swallowed. 'I'd lost him,' he said. 'I went to his cabin to find him. We were friendly enough again by this time. I must have picked it up then.'

'Did you see him?'

'Yes. But I didn't know he'd been stabbed. The light wasn't on and he was on his face. I decided he'd passed out and that was the end of the evening. I closed the door and went to my own cabin. I remember sitting on the bed to take my shoes off but that's the lot. I don't remember any more.'

'Do you possess a knife?'

'Penknife. That's all. I use it to clean my pipe.'

Pel held out his hand. There was no sign of blood on the knife and Cham shook his head.

'That wasn't the weapon,' he said.

'I think,' Judge Brisard said portentously, 'that we'd better

171

take this type into custody and give him time to get over his headache. He might then remember a bit more, because it doesn't look as if we're going to pick up much today.'

Though they didn't know it, they were about to pick up much more than they realized, and Mackay's death was going to open more doors for them than they expected.

14

Darcy was in a foul mood. They had managed to trace Madame François, the former deputy matron at the Hospice de Lugny. She was married and living in Vienne and Darcy had shot down the motorway to talk to her, only to find she was not at home, nor even in the country, having gone on a visit to her son in Quebec in Canada.

Her husband, who worked for the railways, had not gone with her and, learning from him the date of her return, Darcy had gone back eagerly to find she had not turned up. Her husband said she had telephoned him to say she had decided to stay another week in Canada with her son. Without her, they seemed unable to find Madame Weill, the owner of the hospice, and Madame Weill seemed suddenly to have become one of the Chief's Missing Persons.

In addition, Darcy had heard more rumours about himself and knew now that there was a definite suggestion floating about the Hôtel de Police that he'd been taking bribes. It was beginning to get on his nerves and he had picked on Debray over some trivial mistake and bawled him out. Debray was the youngest on the team and the look on his face made Darcy feel guilty, because he knew he had picked on him because of his own frustration and that reason alone.

It had relieved his feelings but it didn't stop the rumours, and Darcy knew what happened when rumours floated to the surface. They had to be investigated and, while they were, the man involved was suspended from duty until there could be an enquiry. Darcy had a feeling that the business was coming close to a climax.

He knew the Chief had been sitting for some time on the decision whether to suspend him or not. The Chief was a loyal type, an honest bull-at-a-gate sort of man, and he didn't want to suspend Darcy, but police work was always in the eye of the politicians and he had to do something, and rumours and the waiting were getting on Darcy's nerves. Moreover, that morning, crossing the square at the Porte Guillaume, he had bumped into an old flame. Her name was Josephine-Héloise Aymé and she and Darcy had conducted a stormy love affair a few years before. He was about to greet her when she turned aside and walked past him, apparently without seeing him.

But he knew she had and it made him think. Even after they'd parted they had remained on good terms and she had always been willing to be friendly. He stood still, staring after the slim figure with its mass of red hair. He had a theory about what was happening. Nothing had appeared in the press about him personally, but he had no doubt the word had got around, because this had been the second incident in two days.

Troubled, Darcy thought it might be a good idea to take his mind off things by calling at the Hospice de Lugny again. As he approached, he spotted the woman they'd spoken to when they'd first arrived there. She was heading for the village, a plastic bag in her hand, an apron showing beneath her coat. He stopped his car alongside her.

'Can I give you a lift, madame?' he asked.

She clearly thought he had nefarious intentions towards her.

'I don't accept lifts from strange men,' she said, hostile and haughty at the same time.

'I'm not a strange man,' Darcy said. 'I'm a policeman.' He flashed his identity card at her. 'I met you at the hospice a few days ago, remember? I'm Inspector Darcy. You're Madame–'

As he paused, she supplied the answer. 'Brouchal.'

'That's it. Madame Brouchal. We talked.'

'What do you want with me?' She gestured with the plastic carrier bag. 'What's in here's mine.'

'What *is* in there?'

'Food. And it doesn't belong to the hospice. I do the cooking there and I sometimes take along my own ingredients and cook for myself and my family at the same time. But I buy it myself and just use their cooker. And why not? It doesn't add anything to their bill because I have to use it for them anyway.'

Darcy didn't believe her. What she carried would undoubtedly be for her family but he guessed the ingredients had come from the larder of the hospice. But he didn't argue. He had better things to do than check for stolen food.

'I was just about to visit the hospice when you happened along,' he said. 'Perhaps you can save me a lot of trouble and in return I can take you home.'

Unwillingly she admitted she had finally recognized him and climbed into the car.

'Well,' she admitted, 'it's a help because I'm late. I've been helping to lay the new carpet.'

'What new carpet?'

'In the television room. They said it was worn out. It didn't seem worn out to me. I expect it was the red wine that was spilt.'

'Red wine makes a mess,' Darcy agreed.

'He knocked over a tray of drinks.'

'Who did?'

'Him. The one who was found dead. They rang up Bertholle Carpets and ordered a new one. It came yesterday. They took the old one away. There were bits of glass in it. What are you wanting to know?'

'Anything you can tell me about him. The man who was found dead.'

She shrugged. 'He was a randy old devil,' she said. 'He liked to put his hand on my backside when he passed me in the corridor. I told him in no uncertain terms that my backside wasn't free pasturage for the wandering hands of dirty old men.'

'Funny he disappeared and turned up dead on the motorway.'

She sniffed. 'He's not the first.'

'There've been others found dead on the motorway?'

'Not that.' She seemed to regard Darcy as having the intelligence of a rabbit. 'I meant that he's not the first to disappear.'

'Do they often walk out?'

175

'Some of them aren't all there. Round the bend. Senile. Their families stick them in the home to get rid of them.'

'And they disappear?'

'They have done. Most come back but there was one old boy eighteen months ago who didn't. Wealthy old boy, too, I heard. His family just didn't want to be bothered with him and they weren't very worried when he disappeared. All they were interested in was getting their hands on his money. They even complained we'd stolen some of his belongings.'

'What for instance?'

'Oh, money he had on him.'

'What happened to him?'

'Nobody knows. In the kitchen we decided he'd chucked himself in the river. He was suffering from depression. I'd have been depressed, too, if I'd had a family like he had.'

'Did he live with his family?'

'Not likely. He lived on his own. His family paid him visits. But not often. I think he was glad to come to the hospice. At least they played cards with him at night.'

'They seem to play a lot of cards.'

'Well, when they're old there isn't much else they *can* play, is there? They certainly can't go in for fun and games. Only a few like old Dupont try that. Usually it's backgammon. Or scrabble.'

'Does Madame Weill play?'

'She used to when she was younger.'

'Did she play with this old man?'

'No. She'd gone to see her daughter in Saint-Trop'.'

Darcy's ears pricked. 'You mean she's been there since God knows how long?'

Madame Brouchal gestured with a limp flap of her hand. 'Well, she was getting on a bit herself. She must be eighty if she's a day. She just leaves it to old Sully. Mind you, I expect she takes her share of the profits.'

'Did she know she'd lost one of her inmates?'

'Madame Sully was going to write to her.'

'But she didn't reappear to hold an enquiry?'

'No. They hadn't an address.'

176

'I think,' Darcy said, 'that we ought to try to find her. So we can tell her she's just lost another.'

Absorbed with his information, Darcy headed for the Hôtel de Police. The cold-shouldering he was receiving was worrying him. And he hadn't finished yet.

Arriving in Pel's office, he passed on what he had learned from Madame Brouchal. Pel seemed curiously uninterested.

Darcy's anger was boiling out of him and, as he finished, he burst out at once with his unhappiness. 'I met Philippe Duche downstairs,' he said.

'What's he want?' Pel seemed preoccupied and kept his eyes on the papers on his desk.

'He came in to complain. His wife was with him. They say one of Goriot's men's been following them.'

'Have you asked Goriot?'

'I saw Goriot's sergeant. He says not. But I don't believe him and I reckon Philippe Duche knows whether he's being followed or not. We've followed him often enough in the past. He says he's being harassed.'

'Harassing an innocent man won't help Goriot,' Pel said. 'I think it's time he had another medical. I wonder, in fact, if that medical that allowed him to return to duty was properly conducted or whether his uncle, Forton, had a hand in it.'

'There's another thing, too,' Darcy said angrily. 'I've just been accused of taking bribes.'

'Who by?'

'Gaston Lerenard. You know him. He's Pierre la Poche's sidekick. I brought him in six months ago. He'd been picking pockets. He was fined. He's just been brought in again. One of the Uniformed boys picked him up. When he saw me he said, "Some people get away with it. It depends whom you know." '

'What did you do?'

'I was going to wring his neck. The Uniformed boy – name of Pinchot – pushed me away.'

'It's a good job he did, Daniel.'

'Yes. I'd probably have hit him. It all comes from this

obsession Goriot has that Philippe Duche did the shooting at the airport. Because I've been behind him, he thinks I'm in his pocket.'

'Hang on to your temper. It can only get you into worse trouble. And you've got enough, as it is.'

'What do you mean, *patron?*'

'The Chief's decided: you've been suspended.'

Darcy's face twisted. 'For taking bribes?'

'The Chief doesn't believe that for a minute but people are a bit sensitive about the police these days and he felt it was best. Full pay, of course. You're innocent until you're proved guilty.'

Darcy managed a twisted smile. 'I always thought *your* view of criminals, *patron*, was that they're guilty until they're proved innocent.'

'You're not a criminal.' Pel snapped the words and Darcy knew he was angry. 'But rumours are going round about you. You know they're rubbish. I know they're rubbish. That's because we know and trust each other. But other people have to be convinced.'

'When does the suspension start?'

'Immediately.'

'Who's been doing all the talking?'

'Goriot, for my money.'

'We've no proof.'

'No. Because Deputy Lax's been opening his mouth, too. But then he always does. He thrives on things like this, even when they're untrue. We're not noted in France for electing good politicians. A man's not usually given power because he's the best. Usually it's because he's just better than the others. If Goriot's been talking, he's in trouble. The Chief won't stand for disloyalty. Unfortunately rumours can't go uninvestigated. But they *will* be investigated. The ballistic report on Gehrer's car's due any time – I've heard that Castéou's almost finished – and that might surprise a few people. In the meantime–'

'I'm off the Dupont case.'

'I can't let you touch it, Daniel.'

Darcy's face was grim as he turned to the door. 'I'll be seeing you, *patron*,' he said.

178

When Darcy left the Hôtel de Police, he made a point of moving among the haunts of his old girl-friends. There were several who worked in the city and he deliberately went there.

He spent the rest of the day not knowing what to do. What had happened had come as a shock to him. He sat in the park and walked the streets and eventually to his surprise found himself in the Church of St-Michel et Tous les Anges. He didn't consider himself a good church-goer and even now he didn't pray, not even that things would come right. He simply sat and stared in front of him, trying not to think. After a while, he found the priest sitting beside him.

'You have trouble, my boy?'

Darcy shrugged.

'The Lord never intended the Via Crucis to be paved with lobster mayonnaise.'

Darcy turned quickly at the words and couldn't help smiling.

'Perhaps you would like to make a confession?'

'I've nothing to confess, Father.'

'Nothing?'

'Well, by the standards of the Church, perhaps I have. But I've done nothing very bad. Do you believe that?'

'The ability to distinguish truth from falsehood is not one of the powers granted by the Holy Ghost, my son. But the Church is more broadminded than you think.'

'I'm a cop, Father,' Darcy said suddenly. 'I've been accused of taking bribes.'

'And did you?'

'No.'

'Then it will come right in the end.'

'I wish I could be sure.'

'Well, the Lord teaches us not to count our chickens before they're hatched, but I'm sure you have God's right arm behind you, my son. Even so, God's grace isn't laid on like central heating. You will need to be patient.'

The talk helped a little but it soon wore off, and when Darcy arrived at Angélique Courtoise's flat that evening, he was in a bad temper again.

'What's wrong?' she asked.

'I've been suspended from duty.'

179

She put her arms round him. 'Why?'

'For taking bribes.'

'What nonsense. Surely they believe you?'

'Do they? Perhaps. Pel does, thank God. But others? You know how it gets around. What a nice flat you've got! Does your boy-friend get a lot of bribes? Do *you* believe me?'

'Of course I do.'

'That's because love is blind. But it's only blind because it's easier than mistrusting.'

She tried to brush his anger aside. 'What are we doing tonight. Shall we try the cinema?'

'Why not the usual? There's nothing a young full-blooded girl enjoys more than the pleasures of the bed.'

She looked at him, startled.

'Virginity should be lost gloriously,' he said.

'I'm not a virgin! You, of all people, should know that.'

'Yes. Virgins are collectors' items these days.'

She lost her temper. 'Stop it, Daniel,' she snapped. 'Don't talk like that. It's flip. It's hard. It's childish. You're not normally like this.'

'Noted for my sense of humour? My laughter? Always in overdrive?'

'Not like this, anyway. This is cruel. You do laugh. You make me laugh.'

Suddenly there were tears in her eyes. 'But you're kind, Daniel. You're always kind. You're a policeman and you have to be tough, but you're never mean.'

'I've been mean today.' Darcy frowned. 'Normal men have their little fiddles. Use of office paper for private letters. Office telephone to contact their wives. Office car to see a girl friend. Not much. Only a little out of your way. But cops are different. You don't have to be a hundred per cent honest. You have to be a hundred and twenty per cent. More, if possible. And you have to be seen to be. There's a saying in France about the police: when a cop laughs at the cop-shop, all the cops laugh. It's true, but it's also true that sometimes they do the other thing.'

'Stop it, Daniel.'

'I'll plead Article 64 of the penal code. "There is no crime or

180

misdemeanour if the accused was in a state of dementia at the time of the act, or if he was driven to it by an irresistible impulse." I'll claim I was mad.'

She was growing angry. 'You're talking nonsense.'

'Perhaps I am. I'd better go.'

'You don't have to.'

'I think I do. I'm not fit to be with decent people and it's better than skirmishing round each other like a couple of terriers, snapping at each other's ankles.'

As the door slammed, she stood staring at it, white-faced and sick-looking, and tears began to fill her eyes.

15

After a long period of quiet, the Tuaregs reappeared. They had lain low for so long, Nosjean and De Troq' had come to the conclusion they had given up, that they had acquired all they needed, or grown scared, or simply bored. Nosjean and De Troq' hadn't forgotten them, but there had been nothing they could do. The alibis of De Rille and Tassigny seemed watertight and the surveillance of Janine Ducassis and the supermarket had produced nothing.

Then, early in the morning, De Troq' appeared on the other end of Nosjean's telephone.

'They're back!' he yelled.

'Who're back?' Nosjean mumbled, cradling the telephone to avoid waking Mijo Lehmann.

'The Tuaregs!'

'What!' Sitting up in bed, Nosjean threw off the clothes so hurriedly, Mijo Lehmann came to life, too.

'When?' he yelled.

'Just now! It's just come in. I took the call. All night garage on the N57. It does well because people from Metaux de Dijon going home after the late shift tend to fill their cars there. They got eight thousand-odd francs.'

'Not much!'

'It'll pay for their petrol and a few drinks.'

'What happened?'

'Big car drew up. Dirty. Looked like the sort of car a worker at Metaux de Dijon might use. Next minute the attendant was looking down the spout of a sawn-off shot gun.'

Nosjean was busy trying to drag his clothes on with one

182

hand and talk into the telephone with the other. Mijo Lehmann climbed out of bed after him and stood next to him, fastening the buttons on his shirt. 'I thought it was to be a bank,' Nosjean was saying.

'Perhaps they're just short of ready cash.'

'Well, it sounds like the Tuaregs.'

But, as it happened, this time it wasn't. When Nosjean ran into the Hôtel de Police, De Troq' met him, making wash-out signs with his hands.

'Not the Tuaregs,' he said. 'Two sixteen-year-old kids. It's a copycat job. They said they were excited by what the Tuaregs had been doing and thought they'd do the same.'

'We've got them?'

'Pomereu's men have. They were making their getaway when they hit the curb going round a corner into the estate at Chenove, and the front tyre burst. The car went out of control, went through a hedge and turned upside down. They're lucky to be alive. Pomereu's boys fished them out just before it burst into flames.'

Nosjean drew a deep breath, feeling the adrenalin draining out of him.

'We've got to nail these damned Tuaregs,' he said. 'If we don't, every kid in the area'll start doing it. All that damned nonsense in the papers making the Tuaregs sound like old-fashioned highwaymen! Romantic nonsense! They're sophisticated, whoever they are. They've got brains. They know what they're doing, and they're experts. These kids aren't. Someone will kill himself. The Tuaregs don't go in for killing people.'

'They might one day,' De Troq' said drily.

He and Nosjean had their suspicions but there was really nothing very concrete about them and the whole scene seemed suddenly to have gone dead. Nobody was talking and nobody was doing anything. Claudie Darel and the other policewoman were still watching for the fawn Sierra. They'd spotted young De Rille several times, often with Dominique Tassigny de Bré beside him, but he seemed to be about his legitimate business. He seemed to frequent the bars near Garages Automobile Europe and twice they'd seen him outside with a Ferrari and a man who looked English discussing the car's points.

183

No further indication had come in about which bank was to be the Tuaregs' next target, but Louis the Limp was still certain that it *was* to be a bank.

'How do you know?' Nosjean demanded.

'I picked it up.'

'Where?'

Louis the Limp gave Nosjean a disgusted look and didn't bother to answer. You didn't ask informers where they picked up their information.

'How do you know it's a bank?' Nosjean persisted.

'I don't. This type told me, that's all.'

'Where did the information come from?'

'These types were heard talking and banks were mentioned.'

'They might have been thinking of drawing out their savings.'

'That wasn't the impression.'

'Who was it who was talking?'

'That wasn't passed on.'

'Why not?'

'Scared.'

'What of?'

'It was felt there might be a shot gun in the earhole and the trigger pulled.'

'That doesn't sound like the Tuaregs. Are you sure it isn't all made up to raise a bit of cash?'

'This one doesn't make things up,' Louis the Limp said. 'But a lot of information drifts by.'

'What's he do?'

'He isn't a he. He's a she.

'So what does *she* do?'

'She works a switchboard.'

Nosjean decided Louis the Limp's informant was a girl-friend but since he was known to have a lot of girl-friends – not only in the city but in the countryside around and, come to that, in a few other towns and areas of countryside, too – it didn't help much. Louis refused to give any more information and even seemed indignant that Nosjean wouldn't believe him.

'What we need,' Nosjean said as he discussed it with De Troq' over a beer in the Bar Transvaal, 'is a flying squad. Two or three cars with radios and several men on tap ready to get away at once as soon as we hear something.'

Pel took the same view as Nosjean: that they needed to catch the Tuaregs quickly because copycat robberies might turn into bloody affairs with someone killed. Guns in the hands of sixteen-year-olds could be messy.

'I'll let the Chief know what's in the wind,' he said. 'Inform Pomereu of Traffic, and Turgot, Nadauld's successor. They'll also need to know. What back-up do you want?'

'Just the cars, *patron*.'

'Arms?'

'Nothing special. The Tuaregs don't seem to go in for violence in spite of the shotguns they use. We think they're spoiled kids who've been used to money who've found they're a bit short and thought up this way of earning some. I expect they regard it as a bit of a prank. But we'll take no risks.'

'You'd better not,' Pel said.

Pomereu provided cars and Turgot provided men. With the flying squad formed, all they now needed was the time and place.

'Just the name of the bank Louis the Limp said they were going to do,' Nosjean said.

Watching from a stationer's opposite where Janine Ducassis lived, Claudie Darel continued the surveillance. There had been nothing to indicate that the girl from the supermarket was involved in any way in the robberies. Her route home seemed normal enough. Occasionally, she stopped to buy food but always she went to her home in the Arsenal area of the city, a district of small houses and flats; the young men who appeared outside later, when investigated, seemed to have no connection whatsoever with the Tuaregs.

Then one night they noticed Janine Ducassis was giving Pascal Dubois, the manager's secretary, a lift, and that Pascal Dubois descended from the little Fiat outside an expensive-looking house in the Rue des Alouettes near the Park de la Colombière, one of the best districts in the city. She didn't

185

re-emerge and Janine Ducassis continued on to her home in Arsenal.

It didn't take long to discover that Pascal Dubois's car was having a service at Garages Automobile Europe where De Rille worked from time to time, and the following evening, when the supermarket closed, there were two cars available. Claudie had arranged for the other policewoman to bring her own car and while she followed Janine Ducassis to her home at Arsenal, Claudie followed Pascal Dubois. This time she drove herself home and her car wasn't a Fiat Panda. It was a Ford Escort, much bigger and better-looking than Janine Ducassis's miniature vehicle.

'She lives near the Eglise St-Paul,' Claudie reported. 'So she must have relations or a boy-friend at the place in the Rue des Alouettes. It's a block of flats.'

It didn't take long to acquire the name of the owner of the block. It didn't mean a thing. It belonged to a man called Bagnolle.

The following night, after Pascal Dubois had driven from the supermarket to the flat she owned near the Eglise St-Paul, Claudie watched for a while from her car, then, just as she was about to pack up and go home, she saw Pascal Dubois re-emerge, climb into her car and drive off. She stopped outside the house in the Rue des Alouettes and went inside.

'There's someone there who's important to her,' she told Nosjean.

'There probably is,' Nosjean agreed. 'Find out who.'

They finally seemed to have a link connecting the robbery at Talant to the two bright young men they were watching.

De Rille's girl friend seemed to be the sister of his good friend, Tassigny, while Pascal Dubois, who worked at Talant and doubtless knew all the procedures there, seemed to be in the habit of having her car serviced at the garage which De Rille had made his headquarters. Finally, Pascal Dubois, though she lived near the Eglise St-Paul, was in the habit of regularly visiting a flat in the Rue des Alouettes. Nosjean and De Troq' had already guessed whose it was.

186

De Troq', as stubborn as Darcy and as dogged as Lagé, came in with something else. He had been prowling round Morbihaux, feeling that somehow he might pick up something. He did.

He almost fell into the sergeants' room.

'That boat,' he said.

'Which boat?'

'That boat they used – De Rille and Dominique Tassigny.'

'What about it?'

'They said they used it. They didn't. It wasn't there that day.'

'What?' Nosjean jumped up. 'How did you find out?'

'I bumped into the owner. He said he'd found out who'd had it and it was all right. It wasn't De Rille and Dominique Tassigny. It was a boy called Mouchotte. Georges Mouchotte. He was with a girl called Santez. Anna Santez. And they were up to the same thing De Rille said he was up to with Dominique Tassigny. But if they were using the boat, De Rille couldn't have been.'

'Have you checked?'

'The Santez girl's mother confirms it. She'd suspected what they were up to and she was waiting. The Santez girl got a good hiding. She's only sixteen. The boy's nineteen. Madame Santez thought they were a bit young for that sort of thing.'

'Go on.'

'De Rille knew the boat was available and that people borrowed it and the owner didn't mind. It was a quick and ready alibi. Unfortunately, they didn't make enquiries. If they had they'd have found the boat wasn't there when they said it was. Ought we to pick them up?'

Nosjean frowned, worried. 'It's purely circumstantial and they'll employ the best counsel there is. Daddy's got the money. They'd get off. I'd rather catch them at it. Let's wait. They may have a go at Louis the Limp's bank.'

Like Nosjean and De Troq', Misset also hadn't given up. He also didn't seem to be making much progress and he would happily have written 'No police action required' on his report, but he had a suspicion that somewhere, somehow, he was

187

missing something. He tried Jouet again, the man who was claiming his garden was being ruined.

'It's sodium chlorate,' Jouet said.

'What is?'

'The stuff Ferry's throwing on my lawn.'

'Have you seen him throwing it on?'

'No.'

'So how do you know?'

'When I'm not here, my wife watches.'

'And has she seen him?'

'No. I think he does it at night when we're asleep.'

'It seems a lot of trouble to go to. Especially when you say you haven't quarrelled. How do you know this stuff you found in your garden's this sodium whatever-it-is?'

'I found some crystals and had them tested.'

'Where?'

'I've got a friend who works at Metallurgie Bourguignonne. They have a laboratory.'

'And he decided they were this sodium thing?'

'No. I told him that. He just checked.'

'So, in fact, he didn't know it was this sodium thing until you told him?'

'That's right.'

'That's leading the witness.'

'I'm not a lawyer. I thought it was weedkiller and I wanted to know, that's all.'

Misset ran out of ideas again. He couldn't just go to the man next door and say 'You're scattering weedkiller on your neighbour's lawn'. He had to have a bit more proof.

He went back to the bar, eyed the girl behind the counter again, and studied Ferry, who was in his drive up the street, tinkering with his car. As he watched, it suddenly occurred to Misset that Ferry hadn't worked much lately, and that it might be a good idea to check up on him a little. It turned out that the truck he'd driven when he wasn't unemployed was one of the little tractors that pulled the carts of suitcases out to the aircraft at the airport, where Trudis had the concession, but that he had been sacked four months before for trying to get into one of the pieces of luggage he was hauling.

Trudis confirmed the fact. 'We got rid of him,' the personnel manager explained. 'He had sticky fingers. Things went missing. And he was found trying to get into this suitcase.'

'Did you inform the police?'

'No. He hadn't opened it so we couldn't charge him with theft. Instead we sacked him on the spot.'

'I bet he was mad,' Misset said.

'You're telling me. He threatened us with firebombs, poison gas, tanks, nuclear weapons, the lot. We didn't take much notice. He was always inclined to go over the top a bit. I think he isn't quite all there.'

It set Misset's mind going again. Because his wife had been on at him again, he went to the Bar de la Petite Alsacienne to do his thinking. The girl eyed him suspiciously as he took his beer to a corner table where he could see Jouet's house and Ferry's house next door, with its battered car in the drive. He could also see the girl behind the bar without turning anything more than his eyes, and every time she bent to the sink he could look down the top of her dress. That was something Misset enjoyed. He was still day-dreaming when Pel appeared.

He was in a bad temper. Darcy had disappeared and Pel was angry with the Chief – though he knew the Chief was right – and angrier still with Goriot. In addition, his cold hadn't improved, his sinuses were worse and he was sure he was dying. What was more, his wife had had to go to Paris for the day on business and that always put him in a bad mood until she returned. When he had left the house, Madame Routy, taking advantage of her absence, had had both the radio and the television on. They had been playing different programmes when Pel had left but somehow she managed to absorb them both.

Arriving at the office, he had had a go at Nosjean and De Troq', complaining that they were getting nowhere with the Tuaregs and ignoring their arguments that they were; then he set about Aimedieu and Lagé. Brochard and Debray were out, and thus escaped, so it seemed to be time to have a go at

189

Misset. Any time was a good time to have a go at Misset because it could be guaranteed that he wasn't doing his job properly.

While Misset was leaning on the table, trying to keep his eyes off the barmaid's bust, Pel popped up alongside him. He seemed to emerge through a hole in the ground. Emerging through a hole in the ground when he wasn't expected was one of Pel's gifts.

His temper was worse. There was a bunch of teenagers outside the bar, smoking in the way only French teenagers could smoke and it made him want to light up.

Misset was staring into space.

'See something?' Pel asked.

Misset jumped enough to jar the table and spill his beer. 'No, *patron*,' he said. 'Thinking.'

'With what?'

Misset ignored the comment.

'Found out about Jouet's lawn yet?'

'No, *patron*. It's got me puzzled.'

'I've seen no reports. Why not?'

'I haven't had time, *patron*.'

'Everybody else finds time. Reports are what we exist on. Without reports, tomorrow's policemen don't know anything.'

Misset's mind fluttered, looking for a good excuse. Pel saw his mouth moving. He knew Misset was cursing him under his breath. It didn't worry him. He liked people to curse him. It proved he was doing his job.

As he stared at Misset, Misset couldn't think what else to say so he jerked a hand at the road outside.

'That's Lax's car,' he said conversationally. 'Councillor Lax. I think he has a lady friend round here. It's always there. The one in front is Senator Forton's.'

Pel's ears pricked. 'Oh?' he said. 'How do you know?'

'I've seen him get out of it. I've seen them talking there.'

'Often?'

'More than once.'

It was Pel's turn to have a faraway look in his eyes and, to Misset's surprise, he didn't pursue the subject of Jouet's garden or Misset's lack of brains and initiative. Instead he ordered a

190

beer – even one for Misset – and stood staring through the open door at the two cars himself.

'Pity you can't hear what they're saying,' he said unexpectedly; then, finishing his beer, he departed, leaving Misset feeling he had been swept by a strong wind.

16

Nosjean was staring at a list of all the banks in the district. He had scored out the names of all the big ones and made a list of small country and suburban branches. It was still formidable and told him little. One of them, he felt, was due for the attention of the Tuaregs.

Going to the supermarket at Talant, he found Janine Ducassis in charge, with no sign of the manager or Pascal Dubois.

'It's her day off,' Janine announced. 'We're open seven days a week here. We take our days off when we can.'

'What about the manager?'

'He's gone to the bank to collect the wages. Everybody gets paid today.'

'Much, is it?'

'I don't know. It must be a lot.'

'Does he go on his own?'

'No. Sergeant Blanqui goes with him. He's an ex-para-trooper.'

'Good-looking? Young and active?'

She grinned. 'No. Ugly, old and randy. He tries to get me in his car.'

'Which bank is it?'

'Crédit Agricole.'

'The one in the Place Dumanoir in the city?'

'No. Monsieur Blond's a bit nervous about the city. He says there are too many crooks about. He uses the branch of St-Florent. There's an arrangement to draw the money there. I've been with him once. When Blanqui's had too many brandies the night before.'

Returning to his office, Nosjean sat, frowning. While he waited, the radio squawked. It was Claudie Darel.

'That flat,' she said.

'Yes?'

'The owner's name is – '

'Arthur Tassigny de Bré.'

'You knew?'

'I wondered.'

Claudie laughed. 'There's movement,' she said. 'Pascal Dubois left. In her own car. So did De Rille. In the Ford Sierra. Twenty minutes ago. I couldn't get through before. The radio packed up.'

'Anything else?'

'I think he's got Tassigny with him. He must have been in the flat with him all night. It begins to link up. Dominique Tassigny seems to be De Rille's girl-friend and De Rille's the owner of the car we think was switched at Morbihaux. Pascal Dubois seems to be Arthur Tassigny's girl-friend. I think she's the one who passed on the information that Monique Vachonnière was in the habit of leaving her till with the key in it. The manager's office overlooks the inside of the supermarket on one side and the forecourt on the other. She could easily have signalled to them if they were waiting across the road. I wonder if they're going to do the supermarket again?'

'Are they on their own?'

'No. There's another one doing the driving. I couldn't see him properly. Small. Red hair.'

'Dominique Tassigny,' Nosjean breathed.

'Who?'

'The one who's crazy about fast cars and never misses Le Mans. She's wearing a wig. What else has she got on?'

'One of those denim caps. Blue. With a peak. Makes her look like Lenin on a bad day.'

'Which way did they go?'

'They took the Savigny road out of the city. Towards Marcilly.'

'St-Florent!' Nosjean said.

'What?'

'St-Florent! It's St-Florent!'

193

'What is?'

'The branch of Crédit Agricole. The bank Louis the Limp heard about. But they're not doing the bank. They're doing the manager. Get out there, Claudie!'

De Troq' was already calling Pomereu and Turgot and telephoning the substation at St-Florent. Then he and De Troq' left a message for Pel and ran for De Troq's big roadster. It was bigger and faster than Nosjean's car, a huge open affair with an enormous bonnet held down by a strap and headlights like enormous eyes. De Troq' might be poor but it often seemed to Nosjean that poverty among the aristocracy was a comparative thing.

They found a crowd outside the bank, all huddled together with the manner of scared animals, and they knew at once they were too late. Propped against the wall was an elderly man wearing a gun and a uniform of sorts. His hat had gone and there was a livid bruise on his head and blood on his face. Alongside him was Blond, the manager of the Supermarket at Talant. He was white and looked shocked and seemed barely able to speak.

'What happened.' Nosjean said.

'They snatched the bag. With the wages.'

Nosjean looked about him, puzzled. The police were represented only by two constables. 'Who's handling this?' he demanded.

As he turned away, Pomereu's car screeched to a stop and policemen poured out. Almost immediately Turgot's car arrived behind it and more men appeared, then a third car hurtled up containing Claudie Darel.

'For the love of God,' Nosjean yelled at the local cops, 'who's in control?'

'Brigadier Maret.'

'Well, where is he?'

One of the constables gestured and they saw there was another crowd of people several hundred metres away down the road. There was a police van there as well as an ambulance.

'Come on!'

They fell into De Troq's car and as it stopped again by the crowd, Nosjean jumped out.

194

'What happened?'

Brigadier Maret, a fat man with steel-rimmed spectacles, gestured at a bloodstained shape in the road. Ambulance men were just covering it with a blanket.

'Not us,' they announced. 'It's the mortuary van you want. He's dead. We can't help him.'

The brigadier signed to one of his men. 'Get on to them. Quick.'

'See we get the blanket back,' the ambulance man added. 'We don't want it getting lost like the last one.'

'What happened?' Nosjean asked him.

'The buggers kept it. It made up their blanket numbers for one they lost some months before and – '

'*Here!*' Nosjean roared. 'What happened *here*? For the love of God, a man's dead and you're worrying about a damned blanket!'

The ambulance man blushed and vanished and, as Nosjean showed his identity card, Brigadier Maret came to life at last. He indicated the body.

'It's Colonel Boileau,' he said.

'Who's he?'

'Colonel Amadéo Boileau. He lives at the other end of the village.'

'How's he come to be dead? What happened? Was he involved in the hold up?'

'Well, yes and no. Some type was just coming out of the bank down there with a bag in his fist. There was another guy with him. Then these two other types appeared from a car that drew up. The first two were clubbed down and the bag snatched. The hold-up men ran back to the car and it shot off down here.'

'And Boileau? Was he one of them?'

'No, he wasn't. He's an old soldier. He was taking his daily walk.' The brigadier indicated a cocker spaniel which was sniffing at the shape under the blanket. 'With his dog. That's it. He comes down here every day about this time. Before anyone knew what was happening, the car was heading this way. The Colonel tried to stop it. He stepped out into the road and waved his arms.'

195

'It knocked him down?'

'They drove straight at him. They hadn't much choice. It was either stop and be caught or knock him out of the way. He was flung into the air and hit the windscreen. The car swerved and he rolled off the bonnet and the wheels went over his chest. We have a witness, an old man coming out of the shop over there. Boileau was still lying in the road when the driver of a car down there backed into the road to stop the getaway.'

'And?'

'The driver of the getaway car saw the way was blocked so they reversed. Fast. They ran over the colonel a second time. Then they set off again and turned right to the main road. The colonel was caught by his jacket and dragged along. He was heard shouting for help. When people got to him his jacket had come off and he was lying in the road. The car had gone. He was already dead. The doctor says his lungs must have been crushed and penetrated by the ends of broken ribs when the car backed over him. He also has a broken neck and fractured skull.'

'Is he married?'

'Yes.'

'Then don't you think you'd better inform his wife?'

'Oh, God,' the brigadier said. 'I suppose I had.' He was obviously not looking forward to the task and Claudie stepped forward.

'Give me the address,' she said. 'I'll go.'

The brigadier obliged hurriedly.

'Who else was in the car besides the two who did the snatch?' De Troq' asked as Claudie vanished.

'Just the driver.' The brigadier seemed shocked. 'A kid with a linen cap on. One of those blue denim things with a peak. He had longish red hair.'

There was little doubt but that it was the Tuaregs, and this time they had gone too far. Up to now nobody had been hurt and people, reading of their exploits in the newspapers, had come to regard them as folk-heroes full of pranks and *joie de vivre*. Now it was different. A man was dead, a decent honourable

196

man decorated by his country for bravery with the army. A woman was widowed. And the killing had been deliberate.

There had been plenty of witnesses who could swear to the clothing of the robbers – thick Canadiennes and scarves tied tightly round their noses and mouths. 'Like motor cyclists.' The phrase cropped up twice in half an hour.

Blond, the manager of the supermarket, had recovered a little by the time they returned to him and the guard was being attended by a doctor, assisted by a woman who said she was a nurse.

'What happened?' Nosjean asked.

'I knew at once what was going to happen,' Blond said, 'because they were wearing the same coats as the men who did the supermarket.'

'Go on.'

'I yelled out "It's them" and old Blanqui reached for his gun. But he's old and too slow. He's got enough medals to fill a cart but he got them a long time ago. I've been on to the owners demanding someone younger but they've never done anything about it. One of them hit him with what looked like a sawn-off shotgun and the other snatched the bag from me. I tried to hang on to it but he kneed me in the balls and I let go.'

'Do you always collect the money at the same time?'

'No. I try to vary it.'

'Who'd know the time?'

'Only me. And Blanqui, of course. Perhaps the office staff.'

The case occupied them for the whole of the rest of the day. The car which had been used in the hold-up was found late in the evening, parked badly, one door open, by a policeman in a prowling patrol car. Inevitably it had been stolen – from Chenove – and was the property of a doctor. It had been tuned for high speeds. There were no fingerprints – they hadn't expected any – but the policeman who had found it had found a plastic carrier bag caught in a bush a few yards away.

'It's marked Supermarket Talant,' he pointed out.

Nosjean and De Troq' had a habit of thinking about the cases

197

they were involved in separately, to see where their conclusions matched.

Nosjean was furious with himself. 'An old man's dead,' he snarled. 'Because I tried to be clever.'

'Not you,' De Troq' pointed out. 'De Rille and his friends.'

'It's as plain as a pikestaff.'

'Now it is!'

'De Rille and Tassigny did the job. The Tassigny girl was the driver. She's an expert. She was probably the one who tuned up the car – at the De Rille family home. In what were the stables, remember? She learned from the people who knew – in the pits at Le Mans. We'll give them time to get bedded down. Claudie's keeping an eye on the place.'

They went in De Troq's car. They had a search warrant. Judge Brisard, who should have been available, was missing and Nosjean suspected he was visiting the woman he kept at Beaune. Judge Castéou obliged with a signature.

'The Tuaregs?' she asked.

'Yes.'

Ten minutes later they drew up outside 17, Rue Barnabas with a quiet squeak of brakes. Pomereu and Turgot waited a little further down the street.

Nosjean gave his instructions. 'Two men on the front staircase, one watching the lift, and two watching the service staircase.'

The block of flats where De Rille lived was silent as they paused outside.

'Ready?' Nosjean asked.

De Troq' nodded.

There was no reply to Nosjean's knock so he leaned on the bell, knocking with his other hand. Eventually they heard movement inside the flat and the door was opened. De Rille was wearing a silk dressing-gown and apparently nothing else. They pushed their way past him.

'What the hell's going on?' he demanded. 'Do you know what time it is?'

'I have a search warrant,' Nosjean said.

198

'The hell you have! My lawyer will want to know about this.'
Nosjean pushed into the bedroom. Sitting up in bed, as naked
as De Rille, was Dominique Tassigny.
'What in God's name's this?' she said. There was nothing
rhapsodic or melodic about her voice this time. It was harsh
and frightened and she looked as if she'd been crying.
'Out of bed, please,' Nosjean said. 'Get dressed.'
'Why?'
'Because I say so and, if you don't want to accompany us to
the Hôtel de Police looking like that, you'll do as I say.'
She got out of bed. De Rille was in the living room pouring
himself a whisky. As he raised it, she took it from his hand
and swallowed it at a gulp. He shrugged and began to pour
another. As he did so, Inspector Turgot appeared, followed by
two of his men pushing in front of them Arthur Tassigny. With
him was Pascal Dubois. They were both only half-clothed.
'They came down the fire escape,' Turgot said.
All four of them were drunk and now that the policemen
could get a good look at them they saw they were all scared.
Their latest prank had gone very wrong and they'd been trying
to calm their nerves. There was an empty whisky bottle on its
side on the kitchen floor.
De Rille made a weak effort at bluster. 'What is this?' he said.
'You have nothing on us.'
'We have a great deal on you,' Nosjean said. 'For instance,
a wages snatch at St-Florent this morning.'
'That's nonsense. We have no firearms here beyond what
you've already seen. Quite legitimate and fully licensed.'
He looked too nervous and ill at ease to convince Nosjean.
'Search the place,' he said.
The policemen went through the flat carefully but they turned
nothing up. By this time, the four occupants, all dressed and
drinking whisky, were sitting in armchairs and on the settee,
beginning to look smug.
'Nice place you have here,' Nosjean said. 'Ideal for two lively
young couples. Two large double beds – king size are they? –
plenty to drink, plenty of money. I noticed a plastic carrier
bag marked "Talant Supermarket" hanging behind the pantry
door.'

'Pascal brings those,' De Rille said easily. 'She works there and keeps us supplied with food and drink. As staff, she gets it cheaply.'

In the main bedroom, De Troq' was studying the bed. It was huge and seemed as large as the Parc des Princes. He tried it. It was solid and heavy and felt as if it weighed as much as a tank. He studied it for a while, then he went to the next bedroom. The bed there moved at his touch, sliding easily on castors across the thick pile carpet. De Troq' gazed at it and pushed it a little further. A moment or two later he appeared in the door of the living room, and gestured to Nosjean.

'Come and look at this,' he said.

'Sawn-off shotguns wrapped in Canadiennes and stuffed under the floor,' Nosjean told Pel when he appeared. 'Together with the wages and a red wig. They'd cut a square out of the carpet and lifted four of the boards. There was no ammunition. Pascal Dubois tipped them off about the time Blond was drawing the wages. The fingerprint on the till at Talant could be Tassigny's, and the driver was his sister wearing a red wig.'

It was almost morning by this time and De Rille, the two Tassignys and Pascal Dubois were sitting in cells.

'They'd been doing it for a lark,' Nosjean said. 'De Rille had worked his way through a lot of his legacy, though there was still a bit left. But he began to grow worried that it wouldn't last and they started this game. The Tassignys, who were always short of cash, fell in with it easily enough. Arthur Tassigny had been going around with Pascal Dubois for a long time – originally because she could get hold of cheap food and drink. They didn't intend to go on with the game, but when the press got hold of it and started to build them up as folk heroes, they began to enjoy it.'

Pel looked puzzled. 'Why didn't they bolt?'

Nosjean gave a contemptuous shrug. 'Because they're amateurs, *patron*. A professional would have thought of that.' He was still angry with himself, feeling he should have worked it out earlier than he had. 'They're a lot of spoiled kids and all they can think of now is to blame each other for what happened.

They thought it was just fun and the guns weren't ever loaded. Fun! With poor old Boileau dead, with crushed ribs, a fractured skull, a broken leg, a broken neck and punctured lungs. Know what De Rille said when I charged them, *patron*?'

'Inform me.'

' "We never intended to hurt anyone." '

17

About the time they were wrapping up the Tuaregs, Doc Cham was staring at the body in front of him on the slab. Duff Forbes Mackay was a strong man just beginning to run to fat. Cham already knew a little from what Lagé, who was standing near by trying not to watch the autopsy, had told him. According to the other members of the barge party he'd spoken to, Forbes had joined the group on the barge trip in the hope of finding a girl. It appeared he was lonely and itching to get married.

The possibility of suicide had crossed Cham's mind. But nobody's going to stab himself in the groin as a means of killing himself, he thought. There were much easier ways.

'Stab wound,' he said aloud for the shorthand writer behind him. 'But relatively shallow. Femoral vein's been severed but the artery underneath's untouched. And what's this –?'

Bending, Cham peered closer, then with a pair of tweezers he removed something from the wound and showed it to Lagé.

'Glass,' he said. 'A sliver of glass. That's a funny thing to stab yourself with.'

Placing the splinter of glass in a kidney dish, Cham turned to Lagé to find him with a scowl on his face and his thumb in his mouth like a child. He was cursing under his breath. He indicated the dead man's clothing he'd been searching and, moving carefully, he extricated from the left trouser pocket a dagger-like shard. 'Glass,' he said. 'More glass.'

Cham and Lagé stared at each other for a moment, then Lagé poked cautiously about in the trousers to produce several more dangerously sharp shards of glass. One of them had a label adhering to it marked with three stars and the name 'Barnez Frères'.

'Brandy,' Lagé said. 'Cheap brandy.'

Pel listened to what they had to say.

'Off you go, Lagé,' he said. 'Check the épiceries and bars round the barge port.'

Lagé was back within an hour.

'He bought the bottle at the Epicerie de la Porte,' he announced. 'It's a hundred metres from the barge. Yachtsmen and people on barges passing through use it for their food and drink. The owner – name of Gaffard – says a big man with a funny accent appeared late at night and persuaded him to sell him a half bottle of brandy. Gaffard wasn't open but he was standing at the door smoking a cigarette when the man came along and talked him into it.'

'They'd made up their quarrel,' Pel said. 'And when Duart produced his bottle of whisky, Mackay felt he ought to show the same conciliatory spirit, so he went out to produce a bottle of something, too. Was he drunk?'

'Gaffard said he was. He said *very* drunk. He stuck the bottle in his trouser pocket and set off back to the barge port.'

'And as he lurched back on board,' Pel said, 'having already drunk more than was good for him, he slipped. Perhaps he just banged against the rail of the gangplank. Either way, the bottle was broken, and one of the shards pierced his groin.'

'Judging by the amount he had in him,' Cham said, 'he'd have been numb with intoxication. He probably didn't realize how badly hurt he was. As he tried to open the cabin door he smeared blood on it and that blood found its way on to Duart's shirt when he came looking for him.'

'And, having collapsed on to his bunk, being drunk, he just passed out and bled to death.'

It seemed to be another one wrapped up.

But it wasn't quite. There was a little more to come.

203

The ballistics report when it came also brought a surprise. Castéou had taken his time but he was in no doubts. 'One bullet,' he said. 'One only.' They all looked at each other. They had been expecting perhaps a mad machine-gunner, but here it was – one bullet only, and that had to be the bullet the sentry Girard had admitted firing.

'Bullets do strange things,' Castéou said as he explained his findings. 'For example, when a bullet travelling at high speed suddenly strikes a firm resisting object, though the tip of the bullet is checked, the rest of it continues at its original speed, so that the rear end can sometimes pass over the body of the bullet like a glove that turns inside out as it's drawn off the fingers. At the same time there's a reverse effect at the point of entrance which gives the appearance of an exit hole.'

There was dead silence. Castéou's audience included the Chief, the Procureur, Castéou's wife who was conducting the case, Colonel Le Thiel from the airfield and two of his officers, and all the policemen who had been involved.

Only Darcy wasn't present. The Chief was still trying to set up an investigation because the constant reports that had been coming in couldn't be ignored. The Chief knew Darcy well, but anything to do with the police, no matter what, was always political in the end and with Councillor Lax asking questions in the council chamber, he had to do something about it.

Castéou paused. 'When a bullet leaves the barrel of a rifle it travels at a speed of about seven hundred and fifty metres per second and is spinning at between two and three thousand revolutions per second. At short ranges – between two and three hundred metres – it can have a degree of wobble before it settles down and spins properly, so that a bullet fired into soft clay doesn't simply pass through it; it produces a cavity many times its own diameter and often smashes into fragments, so that it looks as if it were an explosive or a dumdum bullet. It's the same when one strikes a human body at the same range. It has the same explosive effects.'

They shifted uneasily in their chairs and Pel saw Goriot's face grow dark as all his theories were destroyed.

'It would have been very different if Gehrer's car had been a standard model with a solid top,' Castéou went on. 'In that case, the break-up of the bullet would have occurred outside. But Sergeant Gehrer's Volkswagen had a soft top which presented no obstruction and the bullet went through it to strike Nadauld on the jaw.'

A screen had been set up behind him and photographs were flashed on to it to illustrate what he was saying. 'The appearance of the entrance wound in Inspector Nadauld's head,' he continued, 'indicated that the bullet was intact when it struck. It appears merely to have touched the jawbone but its velocity and spin caused complete fragmentation of the bone. Among the pieces found were some from the bullet which itself disintegrated after striking Nadauld's chin.'

Heads turned as they looked at each other.

'The jawbone's not a very solid structure,' Castéou pointed out. 'But it's solid enough to cause a high-speed projectile with a low-range wobble to break up. That's what happened. It hit the inspector on the chin. There was a clean-cut entrance wound on the right side of the lower jaw and a lacerated exit-wound on the left. The second wound was nine centimetres long and ran from the level of the chin to the lobe of the ear. It had the appearance of bursting outwards. The lower jaw was smashed to fragments.'

Castéou paused to let what he had said sink in. 'When Sergeant Gehrer's car was examined, not one but a number of bullet marks were found. There were two holes in the windscreen, each of them looking as though it had been made by an individual bullet. The interior of the car had also been pierced and there were several other marks that seemed to have been made by bullets. On the upper rim of the windscreen frame there was a dent about three centimetres in length where metal had been deposited. This appeared to have been made by another bullet. More fragments of lead and nickel and fragments of human tissue and bone were found in and around the windscreen, on the facia board, on the front passenger seat and on the hood. A portion of the bullet, consisting of the aluminium tip and the cupro-nickel jacket, was found on the rear seat. All this gave the impression that a number of shots had been fired. From the windscreen alone, it seemed that two or three bullets

205

had struck the car. But all the witnesses insist that only one shot was fired and only one cartridge case was found.'

A picture of Gehrer's car was flashed on the screen. Inside it were four men. 'I set up a reconstruction of the scene with the actual vehicle and with passengers, on the spot where it happened,' Castéou said. 'I'm confident no more than one bullet entered the car. One bullet. It hit Nadauld's jaw. As it disintegrated, fragments were driven through Nadauld's cheek, causing the lacerated wound, and some of them, with human tissue adhering to them, flew in different directions to produce the damage to the windscreen and the injuries to the other passengers. The largest fragment – the bullet tip on the back seat – fitted the dent on the frame of the windscreen exactly. After leaving Nadauld's jaw it had struck the frame and ricocheted to the back seat without touching any of the other passengers.'

Castéou paused and glanced at his listeners. 'Only one bullet was fired,' he repeated. 'The bullet fired by the sentry, the bullet that hit Nadauld.'

So that was that.

There never had been a mad machine-gunner and no attempt to take over the airfield. The only bullet that had been fired had been fired by a drunken conscript.

As Castéou finished, Goriot pushed his chair back with a scrape and left the room. His brows were down and his expression was full of anger and frustration.

'So the killing appears to be manslaughter,' the Chief said as the meeting broke up.

'It was probably even an accident,' Colonel Le Thiel agreed. 'Girard swears he didn't intend to kill anybody. He thought he was doing his duty and he had certainly been drinking. But he hadn't expected to be on duty and wouldn't have been but for the explosion. He'll be handed over to the law in the ordinary way. Although he's subject to service discipline, he can't escape by pleading he's exempt, as his lawyer's suggesting.'

'Assault and culpable homicide,' the Chief said. 'That'll be the verdict when he comes before the court. Coupled with a recommendation for lenience. He'll serve a few months' imprisonment and be discharged. Since he's a conscript, I doubt if he'll consider it severe.'

'You could almost say it wasn't intended.'

Pel looked up. 'The bomb was,' he said drily.

Pel was silent the next day, sitting in his office studying his blotter. Darcy had always known that when he was in that sort of mood it was best not to disturb him. Aimedieu – who was trying to do Darcy's job because Darcy wasn't there and Nosjean, who was next senior after Darcy, was still involved with the paperwork caused by the Tuaregs – didn't understand his methods so well and kept interrupting. In the end, Pel threw the *List of French Advocates and Lawyers* at him.

Cadet Darras, sitting in the office next door, grinned. 'He always does that,' he said. 'He's not a bad shot either.'

Then, from his office, Pel was suddenly involved in a flurry of telephone calls. The man on the switchboard grew hot under the collar at the demands being made on him.

'What's happened?' he demanded. 'Has war broken out?'

Pel was in touch with Records. 'Siméon,' he was saying. 'Adenne Siméon. You might as well also check on one or two other types too, while you're at it. I'll give you the names and what I know about them.'

For a long time as he put the telephone down, he sat staring at his blotter. They had appeared to be on the point of a breakthrough. Dupont's old briefs had set them off on a new track, and they had solved an old mystery and recovered a little of the loot from a wages snatch. Yet there was something wrong. Things didn't fit.

Did Dupont go to Lugny because he knew Siméon was there? It didn't seem so. So did he simply arrive by chance and, having arrived, recognize him? It didn't add up. They had found the money from the wages snatch in which Siméon had been involved in Marseilles in 1959. It had been hidden originally in the attic at the home of Siméon's mother. After three years in gaol, which, thanks to the skill of his advocate, Dupont, was all Siméon had suffered, he had retrieved it and banked it in the city. There wasn't a lot left by this time, though it was clear how Siméon had managed to live in comfort in Lugny over the years.

There were still things that didn't seem correct, however. Blackmailers didn't usually steal things. Blackmail was blackmail. Burglary was burglary. Robbery with violence was robbery with violence. They didn't mix and a man who went in for one didn't usually go in for any of the others. And how was Dupont killed? If he wasn't hit by a car, what was he hit with? And where was it? No weapon had yet been found. And who burgled the house at St-Alban? It was opened with a key. But the house in Dôle wasn't touched and, if a key was available for the house at St-Alban, there must surely have been one on the same key-ring for the house in Dôle, and surely the incriminating briefs would have been removed and destroyed.

So was Dupont murdered simply for his money? He was in the habit of carrying a lot with him. Could Madeleine Bas Jaunes be in it, too? Could she have put the three old rogues up to it? Did Dupont talk to her about what he possessed? Could they have caught him in bed with her, dragged him out and done for him there? Then tried to dress him because they had to get rid of him, but in their hurry made a mess of it and got the buttons in the wrong holes? Pel paused. *And*, he thought, Mailly-les-Temps was a hell of a long way from Lugny for two or three old men to carry a body.

In the absence of Darcy, he called Aimedieu and Lagé in and tossed his questions at them.

'Could he have staggered part of the way from Madeleine Bas Jaunes', *patron?*' Lagé asked. 'Losing one of his shoes *en route?*'

Pel sighed. 'She said he didn't visit her that night. I think that whoever hit him, thought they'd killed him, and they left him somewhere they thought was safe and went to his house to see what they could find. Perhaps both houses. But when they returned, he'd disappeared. He wasn't dead. He'd staggered off. But when they found him again he *was* dead. So they put him on the motorway.'

'Without his underclothes and socks and with his clothes all wrong?'

Pel nodded. 'And without his pyjamas. Where did *they* go to? And why didn't they remove the briefs? I'd like to talk to this Madame François who ran the hospice before the Sullys. She must have known of him. When she turns up she might be able to add a little light.'

Despite Pel's worries, there seemed no alternative to charging the three old men from Lugny with murder. Everything pointed to them and, despite their protests of innocence, they admitted Dupont was blackmailing Siméon.

They were just on the point of completing the case, when Madame François, the woman they so much wanted to interview, finally turned up. Since Darcy was no longer around, Pel went to see her himself and took Aimedieu along as witness to anything she had to say.

She was a woman in her middle forties, far from unattractive. She obviously liked the look of Aimedieu and invited them in at once.

'He looks just like my son,' she said warmly, and five minutes later there was coffee and brandy on the table.

'Madame Weill,' Pel tried.

'Her!' Madame François said.

Pel caught the contempt in her voice at once.

'Why do you say it like that, madame?' he asked.

She flapped her hand in a derogatory gesture. 'She wasn't interested in nursing,' she said. 'She was just an old crook who wanted the money she got from the inmates. Most of them were pretty well off and were willing to pay, but they got a raw deal and she made a lot of money. Unfortunately for her, the Health Department decided she was too old to run the place and insisted she should get a young assistant. It turned out to be me.'

'You didn't stay long.'

'There was always too much for one person to do and I insisted on help. She didn't like that because it cost money, but she got a woman called Sully. She wasn't very experienced and, in the end, I quit. I heard she took over.'

'We're trying to get in touch with Madame Weill,' Pel said. 'She seems to be on holiday at the moment and Madame Sully doesn't know where she lives.'

209

'She should. The address was in the house book. Everybody's address was. Old Weill put her daughter's address in because she liked to take long holidays.'

'We don't seem to have seen this address book. Would Madame Weill have taken it away with her?'

Madame François shrugged. 'She might have. She was up to all sorts of tricks. Perhaps there was something in it she didn't want seen.'

'What, for instance?'

'Well, we entered all drugs in there.'

'Could she have been selling drugs?'

'I wouldn't be surprised about anything she did.'

An elderly woman running a drugs racket! It wasn't new but it was unusual.

'Would you have any idea of her daughter's address?'

'It was in a place called Pierrepol. It's near Saint-Trop'. I used to telephone because she liked to know what was going on.'

'Madame Sully doesn't seem to.'

'Well, I told you. She's not experienced and I bet old Weill could pull the wool over her eyes easily. If I were you I'd get in touch with Madame Weill's daughter. Her name's Luciano and Pierrepol's small. The local police would know her.'

18

Doctor Cham had spent a lot of time thinking of the cases he was involved in. By this time they included Colonel Boileau. He sat at his desk staring at the contents of a line of kidney dishes he had spread across its top. In one of them were splinters of glass taken from Colonel Boileau's face. In another was the shard he had removed from the wound in the groin of Duff Forbes Mackay. In another were splinters from the Dutch tourist's spectacles, broken when they had been trodden on – as they now knew – by Tassigny in the hold-up at Marix. In a fourth dish were the splinters taken from Sergeant Gehrer's eye – like those in Boileau's head, blunt and square but as dangerous as a bullet when flung at full speed. In the last tray was the tiny splinter of glass he'd taken from the head of the man found on the motorway, Achille-Jean Quelereil-Dupont, known as Jean Dupont.

They intrigued him. Some of them had similarities. Some were different from the others. All were puzzles, some solved, some not.

He decided to go and see Leguyader, head of the Forensic Laboratory. He didn't like Leguyader, who was an old bore and liked to correct people and blind them with science but, it had to be admitted, he was good at his job.

Leguyader heard what he had to say, then reached for his white coat. 'We'd better look into this,' he said.

Pel was surprised to learn that a deputation consisting of Leguyader and Doctor Cham was anxious to see him. He had been

211

just about to contact Madame Weill's daughter, and he put down the telephone reluctantly and stared suspiciously at the two of them as they entered his office. He was always wary of visits from Leguyader, but the fact that he had requested an interview suggested something important was in the wind. Pel fully expected it to be a complaint about procedure. Someone, he felt sure, had been contacting Leguyader without going through the proper channels. Leguyader was a stickler for the proper channels of communication. But it was nothing to do with procedure. It wasn't even anything to do with blinding them with science. It was about glass.

'Glass,' Leguyader said.

'What about it?'

'Glass,' Leguyader said, 'is a term which covers a wide range of substances that differ widely in chemical composition and physical properties, but which possess the essential characteristic of having cooled from a state of fusion to become solid without crystallization. Most commercial glasses can be regarded as mixtures of silicates. Window and plate glasses are usually made by fusing silica with substances which differ from those used in flint glass, which is used in cut crystal glassware, and heat-resisting glass. They're coloured if necessary by adding metallic oxides to a colourless base.'

'What are we getting at?' Pel asked.

Leguyader held up hand for silence. It was one of his more infuriating traits that he believed everyone was eager to hear what he had to say. 'Plate glass,' he went on, 'glass used for car windscreens, crystal glass and glass for bottles, which are made these days by machine instead of being blown individually, are all different. They also break differently. When shattered, windscreens break into small thick pieces, almost like cubes, though there are among them tiny, sharp shards. Bottle glass tends to break into long slivers, often dagger sharp. Headlight glass is different again.'

Pel shifted in his seat. 'Am I here to listen to a diatribe on the manufacture of glass?'

'No,' Leguyader agreed sourly. 'You are here in the interests of justice.'

Pel scowled, put firmly in his place, and Leguyader smiled.

212

'I know you consider me a bore,' he went on and Pel's head jerked up because this was something he had never expected to hear from Leguyader's lips.

'So do I you,' Leguyader said calmly. 'But give me your attention. It's usually worth while.'

Pel had to admit that it was and since Leguyader, instead of stamping out in a rage at Pel's comment, had been willing to admit himself a bore to make him listen, doubtless what he had to say might produce something.

'Cham and I have worked together over this,' Leguyader explained, 'so if you find it tedious, you'll have to blame him, too.'

Cham grinned and everything suddenly became easier.

Leguyader indicated the kidney dishes Cham had brought along, covered with transparent film and laid out in a row.

'From left to right. Splinters from Colonel Boileau's face. The shard of glass removed from Duff Forbes Mackay's groin wound. Fragments from the spectacles of the Dutch tourist held up by highway robbers at Marix. Splinters from Sergeant Gehrer's eye, removed by the eye surgeon and preserved by Doctor Cham. In the last dish the splinter Cham found in the wound in the head of Quelereil-Dupont.'

Pel was listening now.

'They're all different kinds of glass,' Leguyader went on. 'The glass from the car Gehrer was driving and the glass from the car that hit Colonel Boileau are practically the same – probably even from the same manufacturer. The splinters from the Dutch tourist's spectacles are of finer glass. Finally, the splinter from Quelereil-Dupont's head wound: one would have expected to find it was the same glass as that found in the wounds of Sergeant Gehrer and Colonel Boileau. But it isn't. Because it isn't glass from a car. We didn't examine it too closely at first because we *assumed* it came from a car's headlight. A great mistake, because it didn't. It's not the same sort of glass at all. We've checked it with various glass manufacturers. Three of them. They all gave the same opinion, despite the minute size of it. It didn't come from a car. It came from a bottle.'

'A bottle?' Pel leaned forward. 'He was hit with a bottle?'

'Not a wine bottle because the glass is colourless and wine

bottles are usually green. Not a gin bottle either because they're often green, too. Not brandy, because they're usually brown unless they're half bottles containing cheap brandy, in which case they're often clear, like the one that supplied the shard that killed Duff Forbes Mackay. A vodka bottle? Litre size, for example?'

'A full one,' Cham put in. 'An empty one wouldn't be heavy enough to cause the injury he received. It must have weighed around a kilo.'

Pel sat in silence for a moment, then he looked up and even managed a smile at Leguyader. For a moment Cham thought he was going to embrace him.

'You've said I think you a bore,' he announced. 'And that you think I'm one. Doubtless we're both right. However, and I've admitted it before, there's nobody better at your job than you are. I think, between you, you've just solved another mystery and I'm grateful.'

'Has he solved another mystery, *patron*?' Aimedeu asked as Leguyader vanished.

'More than one. And with a few splinters of glass.' Pel shrugged. 'I know he likes to think we couldn't function without him and, unfortunately, that's true because he's the biggest bore this side of the grave. But he *is* good at his job.' Pel paused. 'Am I a bore, too? He said so.'

Aimedieu grinned. Yes, he thought, Pel *was* a bloody bore occasionally. Especially when he went on about being ill and not being able to give up smoking. But, like Leguyader, he was good at his job.

'Bore?' he said loyally. 'Not you, Chief.'

Pel studied him gravely. 'I don't believe you,' he said.

Within half an hour Pel was talking by telephone to Madame Weill's daughter.

'My mother doesn't live here.' Madame Luciano sounded surprised at his request to speak to her mother. 'She runs a nursing home at Lugny in Burgundy.'

'They tell me she's visiting you and has been for some time.'

214

There was a long silence before Madame Luciano spoke again. 'I haven't seen her for six months,' she said.

She was puzzled and insisted on flying from Marseilles immediately, while Pel decided to delay the holding charges he'd been about to make against the three old men, and await her arrival. Later that day, the thing that had been bothering him for so long became clear. He'd finally remembered where he'd seen Madame Sully before.

He looked at his wife as they sipped their aperitifs. 'You remember,' he said over the Mahler, 'when we ate at the Relais St-Armand a little while ago, there was a woman there who caught your attention.'

Madame had no recollection of the incident. It had been so long before, it had completely slipped from her mind and Pel had to struggle to bring it back.

'Blond woman going grey,' he said. 'With a big dark man. Curly hair. She wore a red polka-dot dress you said came from your boutique. She had a handbag you said also came from your place. And a hair style you said was one of yours. You said Sylvie Goss did it.'

Recollection came. Seeing it was important, Madame turned down the Mahler. 'I remember,' she said.

'Would it have been an expensive dress?'

'We don't sell cheap dresses.' Madame smiled. 'Snobbery being what it is in the clothing and perfumery business, if you don't charge a lot, they think the goods are inferior. Sell cheap dresses and you have failure. Sell expensive ones and you have a runaway success on your hands.'

Pel was frowning again. 'I ask because I wouldn't have imagined the woman who was wearing it drew the sort of salary that enabled her to buy at your place. Or buy handbags of the quality you sell. What about the hair style?'

'I remember it. Sylvie did it. I recognized her style.'

'Would that be expensive?'

'Our hair styles don't come cheaply either.'

Bertholles, the carpet shop, were also helpful. Sure, they said, they had sold a carpet to the Hospice de Lugny. Not a very good one but the hospice hadn't been particular. They just

215

wanted some floor covering and they hadn't quibbled about the quality or the colour. It had been delivered within a few days.

'What happened to the old carpet? The one it replaced?'

'We've got it here. There's a bad stain on it. Someone's spilt a bottle of red wine on it. There's nothing worse for carpets. They must have had a party. It smelled of whisky.

Soon afterwards Records came back to Pel. They exchanged names for a while then Pel tried one more.

Records were silent for a moment or two, and there was the sound of paper being moved. 'There's a record,' they said. 'Both for fraud. Both in Amiens. And, if you're interested, she still seems to be active. We've been approached by the bank. Crédit Industriel. They wanted to know much the same as you. We didn't tell them anything because our records aren't for public use. But they did say she's trying to negotiate a loan to buy a big house in Toulon. The name given is Weill. Any use to you?'

'I think it might be,' Pel said.

As he put down the telephone, Claudie appeared. 'There's a Madame Odebert to see Inspector Darcy,' she said. 'She's wanting to report a disappearance.'

'Inspector Darcy's not here. Give it to Aimedieu. He can deal with a Missing Persons report.'

Claudie hesitated. 'I think this one might be more than just a Missing Persons report, *patron*,' she said.

'It's my father,' Madame Odebert said. 'Henri Lefêvre. He's disappeared and I'm wondering where he is. Then I read about this man being found on the motorway and that he'd been at that hospice at Lugny. My father was there.'

Lefêvre had gone into the hospice at Lugny for a matter of six months.

'My husband's a professor at the University,' Madame Odebert said. 'He got the opportunity to exchange with a professor from the University of Virginia at Charlottesville. Naturally, he wanted me to go with him. My father, who's eighty-four and lived with us, didn't want to be in our way and he said he'd go into the hospice for the six months we were away. It seemed

216

all right to me. It seemed comfortable and when we left he seemed happy and had money available. He's quite wealthy. But then we stopped getting letters and I grew worried. In the end my husband thought I should fly home and make enquiries.'

'And?'

'I've been to the hospice. He isn't there. They said he left three months ago. They say he announced that he wanted to go home. Well, he might have, but it seems very unlike him, and none of our neighbours has seen him.'

As Madame Odebert left, Pel picked up his cigarettes, slipped them into his pocket and stood up.

'Aimedieu.'

As Aimedieu appeared in the doorway, Pel gestured. 'Get in touch with Inspector Turgot, of Uniform,' he said. 'He knows what I want. I've talked to him. We're going to Lugny.'

When they arrived at the hospice, there were three or four elderly people sitting in chairs in the sun on the lawn. They looked up with interest, as though they welcomed any diversion from their boredom.

'Have they found him?' an old woman asked. 'They said he was in the river and that he was a solicitor who'd defrauded his clients.'

'He was found ages ago,' an old man corrected. 'Some men from the village did for him.'

The youth, Bernard Sully, met them at the door. He was still working on the steps with a trowel and a bricklayer's hammer. He studied them with his blank eyes and vacant expression. At Pel's request he summoned his parents.

Like the old people outside, they'd heard that Siméon, Espagne and Cardier had been taken in for questioning.

'Have they been charged?' Madame Sully asked.

'Not yet. There are a few things to sort out still. Siméon has a record and they knew Dupont had money and valuables in his house. After he was killed, it was decided to take him to the motorway and leave him there so it would look like an accident. They were in a hurry.'

217

'They must have been, the way they buttoned up his clothes.' Bernard Sully spoke excitedly. Then he stopped abruptly, his eyes wide and shocked, and there was a dead silence. Pel stared at him.

'Where did you learn that?' he asked. 'It's not general knowledge.'

Sully was staring at his wife, then his eyes turned to his son. 'You stupid bastard,' he said.

As he lunged for the boy, Pel stuck out his foot. Sully stumbled over it and crashed into a small side table which collapsed into matchwood under his weight.

The boy watched dumbly, his eyes uncomprehending; then, as Aimedieu dragged out the handcuffs and wrenched his father's hands behind his back, he came to life. Swinging round, he burst through the open French windows. But, as he stepped on to the terrace, two of Turgot's men appeared from behind the door. As they grabbed his arms, he gave a strangled shout like that of a captured animal.

'Take him away,' Pel said. 'Don't be too hard on him.'

That bomb at the airport.

Things had been stirring for some time in Misset's not over-alert mind. As he watched Ferry's house from outside the Petite Alsacienne he saw the upstairs window – the window of what Ferry called his study – open, and a cloud of white powder tossed out. It landed on the garage roof below and was promptly swept by the breeze in the direction of Jouet's garden.

Misset frowned. He'd just read the report on the wounding at the airport. One of the substances in the bomb that had caused it had been sodium chlorate, he gathered. It suddenly seemed to be worth looking into.

There was a garden centre down the road. It wasn't a big one, because the French were never enthusiastic gardeners, but they answered his question. 'Sodium chlorate,' the salesman said, 'is no longer sold loose, and it's just labelled weed-killer. In any case, there are better ones these days and sodium chlorate rots anything you put it into – even tins. I had a tin of it and the bottom fell out.'

'Nasty stuff, is it?' Misset said.

'Very. But that's not why they don't label it these days. People use it for making bombs. They mix it with something else.'

'What?'

'It's more than my job's worth to tell you.'

'Come off it,' Misset said. 'I know.'

The man looked indignant. 'Well, if you know, why ask?'

Misset puffed his chest out. 'Because I'm police,' he said. 'And I'm interested.'

It seemed to be time to pick up Ferry. Misset was certain he'd solved the mystery of the mad bomber at the airport. It wasn't terrorists of the Free Burgundy organization. It wasn't the Russians or the Chinese or rioting students. It was Aloïs Ferry, because he'd been sacked and wanted to get at Trudis.

Ferry's car was still in the drive and Misset took up a position by the bar of the Petite Alsacienne to consider what to do. The correct thing would have been to call for assistance because Ferry might react with violence. But Misset wanted any glory that was going for himself and, besides, it was hot and he was thirsty. Calling for a beer, he glanced at the barmaid. Oh, God, he thought, if only she were his wife!

He had a feeling that Ferry was on to him. His last chat with him had been stiff and formal. Ferry had been wary and he had a suspicion that at that very moment he was watching Misset through the window of the upper room where he worked. His car was in the drive below, blue and rusty and looking like a heap of junk. Misset began to regard him in a new light. His resentment at his dismissal had not been obvious but it was clear it was seething inside and he had intended doing something about it. He had tried a few curses against Trudis and when they hadn't produced any thunderbolts or flashes of lightning he'd decided to try something more positive.

It didn't require much effort on Misset's part to reach the conclusion that the bombs at the airport, amateurish as they were and despite the fact that one of them had indirectly been the cause of Nadauld's death, were Ferry's work. No wonder

Jouet had a wilting garden. Ferry had been using the weed-killer to make his bombs in the upstairs room he claimed was his study and had been throwing spilled crystals on to the sloping roof of the garage just beneath, from where it had blown in the breeze on to Jouet's property. Ferry had certainly been damaging Jouet's garden but it had been unintentional. His quarrel was not with Jouet. It was with the airport.

The barmaid was at the street end of the bar. As Misset picked up his beer and stared in her direction, Ferry slipped from his mind. A girl with a bust like that, he thought, shouldn't be serving drinks. She should be in a public harem where, for a small fee, Misset could enjoy her favours. There had been a time, he thought nostalgically, when his wife had had a bust like that. Misset had picked his wife for her physical charms but, he realized now, he ought to have thought ahead and taken a look at her mother. They always said that if you wanted to know what your wife would develop into, you should look at her mother. Misset's wife's mother was an interfering old bag who had nagged her husband to his grave. From time to time she came to stay with Misset and his wife. Those were the times when Misset discovered he was on constant duty in the city.

He stared again at the girl behind the bar, hardly aware of what he was doing. Getting his hands on that lot, he thought, would be like –

'You looking at me, Dad?'

Misset came to life with a start. He hadn't been looking at anyone. He'd been staring into space, his mind far away, imagining erotic happenings, and it startled him to realize he had been staring at the girl without being aware of the fact. With a bust like that, too!

He realized what she had said. 'Dad', he thought. Mother of God, what had he come to?

'No,' he said. 'I wasn't looking at you.'

'Yes, you were! You've been looking at me for days. Ever since you started coming in here. Who are you? Merve the Perve or something?'

'Well,' Misset said gallantly, 'you're worth looking at.'

'Not by a wrinkly like you,' the girl said spiritedly and,

shamed and humbled, Misset swallowed the last of his beer and headed for the door. As he reached the street he stopped dead. Name of God! His senses were brought up all-standing. Ferry's car had gone. Where? The bastard was probably blowing up something else with his weed-killer. Perhaps he'd set off for Charles de Gaulle airport in Paris to blow up a couple of 747s, or some of that plastic tubing they used to contain the moving staircases that conveyed passengers from one place to another.

He ran into the road, barely aware that the barmaid was shrieking that he hadn't paid. Where in God's name, he thought, had the little sod gone?

He caught sight of the rusty blue Renault just as it disappeared round the corner down the road. He was heading for Leu, he decided. Why? Was he heading for the airport again? To the garden centre for some more sodium chlorate? Then, in the middle of his panic and for no reason at all, he remembered Ferry's interest in Pel. 'Who's your boss?' 'Where's he live?'

Hostage, his mind shrieked. He was going to hold Pel hostage or something. Blow him up if he didn't withdraw Misset from the scent. It had often occurred to Misset that it would be pleasant to plant a bomb under Pel's car but, though Misset was a weak character and a bully in many ways, the idea of disloyalty of that kind wasn't in his nature.

He fell into his car, to find the barmaid at the window demanding money. Frantically, he put his hand in his pocket and threw the contents at her.

'Oh, charming!' she yelled.

Leaving with a squeal of tyres, Misset headed for Leu at full speed. The roads were clear and he knew he couldn't be far behind.

Roaring into Leu – Misset's car wasn't new and always roared – Misset saw Ferry's Renault parked in the road outside Pel's house. A small boy with a dog that looked like a rag rug was staring at it.

'He's gone inside,' he told Misset.

'Thanks,' Misset said.

'Is he a crook?'

'Yes.'

Misset just had time to be aware of the small boy's look of excitement, then he was running up the drive. Bursting into the house, he saw Madame Pel, with her back against a small table. There was another woman with her, who he assumed was the dragon housekeeper he'd heard about at the Hôtel de Police. Between them on the table was a large heavy-looking device in shining copper with a long oak handle which he realized was an old-fashioned warming pan. The housekeeper was holding a hammer and nails and it dawned on him that they were on the point of hanging the warming pan on the wall. The hammer was far too large for the job and looked heavy enough to drive stakes into hard earth.

Ferry was pointing a small automatic at them. Misset recognized it as a Belgian gun of the sort people bought for protection. Bank clerks carried them. Commercial travellers carried them. So also, it seemed, did Ferry.

Madame Pel – even in his extremity as the gun swung towards him, Misset noticed she was attractive – looked up.

'Sergeant Misset!' she said.

'Madame!'

Ferry grinned and gestured with the automatic. 'Get over there, alongside them,' he said.

Pel had just unloaded the Sullys at the Hôtel de Police. 'Tuck them up, Aimedieu,' he said.

'What do I charge them with, *patron*?'

'I'm not sure yet. But you won't go far wrong if you make it conspiracy, which will do to hold them for the time being.'

Heading for his office, Pel took the Meissen figures from the carton in which they'd been brought to the Hôtel de Police. Some of the silver from Dupont's house was missing but he suspected that was because it was easy to get rid of. A search round the antique shops would doubtless turn some of it up and then there'd also be a few questions to be answered by the owners about why they'd been dealing with stolen property. He expected a few interesting answers.

He placed the Meissen figures on his desk and studied them.

He knew little about antiques but he was aware they had beauty. They would have to get Mijo Lehmann, Nosjean's girl, in to value them. Madame Chappe would no doubt be pleased to see them. If they were worth what she said they were worth, no wonder they were still around. Property of that value wasn't easy to get rid of. It would need a trip to Paris or Marseilles, even to London or the USA. They would need to be dealt with carefully, and the Sullys had been nervous.

It was pretty clear now what had happened because the Sullys had talked. Pel had had the details right but he'd been looking in the wrong direction and a weapon had not been found because it didn't exist any more. It was a bottle – a full one – and it had been smashed against Dupont's head.

'They'd all been drinking,' he explained to Aimedieu when he returned,' and they tried to dope the old man with sleeping tablets. But he was tougher than they thought and came round while they were standing with his wallet in their hands.'

As he had struggled to his feet, the youth, Bernard Ruffel, had panicked and hit him with the full litre bottle of whisky. It had broken, scattering glass, whisky and blood on the carpet.

'The bottle they showed us when we first went out there,' Pel went on, 'was a new one they'd bought to replace it. What else they hit him with we don't know but we'll doubtless soon find out. They haven't finished talking yet. Bernard Ruffel had been repairing the flagged kitchen floor and had brought his tools to the card game because, he says, he didn't want to stop. There was a cold chisel among them so I expect the hammer he was using on the front steps when we first met him was there, too. I expect we'll find it eventually.'

Aimedieu listened carefully, wondering how anyone as unprepossessing as Pel could have the skills he had.

'The Sullys thought he was dead,' Pel continued. 'And, knowing what he possessed they went to his room for his keys and two of them, the father and the son, went to his house and lifted the Meissen figurines and the silver and the money he kept there.'

'What about Madame Sully?' Aimedieu asked.

'She stayed behind to go through his room. When the others returned they found her in a panic. She'd left the old man on

223

the floor – dead, she believed – but when she returned from his room he'd vanished. He'd come round and staggered off into the darkness. But they found blood and guessed he'd headed for the motorway to get help. When they found him this time, he *was* dead.'

After that it had been a series of hurried expediencies. Because it was growing late, they hadn't known what to do, so they had decided not to cart the dead man back to the hospice and had sent the son, Bernard Ruffel, to collect his clothes. But, because he wasn't very bright, he forgot the underclothes and socks.

'They couldn't delay, though,' Pel ended, 'and they dressed him hurriedly with what they had and, in the dark, buttoned him up incorrectly and with his waistcoat inside out. Then they dumped him on the motorway and went back to Lugny to burn the pyjamas, clean up and arrange to change the carpet. They told the shop it had been spoiled with red wine. Probably they emptied a bottle on it to hide the blood. They didn't go to the house in Dôle and they didn't touch the briefs in the safe because they didn't know they existed.'

Pel lit a cigarette, feeling he deserved it. It would probably be the final nail in his coffin but he was feeling so pleased with himself he was prepared to drop dead on the spot if necessary.

The Sullys had tried hard and probably deserved ten for effort, but they'd been amateurs all along. Still, he thought with satisfaction, they might have got away with it but for the fact that Doctor Cham had noticed that the wounds were wrong.

And he, Pel, had been looking for an old scandal, blackmail and extortion, even drug trafficking, as a reason for the murder, and all they'd found was greed. Marianne Sully had wanted money because she was eager to transfer her activities to the safety of the South Coast. And very nice, too! There'd have been plenty of elderly geriatrics down there with a lot of money and, by using Madame Weill's name, which was known to the bank, she'd been negotiating a loan to do it. She hadn't been without experience, either, because, with her husband, she'd engineered frauds on at least two previous occasions.

As he turned to place the Meissen figurines on his safe, the telephone went. Annoyed at the interruption of his triumph, he snatched it up.

'Inform me,' he snapped.

What he got wasn't what he expected. There was a gabble in his ear that made his hair stand on end. *'What!'* he yelled.

Madame Pel was showing no sign of panic and Misset, still panting after his run, had to admire her for it. The housekeeper type just looked angry – as if she resented having her work interrupted.

Madame Pel looked from Ferry to Misset. 'What's all this about?' she asked.

Misset drew a deep breath. 'He's the type who planted the bomb at the airport,' he said.

Ferry grinned, obviously pleased to be recognized. 'It took you long enough to work it out,' he said. 'I'll do better next time. I'm still only learning.'

Misset was still struggling to get his breath.

'It was to get back at the airport?' he said.

'That's right.' Ferry's smile vanished. 'Somebody had to show them.'

Talking to Misset, he had his back now to Madame Pel. Beyond him, Misset saw she was moving quietly and it dawned on him she was grasping the handle of the warming pan they'd been cleaning. Name of God, he thought, she's going to hit him with it!

Even as the thought crossed his mind, Madame Pel swung. Ferry must have caught the movement out of the corner of his eye and he turned just in time to get the warming pan full in the face. The gun went flying.

Good God, Misset thought. Here was Madame Pel, a woman, supposed to be fainting with terror as any normal woman would when faced with a pistol, and instead she was laying about her with a will. It was time he did something. Even as the thought crossed his mind, he dived at Ferry and got a fist in the face for his trouble. A kick in the family jewels doubled him up and he staggered back. Recovering, he stumbled forward again just as Madame Pel swung the warming pan once more. Unfortu-

225

nately this time it missed its target and hit Misset at the side of the head with a clang that set his ears ringing. Ferry leapt for the gun but as he laid his hand on it, the heavy hammer the housekeeper held came down on his fingers. Ferry screamed and, reeling away, clutching his hand, he was hit in the face with another more accurate swing of the warming pan. As he tottered sideways he was finished off with yet another swing and disappeared under the table.

'Madame Routy,' Madame Pel said briskly. 'Get the clothes line.'

By the time Misset had recovered himself, Ferry's hands were tied behind his back and he was trussed like a chicken. For good measure he was attached to the table leg.

Misset struggled to his feet. 'Thank you, madame,' he said. 'He might have shot me.'

Madame Pel smiled. 'You did well,' she said.

'Did I?' Misset was still dazed. 'I think we'd better telephone headquarters.'

'You'd better do it,' Madame Pel said. 'It's your case.'

There was no need. A police car was just turning into the drive and two of Pomereu's men were falling out of it.

'That was quick,' Madame Pel said as they appeared.

Yves Pasquier was just behind them, his dog barking excitedly. 'It was me,' he said. 'The policeman said he was a crook so I thought he'd need help. I telephoned.'

19

'We seem,' Pel said, 'to have ended up with a murder we thought at first was an accident, and an accident that at first we thought was murder. That airman, Girard, didn't intend to kill anyone.'

'He killed Nadauld,' the Chief pointed out. 'But I suppose the real blame should be laid at Ferry's door. But, despite the fact that one man's dead and three others were hurt, he can only be charged with possessing an offensive weapon, assault on the police, malicious damage to government property, and a few other things of that sort.'

He pushed the brandy bottle across. 'You did well to sort out the Quelereil-Dupont business,' he went on. 'Not that *he'll* be missed. I remember him vaguely.'

'He was probably blackmailing the Sullys,' Pel said. 'Madame Sully had a record and he'd doubtless found out. It wasn't an elaborate plot – he was probably even killed by a petulant dull-witted boy because he'd been interrupted in what he was doing. But the reason was money. Getting rid of him not only got him off their backs, it also made his possessions available. He's another of your Missing Persons who's turned up. I've asked for sniffer dogs. It's something they can do, without biting anything or getting into a fight, and they've started on one or two likely places. I suspect we might turn up one or two others from your list as well because I think we've hit a murder racket – and only just in time, too, because I think they were on the point of transferring their operations to the South.'

227

Pel was just about to leave the Hôtel de Police when the telephone went. To his surprise it was Darcy.

'I've been looking for you,' Pel said. 'Where've you been?'

'Around,' Darcy said shortly. 'I've got news for you, *patron*. Philippe Duche's holed up.'

'Holed up?'

'I've just seen his wife. Goriot tried to arrest him again. He's got a rifle.'

'Where is he?'

'His house at Benoit de l'Herbue.'

Slamming down the telephone, Pel turned to find Aimedieu in the doorway. 'Duche, *patron*,' he said. 'They've just telephoned from –'

'– Benoit de l'Herbue. I know. Who's handling it?'

'Inspector Goriot.'

'I'm on my way. Let the Chief know, then follow me.'

As he reached the car park, a small Renault shot in and Duche's wife almost fell out of it. Seeing Pel, she ran towards him, her hair flying.

'Philippe didn't do it,' she said at once.

'Do what, madame?'

'That bomb at the airport.'

'We know he didn't.'

'He's angry that he's still suspected. He doesn't do that sort of thing these days.'

'If he did, he'd go to prison for a long time.'

'He's a good man.'

'He wasn't always, madame.'

Duche's house stood on its own and round it, behind trees and crouching against cars, were policemen. As Pel climbed from his car round the corner, he heard a few shots. A police brigadier gestured.

'Take it easy, sir,' he said.

'What's the situation?'

'He's quiet. But he's not coming out.'

As Pel turned away, his arm was touched and he found himself facing Councillor Lax.

'Ah, Pel,' he said.

228

'*Chief Inspector* Pel!' Pel snapped. 'What are you doing here, Monsieur le Conseilleur?'

Lax had been just about to launch into a series of questions and demands about the police when Pel's attack stopped him dead.

'What do you mean?' he said. 'What am I doing here?' I represent this district and, as such, I'm responsible to the commune, which in its turn is responsible to the arrondissement and upwards to central government.'

'This is a police affair and you should *not* be here. It might be dangerous.'

'Danger's not important,' Lax said heroically. 'I heard about it and felt my place was here.'

'How?'

'How what?' Lax looked startled.

'How did you hear about it? I've only just heard about it myself and I was in the Hôtel de Police. If you'd step into my car perhaps we can discuss it.'

Lax looked worried suddenly. 'Suppose I don't want to?'

'You'd better, Monsieur le Conseilleur,' Pel snapped. 'I need to talk to you. Aimedieu, get in front. I want you as a witness to what's said.'

When Lax climbed out of the car again, he was white-faced and scared.

'You'd better leave, Monsieur,' Pel said shortly. 'If you don't, I'll have one of my men escort you away.'

As Lax vanished, Pel peered round the corner. Among the parked vans and cars policemen were still keeping their heads well down. Several windows and one or two of the tiles on Duche's house had been shattered by the shooting. Chunks of plaster had been gouged out and there were two holes in the door. Goriot was standing near one of the vans holding a loud-hailer and trying to look like Napoleon directing the Battle of Austerlitz. His smile at Pel was stiff and triumphant. Pel didn't return it.

'What's going on?' he demanded.

'I sent my men to make an arrest.'

'Why?'

'I learned he'd acquired a gun. But he gave my men the slip. He's holed up in the house there.'

'Has he done any shooting?'

'One shot.'

'Where did it go?'

'It hit the roof opposite.'

'If he was aiming at you or your men it was a poor shot.'

Goriot said nothing.

'What about your men. Have they fired?'

'Yes.'

'Much?'

'Not much.'

'Their "not much" seems to have done a lot of damage.' Pel indicated the broken windows of the house and the bullet marks in the doorway. 'You're using a steam roller to crack a walnut.'

'I'm in charge,' Goriot said.

Pel drew himself up to his full height. It wasn't much but he had the gift of making it look more than it was.

'That is something you definitely are not,' he said coldly. 'I'm here now and I'm in charge.'

'The Chief welcomes action.'

'Not this sort. Tell your men to hold their fire.'

Goriot hesitated and Pel snapped. 'Now!'

Goriot flushed and at his gesture his sergeant ran among the trees and parked vehicles, crouching down. The pecking fire stopped.

'Give me your loudhailer.'

With the instrument in his hands, Pel was about to step forward when Duche's wife appeared again.

'Can I come with you?'

'I think you'd be wiser to remain here.'

'What are you going to do?'

'Arrest him.'

'You can't.'

'I most certainly can. But I shall only be arresting him for possessing and using a firearm without a permit. It'll mean a sentence. Will you wait for him?'

'For a lifetime.'

'I don't think it will be as long as that,' Pel said drily. 'And

230

it's better than leaving him where he is, where he might be goaded into shooting someone. *That* would carry a much longer sentence.'

As Pel prepared to rise to his feet, the Chief appeared. 'Where in God's name are you going?' he demanded.

'To talk to Duche.'

'I forbid you to go out there.'

Pel looked at the Chief. His face was a mixture of determination, high dudgeon and anger.

'Lax was here before I was,' he said. 'Perhaps before any of us. As he was at the airport on the night of the bomb. He had information.'

'What are you getting at?'

'He's been seen with Forton.'

'Who by?'

'Misset.'

'Can you rely on Misset?'

'This time I can. Forton's great-uncle to Inspector Goriot. Goriot doesn't like me. He's been using Darcy to get at me. He's probably ruined Darcy's career. Information's been passing from him to Lax via Forton. The stories about Darcy stemmed from that source.'

'You know?'

'Lax's just admitted it. Aimedieu was present and will confirm. Goriot goes and Forton receives an official letter from the Prefect. If not, *I* go.'

The Chief looked worried. Not Pel, he thought. Mother of God, not Pel! He drew a deep breath. 'Leave it to me,' he growled. 'I'll attend to it. It'll take time, of course.'

'Not if Goriot resigns at once through ill-health.'

The Chief gave in. 'Very well. If necessary we'll get a psychiatrist's report. He'll take his pension early.'

'I don't care what he does,' Pel said shortly. 'So long as he does it.' He turned away and blew into the microphone of the loudhailer to test it. 'Philippe Duche,' he said, and the iron voice rang out among the houses. 'Can you hear me? Wave something if you can.'

There was a pause, then a handkerchief appeared in the window of the house and waved from side to side.

231

'This is Chief Inspector Pel. I'm coming in to talk to you. Hold your fire.'

He handed the loudhailer back. Goriot looked shaken. 'You can't do that,' he said.

'Why not?'

'He'll shoot you.'

'If he does, doubtless you'll be happy to try to take my job.' Pel's eyes glittered. 'But I shouldn't bother. You couldn't do it.'

He rose and stepped forward to a point where he could plainly be seen from the house. There was no sound and slowly Pel began to walk towards the door. The watching policemen held their breaths but, as he reached it, they saw it open and he vanished beyond it. Inside, the door slammed behind him and he turned slowly to face Duche.

Duche was scowling. 'I could have shot you,' he said.

'But you didn't, did you?'

'No.'

'Why not?'

'Name of God, I don't want to shoot *you*! You and Inspector Darcy have been decent to me. And with no good reason!'

'Some *flics* are human.'

'I didn't plant that bomb, Chief.'

'I never thought you did. Too amateur. You were always a professional, Philippe.'

'Is that the only reason?'

'No. You've gone straight. I spoke to your wife.'

'She's a good woman.'

'She must be, to convert *you*.'

'Why are you here?'

'To tell you to give up.'

'They'll send me to prison if they get a chance.'

'They certainly will now. But not for the bomb. And not for the shooting at the airport. That's been sorted out.' Pel nodded at the rifle Duche held. 'Is that licensed?'

'You know it isn't. It belonged to my brother. His widow kept it in the attic and I knew about it. When I heard that bloody Inspector Goriot was after me I went and got it.'

'That was silly. You're committing a crime: possessing a firearm without a permit. There's now also another one: you fired it.'

'I wasn't aiming at anybody.'

'I didn't think you were. Especially as you hit the roof opposite.'

'What are you going to do?'

'Arrest you. For using a firearm without a licence.'

'What'll happen?'

'With your record you'll inevitably go to prison. But I'll be there. I'll speak for you. I don't think it'll be for long. But you've committed a crime and the law demands punishment. But not for something you didn't do. I think your wife will wait for you.'

'I'm sure she will.'

'You might even get off with a fine. Could you pay one?'

'Yes.'

'I'll get the press boys to tell your story. I'll also talk to your customers – personally – and explain what happened. Will you come with me?'

Duche paused, then he said, 'I'll come with you, Chief. Not with that other bastard.'

'That other bastard has nothing to do with this. You'll go to headquarters with *me* and *I'll* charge you. For the gun. That's all.'

'Can I see my wife?'

'I see no reason why not.'

Duche thought for a moment, then he nodded. 'I'll come.'

Pel indicated the rifle. 'Not with that in your hand.'

Duche gave him a twisted smile and handed the weapon over. 'I'm ready.'

'Then let's go.'

The door opened and they emerged in silence. Pel appeared first, holding the rifle, then, immediately behind him, Philippe Duche. They walked together, side by side, Pel making no attempt to threaten Duche with the weapon. As they drew nearer, Goriot stepped forward.

'Stay where you are!' Pel snapped. '*I'm* arresting this man!'

As they approached the parked cars, he wasn't very surprised to see Darcy standing by one of the trees.

'Will you drive us to headquarters, Daniel?' he said.

'I'm suspended, *patron*.'

'You've just been recruited as a civilian reservist and it's an offence to refuse to assist the police when called on to give help.'

Darcy grinned and opened the rear door of his car. Duche climbed in. Pel sat alongside him. 'I think that's that,' he said. 'We can go now, Daniel.'

20

The Chief sat back in his chair, looking pleased.

'I'm glad that's all over,' he said. 'Duche won't suffer much. It might even be dropped. The psychiatrist's report blames Goriot entirely. We seem to have done well lately. We've found another of Records' Missing Persons. A boy this time. He was running with a gang in Paris.'

'I think we'll find one or two others before long, too,' Pel said. 'They've already found something at Lugny. It was under the new floor of the laundry. It looks like an old woman. I think it'll turn out to be Madame Weill. We might even find more because it seems one or two others appear to have "walked out" at various times in the past. You'll probably find your Missing Persons list is smaller than you anticipated. You might even be able to call off the search.'

'Probably,' the Chief said placidly.

'Which will mean that I shall want Morell and Cadet Darras back on my team again.'

Trust the little bugger to think of that, the Chief thought. 'Your wife appears to have handled herself very bravely with this Ferry type,' he said.

'She's not a nervous kind,' Pel said comfortably.

'Misset did well, too.'

Pel was still suspicious of Misset's part in the affair. Madame Pel had often heard of Misset but she had a kind heart and, knowing her Evariste Clovis Désiré, had spun a yarn that Misset had put up a heroic fight. Pel didn't believe it but he wasn't prepared to argue with his wife.

'My wife said he did,' he agreed.

'Don't you believe her?'

'My wife is generous-minded.'

That night, except for the Sullys, everybody was happy. Nosjean, recovered from his anger at the Tuaregs, was with Mijo Lehmann. She was talking about marriage again and, as usual, he was trying to fend her off. De Troq' was with the girl from the Palais de Justice. Not only with her, but with her parents too, who were looking him over. They had decided he was quite a catch with his title but that it was a pity he was only a sergeant, and were encouraging him to go for promotion. 'With your background it shouldn't be difficult,' they were saying: De Troq' was thinking that, though the girl was all right, her mother was a bit pushy. Judge Castéou was with her husband. Pel was admiring his wife.

'Goriot's gone,' he was saying. 'We got a psychiatrist's report on him. It wasn't his fault. Being blown up isn't very good for anyone.'

There was a note of compassion in his voice and his wife kissed his cheek.

'The Chief's going with the Prefect to see Senator Forton. He'll get the message. Especially as Lax has already been seen. There's to be an apology.'

'Will an apology help Daniel?'

'This one will. Lax will get his name in the papers but not in a way he'll enjoy.'

Even Misset was reasonably happy, basking in the admiration of his family. His picture was in Le Bien Public. 'AIRPORT BOMBER CAPTURED BY CITY TEC', the headline said. For once, he'd given them something they couldn't complain about, though, as usual, his wife had managed to insert a niggle into the praise. 'You might have been killed,' she said. 'And then what would we have done?'

'Will they give you a medal, Papa?' his youngest asked.

'Probably,' Misset said. But he didn't think they would. He knew how much luck had counted and was aware that Pel knew him too well.

But he sat back, far from dissatisfied as his eldest daughter

236

poured him another beer, though his satisfaction was tempered a little by the news he'd received over the soup at dinner that his wife's mother was coming to stay with them.

Finally, Darcy was happy. He'd been called into the Chief's office and informed that the investigation into the allegations against him had been dropped without any evidence being given or even asked for. He and Pel had celebrated as they usually celebrated successes – with a quiet beer at the Bar Transvaal. There were one or two other cops in there, too, but they were all a bit subdued, because it wasn't all that long since Nadauld's celebratory drink had been cancelled by Nadauld's death.

As Pel had turned for home, Darcy had headed his car for Angélique Courtoise's flat. She was waiting for him.

'You're moving in with me,' he said.

'I thought I might be soon,' she said. 'I've been packed for some time.'

With the car full of her belongings, the suitcases and cartons, the portable TV, video and record player, the half-dozen hats for weddings all girls seemed to possess, Darcy seemed satisfied.

'I'm not a bad cook, too,' she pointed out.

They ate at a restaurant on the edge of the city and, back at Darcy's flat, he passed over a glass of champagne. Angélique's face was full of happiness. She gave him a shattering grin. 'Champagne in bed,' she said.

'Très grande horizontale. Anybody can do it these days.'

'My mother warned me about living in sin.'

'Mine warned me about bringing trouble home.'

'Parents aren't always right.'

He leaned over and kissed her. She stared back at him. 'You're trying it on,' she whispered.

'With you I'm always trying it on.'

'I thought you were a gentleman.'

'I've been known to kick dogs. Have some more champagne?'

She looked up at him under her eyebrows, her eyes sparkling a little with moisture. 'What are we celebrating? Me being here?'

'Not just that. I'm back on the job. Pel fixed it.'

'Good old Pel. I thought he would.'

'Did you really believe I hadn't taken bribes?'

'Of course. Always.'

Darcy drew a deep breath. It was a bit in the nature of the confessional. 'Last week,' he said slowly, 'I crossed the path of two of my old flames. They didn't seem at all pleased to see me. Just to make sure, I deliberately looked up a third. They'd heard the story. They didn't want to know me.'

She kissed him gently. 'Start a story like that and there are always fools who'll believe.'

'They cut me dead.'

She put her arms round him. 'I shan't, Daniel,' she said. 'Never.'

'I'm glad about that,' Darcy said gravely. 'Very glad.'

'Daniel,' her voice was solemn, 'you suddenly sound middle-aged.'

Darcy laughed. 'I think I'm growing old,' he said. 'I've suddenly noticed. I'm getting like Pel. Soon I'll be complaining I can't give up smoking.'